CLARE CURZON

CAT'S CRADLE

W⊕RLDWIDE.

TORONTO • NEW YORK • LONDON
AMSTERDAM • PARIS • SYDNEY • HAMBURG
STOCKHOLM • ATHENS • TOKYO • MILAN
MADRID • WARSAW • BUDAPEST • AUCKLAND

CAT'S CRADLE

A Worldwide Mystery/September 1994

First published by St. Martin's Press, Incorporated.

ISBN 0-373-26151-9

Printed in U.S.A.

★

ANATOMY OF A CORPSE

The body lay faceup as she had been found, but now the clothes had been removed. On each forearm and twice through one wrist, always on the outer side, were the small, dark holes where shot had entered.

"This is one slide that really matters," Yeadings told them sombrely. "In a way, the others are pure theatre. You see, the stripped body shows clearly that when shot the woman had her arms folded across her lower ribcage. Two of those entry marks correspond with reentry into the chest."

He looked round at them and pressed the point home. "What we've been presented with in Farlowes Wood was a rearranged cruciform corpse."

★

"The Cat. He walked by himself... He went back through the Wet, Wild Woods, waving his wild tail, and walking by his wild lone. But he never told anybody."

—Rudyard Kipling,
"The Cat That Walked by Himself"

ONE

BEAUMONT ACCEPTED the heavy glass tankard the woman thrust on him, remarked her thin, flushed cheeks, the flustered movements of her hands, and was then advanced on by his over-genial host. Above the firm handclasp, the expansive grin, hard eyes were quickly assessing, recording, marking him down.

The detective shrugged inside his drab raincoat. Coming straight off duty, he hadn't had time to gentrify his appearance. And here appearance mattered; didn't it just! Turning off into the lane, he might have taken it for any prosperous Thames Valley farmland, but once in sight of the house, oh no. Period residence updated for easy living, down-dated for snobby aesthetics. Everything just too perfect. Front lawn been brushed and combed; not for this one occasion, but daily over decades. The Welches had clearly arrived, and not by way of agriculture either.

'The lads seem to be enjoying themselves,' Beaumont offered, nodding towards the scrum rolling on the grass beyond the open french windows.

'Give them plenty to do,' said 'Farmer' Welch smugly. 'That's the secret. Like to take a look around?' He didn't wait for an answer but strode off, confident as a general among his prize troops, determined this laconic parent should appreciate the extent of his hospitality to his son's friends.

Beaumont hadn't missed much on his slow drive down between the undulating fields, one of which had been set out as a course for go-kart racing. There had even been a pair of

Sinclair C5s for those who'd wanted to sample the Green approach to wheels. But Welch was leading him now round to a side of the house with the inevitable pool, even a two-metre diving platform.

Beyond a light screen of young birches grassland sloped gently down to distant woodland, and half way there he saw the targets; to the left three large straw ones marked out with concentric coloured circles; over to the right four orange-brown cardboard outlines of enemy soldiers hunched over rifles. The bloody man had actually had the kids target-shooting.

'Using what?' he asked, eyes narrowing with the wariness of a man who knew and detested firearms.

'Archery,' said Welch, waving a casual hand towards the left. 'And over there air rifles. A country lad needs to learn to handle the things properly. One or two steady hands I let try with my shotguns.'

Beaumont said nothing. Well, spilt milk, wasn't it? How many incompetent townee youngsters were going to bludgeon their dads now into forking out for firearms? Just another phased need in the 'gimme' progress of today's juvenile, midway between skateboards and condoms. Soured cynic?—maybe he was, but he'd had cause to learn the hard way, his boy subject to two-way pulling from separated parents, and shrewd enough to be on the make because of it.

'Which is yours, then?' asked 'Farmer' Welch with assumed jollity, tiring of the anonymous man's dourness.

'Beaumont. Stuart of that ilk. At present sitting like a gargoyle on the roof-edge of your barn.'

'The stables? Bloody hell! He could have the tiles off.'

'Or the guttering down,' Beaumont agreed darkly.

'Well, let's go get him.'

But by now the boy had slid away and mingled. He was standing, hands in pockets, presenting a casual profile a few yards short of the french windows his father had left by. Observant if nothing else, Beaumont *père* noted: not always a comfortable talent to have about.

'Time to go, lad,' he greeted him.

So directed, Welch switched his attention to a single member of the mob, as indistinguishable as one frozen pea in a two-pound packet. 'Said your goodbyes to Rory? Where is the boy?'

Apparently he wasn't available, but his sister was. A neat ten-year-old with a china doll face and blonde plaits stepped out of the house and solemnly offered a hand. ''Bye, Stu. I hope you can come again.'

In some confusion, but with rebellion squashed by the warning flash in his father's eye, Stuart allowed his limp hand to be shaken. He mumbled some reply, eyes downcast.

Beaumont managed a twisted smile. 'Well, thanks, Mr Welch. Thanks a lot. For the lager too.' Then they were off.

In the car Stuart shoved a gift-wrapped package down between his feet and glowered at the other occupant. WPC Rosemary Zyczynski's eyebrows twitched humorously at the expected reaction. She had no need to stress that she was merely being dropped off on the way back from the job. Stuart knew that all right; knew by now there'd be no evidence of her presence back at the house, guessed there'd equally be no trace of his father wherever she lived, but he kept up the charade on principle. Sod it, you couldn't tell what they might get up to if he didn't keep the pressure on.

'Good party?' Beaumont inquired flatly.

'It was a *rally*. Parties are for kids.'

'Adults have 'em too, I'm told. You may do when you've rejoined the human race.' Beaumont shifted to catch a

glimpse of his son's superior face in the driving mirror. He
was tempted to stick out his tongue and catch the boy off
balance, but he suppressed it. Too busy squeezing past the
inflow of Jags, Mercs and Rollers now crowding the narrow lane as more parents came to pick up their offspring.

'Money, money, money,' murmured WPC Zyczynski,
eyes all round her. 'Where does so much come from?' She
sounded flattened rather than envious.

Beaumont gave his perky grin. 'They call him "Farmer"
Welch because it amuses him to act the countryman, but
he's MD and principal shareholder of a small electronics
firm in Slough making intricate components for the international giants. Astute businessman from all accounts, and
he fields a good team.'

'You've had him checked out.' Her voice mixed surprise
and amusement.

'It came up in another context. Something Inspector Mott
was interested in. Nothing there, though.'

Rosemary Z turned to ask Stuart over her shoulder, 'Did
you get a turn at the go-karts? I've always fancied one myself.'

'Yeah. Came second in my round. Six laps.' He checked
himself and toned down the enthusiasm. 'The others were
pretty feeble anyway.'

'What about the archery?' Beaumont pressed. 'Crossbows, I suppose?'

'There was a longbow too, but only Mr Welch could load
it. The crossbows were all right.' (High praise indeed from
Stuart.) 'Expensive, I should think. Shouldn't mind an air
rifle, though.'

There it was, the demand: fine technique sharpened by
practice. First the wistful admiration of the unattainable,
then the settling for something more in their financial range.

'Well, you won't be getting one,' said Beaumont.

Abrupt end of conversation.

SOME OF THE REPORTS had come in from patrol cars, some via 999, and others were phoned in to local stations, and whatever interpretation was put on the sightings by Tom, Dick or Harry—whether of flying saucer, foundering air-craft or burning glider—all agreed that there had been a bright light in the evening sky moving slowly in a generally ESE direction. At Maidenhead sub-divisional station the duty sergeant, roughly plotting times and sightings, looked up with a groan. 'Hell's bells! Whatever it is, it's making straight for Heathrow! And possibly rising. Samways, get up the fire-station tower and see what's going on.'

The PC addressed picked up the station field-glasses on his way and went off unimpressed. 'Wotcher looken for?' demanded the Brum recruit who followed him up.

'Martians, lad. Every second Saturday at just this hour we make a check and log it. Just in case.'

'Yer haven me on. Jes' in case of what?'

'In case something weird escapes from the kids' Satur-day matinee film shows. Lordy, there it is!'

He swung up the glasses and took a magnified look, but this merely intensified the object's glare against the evening sky. No way could he make out the precise outline of the flaring mass.

'Let's hope Heathrow Control Tower has a better fix on it.' He watched a moment while the distant blaze seemed to hang unmoving, then he dived below to inform Sergeant Hatch.

Eventually, as the result of a series of radio calls, the mysterious object was written off as a Chinese hot-air bal-loon—and an unmanned miniature at that—which, rising to some thousand feet, had taken fire and continued to burn steadily until the supposedly fire-resistant fabric had acknowledged defeat. It was finally consumed over Datchet, and any remains could well have fallen on royal reserves. Irreverent voices debated the chance of receiving a soprano complaint from Windsor with a background yapping of Corgis, but none came.

The earliest sightings having originated from high ground near Christmas Common and Turville Heath, a patrol car was dispatched on Sunday morning to interview locals in the north of E Division. At about the time that the balloon's ascent was traced to a young people's party at a country house near Henley, a more crucial message came through to Reading divisional station concerning a violent death. Any interest in the hot-air balloon was overshadowed by a call for a murder team turnout, notably Detective-Superintendent Yeadings and DI Angus Mott.

MIKE YEADINGS was at home wrestling with the cold-water tap in the downstairs cloakroom. Nan, who understood that DIY plumbing was best exercised in decent seclusion, had taken the baby for a swing in the garden, having checked that the stop-cock for the mains water supply was actually turned off. Sally, the Yeadings' older child, however, was seated on the tiled floor behind him, wearing a worried frown and making mouth movements sympathetic to the antics of the wrench. Mike would have preferred her absence since things were not going his way and patience was wearing thin, but he knew that any interest displayed by a Down's Syndrome child must be positively encouraged, so he rested, gave her a smile, said, 'Not easy, this,' and then resumed.

He completed fitting the new washer and stood back in admiration of his handiwork.

'Spla-a-ash!' Sally commanded, waiting for the water to flow.

'I have to turn it on again at the mains first,' he explained. 'Back in a minute.'

Sally waited, and sure enough with a rush and a gurgle water suddenly gushed from the mended tap. In the hall outside came the cooing of the phone and her father's voice as he answered.

She watched the level rising in the basin and at first it didn't worry her. When it reached the overflow she reached for the bung, but it was already swinging loose on its chain. And still the water rose. She knew it shouldn't. Sally whimpered and moved away.

The water came up to the basin rim, levelled and began to slop over. Bravely she moved in and seized the tap, turned it until it tightened. The flow continued unchecked, water spurting and cascading on to the cloakroom floor. She let out a wail of despair, then covered her mouth because Mike was still talking into the phone. She had to be quiet as a mouse then.

And now the tiles were showing shiny through a creeping tide of water and her sandals were letting the wet in. She watched her pale blue socks go darker blue and felt the shock of cold go up her legs in shudders.

At last the receiver went down and she gave a plaintive cry. Mike came swooping down the two steps to lift her, depositing her on high ground.

'Oh hell!' He plunged one hand in the basin, slopping even more on the floor, and struggled with the other to stop the flow. Nothing new happened. Then his fingers had freed the bung-hole of the blackened debris of the perished washer previously removed. More indignant gurgles, and the water began to subside, flowing in now at a rate rather less than it was getting away.

Mike Yeadings shook most of the drops off his hands and lifted Sally again in his arms. 'Nan,' he roared. 'I've got to go out. You'd better ring the plumber!'

DI ANGUS MOTT reached the death scene some twenty-five minutes ahead of Yeadings. He had rung DS Beaumont at his home but there was no reply, so he left a WPC with instructions to go on ringing. On her second try the receiver was lifted and a boy's gruff voice answered her query. 'He's washing the car. Shall I call him?'

'Tell him there's a body.'

Beaumont came on for directions. 'Yes. Yes, I know the area roughly. Was near there yesterday. Who's been notified? Right. On my way.'

He slung the soapy sponge in the bucket of water and backed out on to the road. Stuart called after him and he put his head out of the car door to demand, 'Whassat?'

'Can I come?' the boy demanded hopelessly.

Of course he couldn't, but dammit it was his holiday, and leaving him in the house idle was just the programme that had got up his mother's nose. 'Get in,' Beaumont ordered shortly. He'd have to think up some alternative on the way there, drop him off where he'd do least mischief. Poor kid; Cathy couldn't cope with him and Granny wouldn't. A human shuttlecock, more in the air than on the bat. Small wonder he'd got that set, broody look.

Beaumont darted him a glance as he waited to turn into the main road. The boy was no end chuffed at the invitation, though he was putting a blasé face on it. 'Map in the glove compartment. You can navigate me to Farlowes Wood.'

Stuart refolded the map and scowled over it. 'Hey,' he said suddenly, 'it's right near Welches'. Only you need to turn off left just before the farm lane. Then it's on your right, half a mile along Battels Lane.'

'Think Rory could stand you turning up there this early?' his father asked.

'Can't I go and view the bod with you?'

Beaumont closed his lips over a snappy answer and grunted. 'We've enough big boots trampling the scene already. It makes things more complicated.'

'Will Rosemary Z be there?' Deadpan.

'The scenes-of-crime team were picking her up.'

'If women are let in on it, I don't see why—'

'You stick to your GCSE dogfish. We don't need a teenage vampire picking over the corpse.'

Stuart sat back. 'Actually I wouldn't mind that. Specializing.'

'Mind what?'

'Pathology.' He looked smug, knowing he'd dropped a bombshell.

The car took a bend rather wildly. 'Study medicine? That'd mortgage a few years, lad.' Cost the earth, too. 'How about your grades?'

'Old Bawdy thought I could get them up by next summer.'

So he'd even discussed future O-levels with his previous form master. 'You're looking a long way ahead. What about this half-term's report?'

'Well, that'll go to Mum, won't it? I mean, since that's my present address . . .'

'I'll ring her, tell her I need to see it.' He slowed and braked. 'You can walk from here. Hang on to the map and get yourself home on the hoof. Got enough money?'

'A fiver inside my sock.'

'That'll improve it! See you, then.' He watched the boy decant himself into a spiky patch of desiccated cow parsley, leap to avoid the ditch and assume a countryman's plod as he went on ahead without a backward glance.

Having me on, Beaumont told himself, but didn't quite believe it. Maybe Stuart did want to become a doctor. Or maybe he wanted to take a rise out of his father. Whichever, he'd grown up somewhat since Cathy had walked out of the marital home taking their son along. Cut off, Stuart could be settling to the life of a loner. Wolf or Ranger, though?

Still mildly shocked, he arrived among the police cars and a morgue wagon. It seemed almost a relief to make the switch and be dealing with someone dead.

WDC ROSEMARY ZYCZYNSKI had been at Reading when the call came in and so went straight out with the SOCO unit. It was the first case of violent death since she had officially joined the Yeadings team, turning down promotion to uniform sergeant for the chance of a transfer to CID. Since making her mark while on temporary secondment to Yeading's team for the Sefton murder investigation[1], she was determined to show that she could fill the space made for her, even if it meant coming last in the promotion queue.

At first half her energy had been used, she reckoned, in batting off assumptions that she was there to type and make the tea, but gradually she was overcoming male prejudice and gaining respect for the less sinewy, more sinuous, female arm of the law. This case, she vowed, should be as much a challenge to her colleagues as to herself as squaddy.

The report of this death, phoned in at 07.58 hrs from a neighbouring cottage, stated baldly that the body of a woman was lying some twenty yards inside Farlowes Wood, to the left of a pathway worn as a short cut to the main road

[1] *The Blue-Eyed Boy.*

which they'd left half a mile before. Skirting the path, Rosemary followed the SOCO in among the trees and out at the far end near a country bus stop. There she saw that fifty yards to the left the recently straightened main road had by-passed Swardley village, the church tower of which just topped some tall trees on the far side from where she stood. That would be St Mary's, where the witness had been bound for the 8.0 a.m. service, coming from a group of estate cottages near the beginning of this woodland path.

This end of it was no more than a break between hazels and brambles which screened the by-pass. It wouldn't be noticeable to strangers passing at speed, except for a patrol car run up on the grass verge just opposite.

Knowing that soon the rest of the CID team would be crowding in, she went back to view the corpse before the brass arrived, standing off with her hands behind her back, eyes and ears open, feet well out of the line of approach.

The dead woman, fully clothed, lay on her back, arms and legs outflung, and the black-brown stains of blood were all over her cardigan and neck. The face, Rosemary observed by leaning close over a bramble patch, was almost untouched except for an entry hole under her cheekbone; a severe, elderly, weathered face, brown and wrinkled as a shelled walnut. And somehow familiar. Not a reassuring face, even when she'd been alive, Rosemary considered.

And why was it that, a stranger to this neck of the woods, she felt she had seen it before?

TWO

WHEN YEADINGS WAS a mere DCI there had been no thinking twice about viewing a body *in situ*. Then Angus Mott had been his sergeant. Promotion for both had meant that Angus must be allowed more initiative, and by rights Yeadings should be shining the seat of his suit on an office chair rather than pulling his wellies out of the Rover's boot and stomping in there among the preliminary investigative team. But DCI Atkinson having such a flair for the collation side did mean that an interchange of roles was often beneficial; Yeadings as pure jack, Acky on the admin end.

And on such a perfect autumn morning what better place to be than out in the rolling Thames Valley farmlands (what was left of them between all the motorways!) with a taste for detection? Except for the sobering thought that there was a death involved, a woman dispatched before her time, and someone to be clobbered with having done it.

Both his DI and Detective-Sergeant Beaumont were there before him, and now he remembered that Mott would be off on leave, starting tomorrow, so it was as well he'd turned up in person. CID would be a bit thin on the ground for a murder investigation if that was what it turned into.

'Beaumont!' he called, recognizing the other's back ahead. He moved up and came alongside, observed that the DS literally had his tongue in his cheek. 'What have we got, then?' They were looking down at a scarecrow figure, elderly if not actually old, dimly female.

'Gunshot wounds, fairly widespread. Once they've measured distribution we'll ask Firearms to let off a few to fix the likely range. Blew her off her feet. Half way out of her wellies. She took a full frontal. No sign of powder burns, of course.'

Yeadings swivelled and peered through the undergrowth. 'What's out there?'

'Open field. It leads up to a converted farmhouse.'

'Converted to what?'

'Gracious living,' Beaumont sighed. 'I've just worked out the topography, and surprise, surprise, wasn't I there only yesterday. Nor is that all.'

'Tell me, then.'

'A kids' party—thirteen-year-olds' half-term reunion— once fought each other over conkers, and now all dispersed, but Pater decided to put on a success-story display.'

'And?'

'And turned that field into a competition range, archery, air rifles and a couple of shotguns. Shooting downfield, towards this wood.'

As he turned, a spiky loop of bramble swore across the sleeve of his jacket. He looked at Yeadings, mouth pursed and with strangely blank eyes. His round, sharp-nosed Pinocchio face looked pinched. 'Not nice to think my kid could have been the one to do this.'

WHEN THE PHOTOGRAPHERS had finished with the body and the immediate surrounds, Yeadings went carefully forward by a narrow route exposed by roping back the undergrowth. Closer to the body soil samples were being taken. Not that the ground round the recently dead woman would tell much after two rainless weeks. Scuffings nearby in the layer of fallen beech leaves would have been made by the woman who discovered the body, or possibly by some rooting wild animal.

A distant car door slamming announced another arrival.
'Dr Littlejohn, sir,' called a constable out by the road. 'Shall
he come through, sir?'

Yeadings waved assent and stood waiting while the pathologist approached. ''Morning, Yeadings. Dear, oh dear,
what have we now?'

'Nothing known,' Yeadings said flatly. 'Up to you to fill
in the blanks.'

Littlejohn knelt beside the woman's body and placed his
fingers on the neck. 'Well—certainly dead. Surprisingly
proper of you not to pre-empt me on that, Mike. I take it no
police surgeon's beaten me to it this time? Female, of more
than a certain age. Late seventy-somethings, shall we say?
Outdoor appearance. H'm, take a squint at that.'

Yeadings moved in and looked where the doctor pointed.
He had pulled the baggy sleeve of the woman's cardigan
back to disclose several shot marks and a three-inch red
scratch running up the inside towards the elbow. 'Here too,
see? And there again. Brambles? No; too late for blackber-
rying. Cat, I'd say at a wild guess.'

'*That's* it!' The voice issued from a hazel bush to their
left, and the branches parted carefully to reveal Rosemary
Zyczynski's bright face. 'I knew I recognized her from
somewhere. It was a photo in the local newspaper: the Cat
Woman. She has a big house somewhere round here and
lives alone, with about fifty cats in varying stages of ill
health. Some local bigwig wrote a letter to the editor, wanting the animals put down. They sent a reporter and photographer out to interview her and she saw them off with a
shotgun. It was quite a fearsome picture they got.'

'Keeps cats, does she? Or *did* she? 'Morning, Z. Have you
met Dr Littlejohn?' Yeadings effected the introductions. 'Z
is officially on the team now,' he explained.

'I've heard of your exploits,' said Littlejohn, nodding since his hands were otherwise engaged. 'Didn't picture you quite as you are.' He smiled up at the pretty face from his kneeling position.

If the chief hadn't been there Rosemary Z would have said something about not judging a sausage by its skin. As it was she smiled, stepped back and let the bush resume its natural shape. She hadn't much experience of guns but knew enough to guess that what she'd been sent in a straight line unspecifically to search for would be a spent cartridge case. When found, it would have to be left for a photographer, then the distance measured back to the corpse and finally it would be bagged for fingerprinting.

She worked in the general direction indicated until stopped on the wood's edge by three strands of newish barbed wire. Beyond this fence lay a dried-up ditch with the stiff, buff remains of seeded cow parsley on its edge, then the gentle upward slope of a grazing-field. In an almost shoulder-to-shoulder line across it and working down towards her were a score or so of uniform constables scanning the ground ahead of their feet. And as she watched, one stopped in his tracks, put two fingers to his mouth and gave a piercing whistle. A sergeant evidently gave the command for the rest to continue. There might well have been more than one shot fired, more than one person hunting game on the edge of the wood. She went back to DI Mott and reported her own negative find.

'Can't really see much here. Too cramped,' the big doctor was complaining. 'You can zip the lady away now, but I'd like hands, head and boots bagged separately.'

'Remove the boots completely, sir?' asked one of the SOCO team cautiously.

Dr Littlejohn looked at him deadpan. 'But not the other parts if you can help it.' The man bent over the body to hide his red face.

When Rosemary came out into the full sunlight again she found Beaumont waiting. 'All right, Z?'

'Sure. Nothing to it.' Then she felt she'd choked him off. 'I'm glad my first body wasn't a young one,' she admitted.

'Yup. Had a good innings, that old girl. An accident, anyway. All the same I'll be glad when the inquest's over.'

'That was the Welches' place up the hill, wasn't it?'

'And the field they found the cartridge case in is the very one Stuart, among others, was using a shotgun in yesterday afternoon. Did you happen to overhear anything the doc said about time of death?'

'He wasn't giving. And the chief wasn't pushing it. Didn't mention what rectal temperature he got either, nor the extent of rigor.' She pointed up-field. 'What are they taping-off up there?'

'Can't be sure, but they could have found marks where yesterday's targets were set up. Roughly at the level where the single cartridge case was found, I should think.'

'So where were the boys standing to shoot?'

'About twenty yards above that, I'd say.'

'So that's all right then, isn't it? The shot that killed her couldn't have come from them.'

Beaumont shrugged inside his raincoat. 'I'd like to think so. But shooting downhill?—and with rank amateurs you can't be sure of anything. The cartridge case could have been one of theirs that they miscounted on, found after they'd cleared up, and just checked away.'

They watched the photographer set up his tripod afresh on the supposed spot the hunter had shot from and aim his lens towards the tree under which they'd found the body. 'Checking how well the woman would have shown up,'

Beaumont explained. 'Most people who go out after bunnies and pigeons should have better than average eyesight.'

'But at dusk, say? And the woman in such drab clothes? The hunter might just have caught a movement and taken her for a deer.'

'If they get deer in that spinney. One thing I know is that they do get people in there. Don't forget the footpath worn right through to the main road. All the locals must know about it. So—unless we're looking for a stranger to the district—there's a chance it wasn't an accident after all.'

STANDING BY his chief's car as the experts began to disperse, DI Mott asked, wooden-faced, 'Think it's an accident, sir?'

Yeadings was being cautious in both directions, but he saw no reason as yet for Angus to put off his leave. He knew it had been booked months ahead and that a cancellation now would be a let-down for Paula too, the DI's barrister girlfriend. There'd be hell to pay with Nan if he stymied this holiday for them; she'd great hopes of the outcome, marriagewise.

'Could be,' he offered. 'We'll know better when Littlejohn's done the post-mortem and we find out who saw the lady last, and when. It'll take a little while to get round all the locals, and by then you should be safely airborne. Meanwhile get Beaumont and Z visiting the cottages we passed, see if anyone heard or saw anything; who used the path last before the body was found; all the usual. I'm going to call on Beaumont's plutocratic friend up yonder, then have a look at the dead woman's house.'

'Better take her key then, sir. It was on a cord round her neck.'

'No, you can hang on to it, Angus. Meet me outside in half an hour. If everything seems normal there, you're off the hook. Then I'll say "bon whatsit" and suggest you keep your head well down until tomorrow's officially arrived.'

All the same, he thought, leaning against the Rover's door while he pulled off his wellies, it could still turn out to be murder. Which would be a damn sight more interesting.

IT WOULD HAVE BEEN more direct and probably quicker to walk up the field his men were still searching and approach the farmhouse from the rear. (Certainly the Welches must be aware of what was going on, unless they were away and the uniform officer in charge had found no one to warn of the invasion.) But this was going to be an official visit, so it meant returning to the main road, then driving on to the farm lane and approaching the more seemly front of the house.

Back doors, farmyards, sculleries, fire escapes, kitchens, they were the uncosmeticized side of living, he reflected; therefore more revealing. People so caught out were more likely to bridle and go on the defensive.

Yeadings grinned. Well, since he was into generalizations, how about one on how people spent their fine Sunday mornings? He knew where he'd choose to be in such autumn sunshine: out in the veg plot with a garden fork in his hand, an ear pricked for Nan calling that coffee would be up in ten minutes.

The Welches, he found, were not so employed. As he drove slowly down the curves of the hawthorn-hedged lane he caught his first sight of the house in three-quarters profile. And, elbows on the outer sill of an attic window, with a pair of field-glasses to his eyes, a teenage boy absorbed in the activities of the line of dark blue figures now working back uphill in the grazing-field.

It took some moments for the purr of the Rover's engine to disturb his concentration, and when the lenses swung round to focus on him Yeadings leaned forward over the wheel, raising a hand in acknowledgement. The glasses were instantly lowered. Uncertainly the boy waved back, then withdrew and closed the window. Curiosity transferred, Yeadings guessed, to the advent of supercop.

He didn't need to knock. A well-built man in his middle forties, tall as the Superintendent himself but red-haired where Yeading's thick crop was badger-streaked near-black, opened the front door and came out on the porch, eyes narrowed against the sun. 'Police, I take it?'

'Superintendent Yeadings, Thames Valley CID, sir.' He produced his card. 'And you are?'

'Welch, Franklin, but known locally as "Farmer".' It was meant as humour, but from a definite height.

Yeadings took in the cream silk shirt, well-cut Bedford cords, expensive calf brogues.

'A joke, Superintendent. Rural sarcasm might have stretched to "Squire", but they probably think I don't know the word. Being to them a townee.'

'I see, sir.' Not acknowledging any humour. 'Perhaps it was on account of your initial. Or because part of this house must once have been a farm.'

'F for Farmer? Never thought of that. Yes, this was originally the Home Farm to Malmsmead Hall. Been very much enlarged since then, of course.'

Welch stood back and indicated the hall for Yeadings to come through. He had a rapid impression of white walls, gleaming copper, and golden chrysanthemums big and shaggy as the heads of sheepdogs. Brick floor, but not the original; expensive-looking rugs in glowing colours. Lord Almighty!—a Canaletto! Must be genuine, with that electric cable almost concealed by the frame. He assumed the 'Farmer' was well boned up on security systems.

He was being ushered now into a south-facing room full of sunshine. On a window-seat, sharing it with a heap of scattered Sunday newspapers, a fair-haired woman was pouring coffee. She looked delicate, with mauve shadows under the eyes, but her hands as she lifted a heavy silver coffee-pot were firm and muscled. Beside her a pretty child with blonde plaits stood waiting to pass the cups and saucers out, earnestly two-handed. She glanced at the policeman from the corners of her eyes because she wanted to stare but knew that was rude. Yeadings let his smile cover them both while Welch made the introductions.

'And this—' turning back as the door to the hall opened again—'will be—yes, it is—this is our son Rory, home for half-term and bursting with questions about the accident, if I'm any judge.'

'Mrs Welch, Amanda, Rory.' Yeadings shook hands all round and took the easy chair offered. Welch moved a little aside on to a second broad window-seat, in silhouette like his wife, while Yeadings blinked in the sunshine.

'If you don't mind, I'll ask the questions, at least for the present. I gather then that you've heard why there's so much activity round here at the moment.'

'One of your men said a body...found in Farlowes Wood. But he didn't say who.' It was Mrs Welch rushing in rather breathlessly while her husband's mouth was opening to reply.

'I'm afraid so. You haven't heard of anyone missing locally?' He was in no hurry to admit that the woman's identity was known.

'Has it been there a long time?' the boy asked in the following silence. He had a light, clear voice, sounded like a choirboy. Looked like one too with that innocently rounded, pink and white face. He'd inherited his father's thatch but toned down to the warm red-brown of fresh conkers. His

eyes were a pale grey and long. A beautiful, sexless, medi-
æval face.

'We don't know. The pathologist will say when death actually occurred, but that isn't quite the same, is it?'

The boy frowned, working that out. 'Because she may not
have been killed there?'

'Because people who use the path regularly will know
better about when the body appeared. But you said "she".
How did you know it was a woman?'

Welch got the answer in first. 'We all know it's a woman.'
He sounded ruffled. 'It must have come from your man who
came up to tell us they'd be searching the field.'

'I don't think so, sir.' It was the experienced Sergeant
Buller who had done that, and he was well versed in how
much not to tell.

'Actually,' Rory admitted, 'it was Stu told me.'

'Stu who?' Yeadings asked and saw the boy's mouth
twitch in an attempt not to laugh at the daft sound of it.

'Beaumont,' Rory said. 'He was here yesterday at the
rally, and his father dropped him off early this morning on
the way. Maybe he shouldn't have told me. I don't suppose
he knew it mattered. Sorry I spilt.'

'I'm not sure that it does matter really. It will be public
property soon in any case. But maybe you could hang on to
the information until it's official tomorrow.'

There was a general rumble of agreement. 'Was she—I
mean, had anybody...?' Welch looked quickly down at his
daughter and thought better of finishing the question.

'She was shot, Mr Welch. I understand from DS Beaumont that there was some shooting going on here yesterday.'

'*Shot?*' The woman's voice was full of alarm. 'What
with? Oh my God, you don't imagine—'

'With a gun, Mrs Welch. Perhaps I could see all the fire-arms used here yesterday, for purposes of elimination.'

The temperature seemed to have dropped by several degrees. There was a shocked silence, then Welch rose and led the way out into the hall. 'I don't think you will be able to fault the precautions we take, Superintendent. For the guns there is a proper steel cabinet bolted into floor and wall, and all ammunition is under lock and key separately. I hold the only keys. If you'll wait a moment I'll fetch them from upstairs.'

Yeadings turned to find the little girl close behind him. She was carrying his coffee-cup with a wheatmeal biscuit in the saucer. 'You didn't drink your coffee.'

He took it from her. 'I was talking too much, I'm afraid.'

She didn't move away as he drank, but stood watching him with eyes that were almost circular and of the same pale grey as her brother's. She murmured, barely voicing the words, but surely with the identical inflection he had used, '. . . for purposes of elimination.'

She wasn't mocking him. It was the sound of the words that had fascinated her. She had savoured the phrase, put it carefully away in some mental store.

On an impulse he asked, 'Do you like poetry?'

'Oh yeth, do you?' Eagerly.

There was only the slightest hint of a lisp, not an affectation he was sure. Such an earnest little girl would be at pains to get rid of it. He nodded. 'I like most poems, but especially gallopy ones.'

'John Gilpin,' she said quickly, marking him down, as he'd hoped, as an earthbound type.

'And Masefield. You know that thing about—'

'Cargoes.' On the single expelled breath there had been no lisp.

'Thank you, Amanda.' Her father had come downstairs and was dismissing her. The hand-over was as smooth as the Ceremony of the Keys at the Tower.

Yeadings passed back the empty cup and saucer. 'I'll save the biscuit for later, if I may.' She smiled at him, showing a gap between her front teeth.

'What a polite little girl,' he remarked to Welch as they threaded passages and went down a short flight of steps to reach a rear office.

This seemed to discomfit the other man somewhat. 'Have you children, Superintendent?'

'The same as yourself, two.' Not quite like Welch's advantaged pair, though. Luke still a toddler, a late venture because after Sally's Down's Syndrome they'd been long afraid of lightning striking twice.

'We had the son of one of your men here yesterday,' Welch led. 'Name of Beaumont.'

'Young Stuart,' said Yeadings, cautiously admitting acquaintance. 'The one who turned up this morning and told you all that the victim was a woman.'

'Told Rory actually. They met outside. The rest of us were still getting up.'

Funny he should reintroduce the Beaumont boy, and as though it was the first mention of him. Yeadings had the feeling there was a specific reason. Something more to follow?

'Bit of a wild lad, wouldn't you say?'

He wouldn't actually, not having enough knowledge. But if Stuart had inherited much from his father, he could be more than a bit original. 'How d'you mean?'

'Oh, general attitude. Stand-offish without having anything to be superior about.'

A tendency to sneer, Yeadings translated this. Which might well be the lad's way of refusing to be patronized and insulating himself from a world in which the trauma of parental separation loomed large. No call to gossip to this man about that, though. 'Oh, really?'

'Bit of a loner. Don't like to see that as they come up to puberty. A boy should learn to mix.'

The Superintendent made no comment, leaving it to Welch to say more. Which he did. 'Not easy being a policeman's son, I imagine.'

There it was. Back to Beaumont senior. He was the one who'd gone down like a rat sandwich with Welch. And the DS had been here only yesterday, probably the day of the fatality in the adjacent wood.

The hell of it! Would Beaumont have to be dropped from the team now because of a social connection? With Mott due to leave, that would mean Yeadings covering DS and DI as well as the fieldwork for DCI Atkinson. The Assistant Chief would have every cause to insist on him returning to his Superintendent's desk and drafting in an alternative team.

Over my dead body, Yeadings resolved. Once there's any indication that the Welch kids' party is in the clear, I'll be hanging on to Beaumont, as my acting-DI if need be.

THREE

WITH WELCH'S TWO SHOTGUNS (plus his stable-man's one) locked in the Rover's boot and a hand-written receipt left in exchange, Yeadings continued by road to the dark square marked on his ordnance map as Malmsmead Hall. The journey clocked up 4.2 miles on the dashboard, but the map showed it lay over a shallow ridge, perhaps a brisk walk of only twelve minutes. The back drive of Farlowes Farm connected with Battels Lane, and the rear of the Hall was almost directly across two fallow fields from there. By car, however, he was obliged to regain the main road and return to a roundabout beyond the Battels Lane turning. There he followed a narrow track skirting a brick wall some eight feet high but at places crumbling or destroyed by leaning tree-trunks, until he reached iron gates rusted permanently open and wound about by dried stems of bindweed. Dense undergrowth of a neglected spinney obscured the house itself. The curving driveway, originally gravelled, had worn bald and was distinguishable from the verge mainly by a drop of some four inches. Every kind of wild flower seemed to have bloomed there at some time, died and gone mummified.

Spooky place, he felt; neglected like the poor old thing whose death they were to look into. He wondered who would now be giving an equivalent *coup de grâce* to her home. Demolition experts for some property developer? Or had the place a preservation order on it?

He still couldn't decide when it loomed suddenly before him, a dark brick monstrosity made more gloomy by the closeness of skeletal, black trees. High against the pale Oc-

tober sky swayed the lumpy nests of a rookery. Disturbed by
his arrival, the birds wheeled above the angled roofs with
raucous cawing, hostile as vultures to his mind.

Mott's most recent mechanical obsession, a near-vintage
MG, was parked beside three stone steps that led up to central double doors. The house appeared asleep, all downstairs windows masked by curtains or closed shutters.

As Yeadings cut the engine and reached in the glove
compartment for his torch, Angus came round the corner of
the house to meet him. 'The key was for the back door,' he
announced. 'It looks as though she lived alone right enough.
And see this.' He held out the shining, round-shafted key.
'Practically brand-new. So is the string it's on. I've looked
inside and I'd say she's recently had the lock changed.'

'Did you try the front door?'

'Yup. Tight as a drum. Locked, with bolts shot top and
bottom. From the look of the steps she hasn't used that way
in for years.'

'Right. Let's go round and look inside, then.'

There were five assorted cats curled up in the courtyard
at the rear. Another came sinuously out through a flap in the
door as they approached, stretched, arched its back and
walked off contemptuously, tail flicked stiffly high.

'If she did live alone we'll have to give the RSPCA a call.
Pity; they look good enough beasts to me.'

'If you happen to like cats.' DI Mott clearly did not. 'Fifty
of them, according to what Z saw in the paper.'

'Probably exaggeration. How could you ever count such
independent creatures?'

'If Beaumont was here he'd suggest a pongometer.'

By now they had the door back on its hinges and were in
a glass-sided passage that gave entry to the scullery. On its
stone-flagged floor were cardboard grocery cartons and
every kind of basket lined with old clothing. Few had oc-

cupants, and those were engaged in geriatric slumbers. Only one cat approached the two men, a ginger of indeterminate sex which rubbed itself intimately against Mott's leg until firmly shoved away by his shoe.

'Anything specific we're looking for?' he asked to cover his distaste.

'You heard what Z told us. The newspaper mentioned the old woman chasing reporters off with a shotgun. That's the way she was killed, but there was no gun by the body. So let's find hers.'

They didn't have far to look. It was leaning in a corner of the kitchen between an old-fashioned built-in cupboard and a rather fine long-case clock. Holding it through a handkerchief, Mott broke it open and sniffed. 'Well, whatever else she neglected, she knew how to take care of a gun. Clean as a whistle and decently oiled.'

'Let's not assume she had only the one. There must be someone who knows the old lady's habits. I'm going to tour upstairs. You take the ground floor. Shout if there's anything of note.'

'Well?' Yeadings demanded when they met up again in the hall. He was carrying a second gun, a double-barrelled over-and-under 12-bore.

'She hasn't used the downstairs rooms lately. They're mostly in half-darkness. There are just patches on the walls where pictures hung. Lots of empty spaces to show where furniture once stood. Only the library seems complete. It was locked, with the key on the outside. Come and look.'

Again the heavy curtains were drawn here, and when Yeadings went to pull them back he was showered with dust. Behind them there were solid wooden shutters held firm by an iron cross-bar. 'No go. Can you find the lights, Angus?'

'Found the switches, but the current's off. Maybe she couldn't pay the bills.' There followed a few fumblings and a grunt of satisfaction. 'Ah, this seems to be an oil lamp. Hang on while I get it alight. Dammit, people shouldn't be allowed to get in a state like this.'

'She wasn't of your generation, lad. Too proud to take handouts, probably. I suppose what money she once had dried up and if the DSS tried checking on her she could have seen them off in the same way as the local press.'

'But she can't have existed totally cut off.' Mott sounded exasperated. 'There must have been times she needed a doctor, even a lawyer. There were cartons she used for cat boxes. Who would have delivered the goods that were in them?'

'That's where the locals can help. Some of the answers may be with Beaumont and Z by now.' Yeadings was eyeing the impressive stack of books which covered three walls of the room right up to ceiling level. 'She seems to have lived in here.' He nodded towards a divan bed in one corner.

On the floor by its head stood a shallow basket lined with quivering swathes of soft flannel. From within came a feeble mewing. Gently Yeadings explored with his fingertips. 'Three of them, just a day or two old. And I think one's dead. Angus, we'd better close the place up temporarily and send the SOC team in, plus an animal care officer to collect the moggies. If we can't locate Mum Cat I'd better take this little lot with me now.' He lifted the basket by its handle and, preceded by Mott carrying the oil lamp, returned to the scullery and an expectant reception committee of felines. 'I wonder when they were last fed.'

'Recently, I should think. Some of those bowls down by the sink have stuff still in them.'

'You can't always go by that. Cats aren't like dogs, scoffing the lot and anything else that they can scrounge. Cats eat just as much as they need for the moment and will come back for the rest when hungry. None of those we've seen

look undernourished. Just the skinniness of old age in one
or two cases. I'd be more interested to see what the old lady
herself lived on.'

He went across to a row of high cupboards, opened doors
and pushed things about. 'M'm, wholemeal flour. Baking
materials all carefully sealed in containers. Made her own
bread, would you believe? No sign of weevils or ants. She
wasn't quite the derelict she first appeared. Another thing,
the one and only bathroom upstairs was scrupulously clean;
in regular use, I'd say. No bleach, though. I have a feeling
the lady was more than just hard-up: a forerunner of the
Greens maybe.'

'That figures. There's a sizeable vegetable plot round the
south side, with fresh drills ready for sowing.'

Yeadings closed the last cupboard and stood a moment in
thought. 'You questioned her needing a doctor. It seems she
treated herself, herbally. There's a collection of remedies in
labelled tins. We're getting quite a clear picture of her now.
More than keeping her end up, for all she was old. Let most
of the house go, but saved her energy for what she considered priorities. A person of principle, wouldn't you say,
Angus? Knew exactly how she wanted to live and in what
company; independent and determined to stay that way. I
wonder if she happened on someone equally determined but
at cross purposes.'

'Irresistible force and immovable object? Your nose opt-
ing for murder, then?'

Cat basket in hand, Yeadings stopped short on his way
out of the door. 'Thinking aloud, lad. Sign of old age.
Lucky you went suddenly deaf then. Get off home and finish packing. Nan'll give me no peace if you and Paula don't
get away!'

In the car he disposed of the dead kitten in a large envelope previously used for maps. The other two looked healthy

enough, one fastening its blunt little mouth blindly on his finger end when he explored it. He had intended returning to his Reading office but there was no great hurry. Reports from the uniform branch and his two CID juniors would take time coming in. Meanwhile he'd drop the kittens in on Nan.

They were received with leaping excitement by Sally and round-eyed wonder by little Luke. Nan warmed diluted cow's milk and fed the newcomers from a baby's bottle fitted with a teat.

During the night a teasing wind blew up, sending flurries of dry leaves scudding to all points of the garden. By morning they lay thick along the edges of the flowerbeds. Across the terrace a single sycamore leaf cartwheeled along with a staccato ticking that made Sally roar with delight. Diagonally over the western sky was drawn a sharp white line, and behind it a solid front of cloud bringing rain.

'The end of our Indian Summer,' Nan said regretfully, looking up from care of the kittens. 'Tonight's Hallowe'en and the children will get soaked.'

'It might keep them indoors out of mischief,' Yeadings said darkly. There were a dozen jobs in the garden he'd promised himself to finish before the weather broke, less likely now if the Cat Woman's death made demands on CID's reduced man-power. He'd have no free days before the case was cleared. It might still prove no more than an accident, but he felt in his bones it would turn out a stinker.

WDC ROSEMARY ZYCZYNSKI had celebrated her official transfer to CID by extending her wardrobe. *Plain* clothes, of course, but no more navy blue! She appeared at the Monday conference in a tan jacket and skirt that made Yeadings think of bright conkers, and his mind jumped back to the previous day when he'd been struck by the same colour. The young Welch lad's hair, that was it! After a report of the body's discovery—by a Mrs Barrow on her way to early service—he'd get Beaumont to report on Saturday's half-term party.

Laconic as ever, Beaumont obliged. He hadn't actually seen Welch's boy Rory when he dropped in, being pushed to deliver Z and get home to cook supper. Just swallowed the obligatory drink from the over-affable host and made off. Stuart hadn't been very forthcoming about the day's activities, a bit heavy on the blasé touch at present. Maybe he'd open up more if pressed. As confirmed by Welch, there had been separate targets for crossbow archery and air rifles. At the end of everything he had allowed three of the more promising lads to join Rory in trying out his two shotguns, firing at toughened plastic screens. Stuart had been one of them. They were given a short range, possibly fifteen metres. It wasn't known whether any of the shots had been badly off target, but the direction could have been right for any very wild effort to reach the wood about where the body was found.

'With it happening at the weekend, we've not yet sent off the cartridge case and guns to Ballistics at Huntingdon,' Yeadings told them, 'and we all know how long they'll take. But I asked our Firearms people to take a look at photographs of the dead woman.'

He picked out a paper from a bundle before him. 'In short, the spread of shot indicates medium range, which could be consistent with a shooting-point level with the targets, where the single ejected cartridge case was discovered. Now, Mr Welch has assured me that forty 12-bore cartridges were issued and forty cartridge cases, plus their wads, scrupulously collected after the shooting. (That was partly an exercise to impress the boys but also because it's a grazing-field and they don't want trouble later with the cows.) On my insistence he retrieved these from the bin and we checked numbers as correct. There were no other spent cases binned. Welch couldn't account for the presence of the odd one of the same kind found in the field, hadn't himself shot anywhere near there in a matter of months, and Fire-arms say the case was from a cartridge probably fired within the previous twenty-four hours. Incidentally it was a ''Western'' 6-shot. It would have been packed with a plas-tic cup-wad which—despite a thorough fingertip search in field, ditch and wood—we haven't yet laid hands on. They do butterfly off but we should expect to find it somewhere near the body.'

'So the cartridge case could have been a plant,' offered DC Silver.

'But also it *could* have come from a gun aimed in the di-rection of the dead woman. Whether with the intention of wounding her, or bagging some other creature, won't be clear until we know when and under what conditions it was fired. Significantly it wasn't fired from as far away as where the boys stood to shoot.'

Yeadings looked round at them. 'The inquest opens on Friday. After evidence of finding, identification and medi-cal report, we'll ask for the usual adjournment.

'So, facts as we have them this far—' He pulled another sheet from the file. 'The dead woman is named as Lorely Pelling, unmarried, born 1912, only surviving daughter of the late Squire of Swardley, Brigadier Howard Hedley Pell-ing, Royal Engineers, born 1880, died 1962. Retired from army 1934, but stayed on in Poona as civil engineering con-sultant; returned to UK 1945. Ironic that he survived the Great War and numerous frontier skirmishes in North-West India, to contract Parkinson's Disease and fall downstairs to his death at home. Said home is Malmsmead Hall, an in-herited 23-roomed red-brick mansion roughly half a mile south-south-west from where the body was found and marked on Ordnance Survey map L 175. The following notes on Miss Lorely Pelling have been prepared for us in confidence by her late father's solicitor, now retired, who formally identified the body.

"'Lorely was independent-minded almost to the point of aggressiveness, and early on in India rebelled against being schooled for what she termed 'marriage fodder'. She was very fond of her widowed father and cared for him devotedly on his return to England until his death when she was fifty years of age.

"'Miss Pelling was sole beneficiary under the Brigadier's will. Assessment for Death Duties on the estate was complicated and prolonged. Throughout the proceedings Miss Pelling expressed a measure of disdain for all parties necessarily involved, proving regrettably uncooperative during assessment for probate, and finally a presumptive valuation was agreed with the authorities by my partners.

"'From the time of her father's death Miss Pelling withdrew from a number of charitable services in which she had been voluntarily engaged part-time and became progressively a recluse. She took to poultry-farming and even bred from two Large White prize sows, with the assistance of a simple-minded boy from the nearby cottages once part of the estate; she also practised organic arable farming on a small scale.

"'With increasing age she became less capable of hard physical work, finally selling off the livestock and some of the unprofitable land. All dwellings on the estate had been parcelled off during her father's lifetime. She did, however, retain some rough shooting and a few acres near the Hall which by then she had turned into a refuge for stray cats. Farlowes Wood, in which she was so sadly found shot, was an extremity of her land, the boundary being marked by the triple-wire fence below the property now owned by Mr Franklin Welch, whose house—Farlowes—was once the Home Farm of the Malmsmead estate. The precise extent of the existing estate can be ascertained from my sometime partners.

'"Over recent years communications from various government departments including the Inland Revenue, the Ministry of Agriculture, the DoE and the DSS were persistently ignored by Miss Pelling. Complaints of her increasing eccentricity were passed to my partners and several attempts were made to persuade her to use our facilities to negotiate with the authorities. Eventually, after summonses had been issued for non-payment of local authority rates and Income Tax, my partners were successful in obtaining limited powers of attorney to settle outstanding debts, and a single large sum was deposited with them in Trust by Miss Pelling for this express purpose.

'"To our general consternation this money was presented entirely in treasury notes of medium and large denomination, which fact may, despite my partners' utter discretion in the matter, have formed some basis for the subsequent rumour locally current that a considerable amount of negotiable currency was being held in Malmsmead Hall. It is my personal belief that this was a completely mistaken notion and that Miss Pelling had raised the sum of money deposited for the payment of her outstanding expenses solely through the sale of art works and antique furniture from her home. My nephew, the present senior partner, expressed his serious misgivings over the probable conduct of these sales and the type of persons involved, but to no avail. Miss Pelling replied, in the only written communication ever received by us from her (I quote the entire message)—'They were only things. I do not need them. Lorely Pelling, spinster.' The letter was undated and the envelope simply addressed to *The Solicitors, Henley-upon Thames.*' "

'Nutty as a fruit cake,' DS Beaumont was heard to observe.

Yeadings glanced at him over his reading lenses. 'Perhaps you would add extra titbits gleaned from the cottagers. No need to quote sources at this point.'

The DS produced his own notes and read in a rapid monotone. 'Miss Pelling was variously described as "weird as two left boots", "With more marbles than you'd credit", "a wily old bird, but you couldn't help admiring her", and "gutsy as the worst of her old tom cats". Nobody *ever* (and this includes her labourer, who was simple) has been known to get inside the house since a few years after her father's death. A Mrs Lammas from the onetime estate cottages did her shopping and left it in an outhouse cupboard, from which she took the list every Wednesday morning. On several occasions she found other packages left in the same cupboard and believed these to be offerings from unnamed superstitious villagers who thought Miss Pelling had supernatural powers.'

There was a general titter. One of the uniform constables present marvelled, 'In this day and age!'

Yeadings asked, 'Lammas, Sergeant? Unusual name, that.'

'Yes sir. I queried it at the time. Mrs Lammas's husband was an abandoned baby dumped without identification in the parish church porch—'

'At Lammastide, August 1st, date of the original Harvest Festival,' Yeadings completed. 'My, my! A suspected witch, ancient religious feasts, and foundling cottagers: we appear to have struck a rich vein of folklore here. Go on, Sergeant.'

'Well, as the solicitor said, there was constant trouble with officials trying to get in or to get bills paid. Gas, water, telephone and electricity had all been cut off at different times. Miss Pelling had a well in the rear courtyard, and the paraffin man called once a month. But in the main it seems Miss P got up and went down with the sun, and spent most of her waking time outdoors. Her kitchen had a wood-burning stove to give hot water, and there was no shortage of dead trees to saw and chop up.

'She aimed to be self-supporting, made her own candles and even supplied the cottagers for emergencies. Used beeswax which she took herself from wild swarms in the grounds. She must have been mainly vegetarian but would shoot, skin and cook the odd rabbit to share with her cats, of which the RSPCA has rounded up twenty-three.'

'Plus my two surviving kittens,' Yeadings murmured.

'She also potted at pigeons or rabbits and she'd take a pheasant off her own land, but only in season. She kept two goats and when there was a surplus of milk she pressed it into cheese.

'Either she wore the same clothes all the time or had several versions of the one outfit—long hobble-type skirt of darkish tweed topped off with any number of sweaters and such, some of them cheap, department-store numbers and others ancient cashmere. She always looked bedraggled and frequently dirty. Outdoors she put on cut-down black wellingtons over the two pairs of thick woollen socks which were all she was thought to wear on her feet indoors. Sometimes she was observed with a green, heavy plastic apron over her costume, rather like a surgeon in the operating theatre. Outdoors she wore an old tweed fisherman's hat of murky greenish-browny-grey, and the man who described it said that her hair stuck out in tufts each side of her neck and was much the same colour. All her neighbours were agreed that she hadn't stepped outside her own grounds for at least eight years.'

'Thank you. That's a good enough picture to be going on with. Any impression of resentment against the dead woman?'

'I didn't get any.'

'Z?'

Rosemary stirred in her seat. 'The general attitude was a sort of communal pride in her eccentricity. One or two of the men wanted me to think they found her rather a joke, but to my mind it was bravado. I think she made her presence felt and they all toed the line, at least in her presence. Some of them spoke with real affection of her dead father, the Brigadier. He'd been their Squire, and he'd freed their tied cottages, probably for a song. I think, partly because of him, they respected the daughter, and certainly everyone seemed very shocked at her violent death. When a woman supposed out loud that she'd had an accident with her own gun she was shouted down at once. Those who knew about such matters said she was competent and careful.'

'Did either of you sound them out about the possibility of suicide?'

'I did.' Beaumont grinned ruefully. 'Nearly got thrown out on my ear each time. Just not on the cards.'

'But at medium range it couldn't be suicide, anyway,' DC Silver objected, 'and even if she'd rigged it, someone would have had to come along afterwards, dismantle the device and take away the gun.'

'It's certainly the least likely of our three options.' Yeadings looked round his team and waved the next sheaf of papers. 'So now we come to the preliminary path. report. If you'll drop the screen, Jim, and one of you sees to the windows, I'll show some stills of the death scene. Later we hope to prepare a video, in which some of you will be asked to take part.'

There was some shuffling of chairs while things were got ready. 'Right? First, Farlowes Wood, looking north-east from Battels Lane entrance.' *Click.* 'The path leading towards the main road, body just visible, left background.' *Click.* 'The body as approached from the path.' *Click.* 'Close-up of boots. Notice how they have come loose by a good two inches.'

'Blasted backwards out of them,' said a knowledgeable voice from the front.

'Torso. Arms outflung. Head back. Notice the extent of shot wounds, particularly in the neck and upper chest. Spread circular, not displaying much of the elliptical drop you'd get with long range. Face untouched but for one entry under the left cheekbone. Nothing below the waist.' *Click.* 'Trunk of beech tree behind and to one side of body and in almost direct line of fire.'

Yeadings let them linger over this one, taking in the entry points of the shot ringed with chalk and the rigid white-faced ruler showing height above ground.

'How tall was the dead woman?' one cautious PC asked.

'Five feet two inches.'

There was a rumble of quiet comment, apparently assenting on assumptions. Without commentary Yeadings nodded for the next slide to come up. It showed the distance between the hatted head and the left side of the tree-trunk, the metre rule now horizontal.

Yeadings gestured towards a ground plan drawing-pinned to a peg-board. 'You've all had a chance to examine that. So, there it all is. Just as our SOCO saw it. Now tell me what happened.'

An invitation to put one's foot right in it up to the thigh, but it all fitted together so well. It had to be what it seemed.

A bright boy near the front waded in. 'By the spread of shot I'd say she received a blast from medium to long range, face on. It blew her back, out of her boots, and sprayed one side of the tree at chest level.'

'So?'

'So by extending the line of fire backwards you get the level at which the gun was held. And since the field out there is a slope, taking the killer as of average height, that gives the point at which the killer stood. Which may or may not be where the discarded cartridge case was found.' The man was perspiring with the effort and consciousness of Yeadings's unyielding stare on him.

'Any comments on that?'

There seemed to be cautious agreement.

'Right. Well, I propose showing you only one slide from the mortuary slab. Then you may appreciate what we're up against.' *Click.*

Harshly lit, the outline of the woman's thin shoulders showed white against some grey background. The body lay face up as she had been found, but now the clothes had been removed. A sheet was decorously drawn up to cover the waist. The arms, previously outflung, were now folded across the flattened breasts.

On each forearm and twice through one wrist, always on the outer side, were the small, dark holes where shot had entered.

'This is one slide that really matters,' Yeadings told them sombrely. 'In a way, the others are pure theatre. You see, the stripped body shows clearly that when shot the woman had her arms folded across her lower ribcage. Two of those entry marks correspond with re-entry into the chest.'

He looked round at them and pressed the point home. 'What we've been presented with in Farlowes Wood was a rearranged crucifon corpse.'

FOUR

His minor bombshell had the effect Yeadings was hoping for. Every officer present came up mentally on his toes, aware that the case had grown a new dimension. Someone, probably the person responsible for the death, was treating them as wallies, would be pursued now in a more alerted and vengeful manner.

However much one stressed that hunting a killer should be an exercise outside red emotion, the personal element was always present. Whenever they looked for the attacker of a child or of a fellow-policeman, Yeadings became conscious of the added keenness in his men which carried them beyond normal limits of energy and patience. Now he'd fed them a challenge; they'd glimpsed a killer's face smirking at their implied incompetence.

He hadn't wanted his team, even unconsciously, to feel the case was less vital because the victim was old, soon for the push anyway. For himself, he admitted a distinct empathy with the dead woman. She might have been a headache to some, but he admired her single-mindedness, her simplification of life, paring away all inessentials whatever the pressures intended to divert her. No one had the right to cut off a courageous spirit by violence.

'Yes,' he said, surveying the watchful faces, 'Chummie is a devious bugger. We aren't dealing with a dead duck here.

'Right then, the preliminary path. report: I'll summarize. The body was female, aged between seventy-five and eighty years of age: spare, but in Dr Littlejohn's words—"a singularly healthy corpse". The cause of death is complex, given here as a combination of shock, hypothermia, and asphyxia due to the inhalation of her own blood following injuries to the neck from the entry of lead shot. The time of death somewhere between 2.0 p.m. and 6.0 p.m. on Saturday, into which period comes the use of shotguns on Franklin Welch's adjoining land.

'I'd like you to note the exemplary caution of the pathologist's claim. He has not mentioned any discharge of firearms, because there were no powder burns and he has not come across a weapon.

'However, we may assume the shot entered the woman's body from a shotgun rather than a pea-shooter, but it is no more than an assumption until we have the actual weapon in our hands. And I'll remind you that lead shot does not, like a metal-cased bullet, carry the signature of the gun it was fired from. We have a single used cartridge case which may or may not have come from the gun the killer employed, and we may in time make that useful connection, but since the cartridge was of common manufacture it can form no positive link between any such gun and the shot found in the corpse.

'As shown in the post-mortem slide, entry wounds on the outsides of the arms indicate that the arms were crossed over the lower ribcage at the time of the shooting, so we must question *why* the body was later rearranged. Also how far such rearrangement went. So our first priority is further expert examination of the area the body was found in, and that PDQ before the rains wash all evidence away. SOCO has made a good attempt at roofing over the immediate area, but because of the trees it isn't entirely waterproof. For most of you, under DS Beaumont temporarily acting as DI, it's the open fields and buildings in an area marked on the handout sketch-maps.

'From approximately 10.30 hrs, after I've had a word with the ACC, I can be reached at Malmsmead Hall. Until then messages for me to WDC Zyczynski there. Briefing at the Incident Room caravan tomorrow, same time. If no questions, dismiss.'

He caught Beaumont's eye and pushed a page of the pathologist's report towards him. One passage was high-lighted, and it wasn't one he'd made public. 'Just glance at this before you go, then pass it to Z.'

The DS read quickly and frowned. 'Nasty. How long do you think... ?'

Yeadings shook his head to discourage questions. 'Bear it in mind when you're searching. Drop Z out at the Hall, will you? And check Allocation have sent a replacement PC along. Have to go now. I'm late.' He nodded and departed.

'Right, Z?' Beaumont clearly wanted to be on his way.

'Can you bear to wait by the supermarket while I pick up provisions?'

She saw his look of scorn gathering and got in first. 'The Hall's cupboards could have only dandelion-and-burdock tea. Not quite the Super's cuppa.'

'Just the minimum, then.'

She rushed off, grabbed four mugs, sugar, biscuits, ground and instant coffee, tea-bags and powdered milk, then had to queue at the check-out behind doddering pen-sioners counting out the correct amount in elusive coins. When she rejoined the DS he was in no mood to suffer questions. Just the same, she ventured to ask, 'Who do you think will be drafted in to replace DI Mott?'

His face went more wooden. The Pinocchio resemblance was quite uncanny. 'One's as bad as another.'

She settled back, checking her seat-belt. Resentment of the outsider: she'd had to face it herself in their previous case together. Now it seemed that the team had mostly accepted her, although Beaumont would never forgive her for being a woman. The weak link, and all that; blow the fact that a woman could do some things better and provide a differently angled view. She'd be damned if she was going to stay shut, though, when her opinion and his differed materially.

'I can walk from Farlowes Wood,' she offered quickly, as the turning came up for Malmsmead Hall.

'I want a look at the place myself.'

Well, of course he would. He was going to push the acting-DI role as far as possible, if only to make whoever took over Mott's place feel inadequate.

Lucky Mott. He and Paula would be in Italy now, scorching up the Sunshine Highway in an Avis rented car, bound for Tuscany. She shivered, looking out at the blowing rain mixed with gritty leaves and the trailing branches of the headgerows whipping and bowing as the wind worked up to gale force. The lanes were pot-holed and puddled. From what she'd gathered of Malmsmead Hall, it would be total squelch.

Across a field to the right she counted the rear of the five cottages they had visited the day before. 'Gash, Greening, Lammas, Medlam and Barrow,' she identified the families. The dead woman had been their old Squire's daughter, and some of them were half-convinced she was a witch. Perhaps in fact less of a black witch or a white witch, Rosemary considered, than a green witch, a conservationist who actually practised the simple life, even though it made a hermit of her. Drove neither car nor tractor, protected cats but used a gun on wildlife. Potty, some thought. Did she? Well, the house should help her decide that.

She reserved judgement until they were inside and then she was gratified to see that the uniform man left on duty

had made free with the wood stocks and the kitchen stove
was pulsating with heat.

All the reported cats had been removed and their collection of boxes and baskets stacked at one end of the scullery. There lingered a dank odour of elderly feline mixed
with canned fish and the bitter scent of some unfamiliar
herb which hung in dried bunches from the smoky ceiling
beams.

Rosemary followed Beaumont on his tour of the downstairs rooms. He pulled back some of the heavy curtains, in
places tearing the worn fabric from its rings so that they
sagged more sadly than before daylight was let in.

'Only *things*,' the girl repeated in her head. Yes, that attitude had been genuine enough. Miss Pelling had not set
great store by any of the elaborate pieces of furniture still
scattered about the rooms. Marks in the carpets showed
where others had gone missing, and in one or two places the
carpets themselves had been removed.

Upstairs all curtains were left open, and dust lay thick
everywhere except in one bedroom and the adjoining bathroom. But it didn't appear that Miss Pelling had slept up
here. It was a man's room, furnished with old pieces of dark
oak. The high bed was a tester with a heavy brocade cover-
let. In one corner stood the steel locker where the Brigadier's gun had been kept. Arranged on an oval linen cloth
on the dressing-table was a man's toilet set. The old-
fashioned silver-backed brushes were quite untarnished.
Beneath them the drawers ran out stiffly but were full of
laundered shirts and underwear scented with sprigs of rosemary.

'Your namesake,' Beaumont said laconically.

'For remembrance. It's rather sad, isn't it? These are only
things too, but they mattered to her because of who'd once
used them.'

'All past. No future,' said Beaumont irritably.

The girl disagreed. What about the cats and the vegetable plot? But she didn't argue. She followed the DS down the branched mahogany staircase. 'I'll leave you, then,' he said abruptly. 'Check your handset works from outside here.'

She watched his car disappear round the curve of the drive and went back in. Because the duty constable had taken over the kitchen she set up the library for Yeadings as an office. A couple of miles away they would be parking the Incident Room caravan on the main-road side of Farlowes Wood, because it was a violent death, even if not yet proved a homicide. She supposed she was lucky that her second case with the Yeadings Team promised to be as challenging as the first.

There was plenty of time to familiarize herself with the house and draw a ground plan before the Superintendent arrived grim-faced. 'You made good time from Kidlington, sir,' she greeted him.

'The ACC came down to meet me,' he said shortly. 'Insists we take on another DI, but I've asked for one from Bicester. He'll be along this afternoon.'

Rosemary considered this. 'Someone special, sir?'

'No.' He waggled his famous bushy black eyebrows, relaxing into better humour as the wood-burning stove thawed him out. 'Do I have to spell it out, Z?'

'Anonymous outsider,' she suggested, and was rewarded with a low chuckle.

'Want the best out of everyone, don't I? Competition shouldn't harm any of you.'

Poor beggar, she thought. She'd try to accept him, whoever he was, and however the others froze him out.

She set about making the first brew-up of coffee, good
and strong, with a couple of ginger nuts in the saucer for the
Super.

'Put your expenses in to Mr Atkinson,' he said, rising
satisfied. 'Now our first job is to find where she left her papers, if she had any. It sounds self-evident that everyone has
something in the nature of records, but given her reluctance to correspond even with her own solicitor, it could be
we'll find very little.'

'There'd be birth certificates, her father's death certificate and so on, surely, sir?'

'Why, Z? She knew she was alive and she knew he was
dead. What use would paper proof be to her? She could
have used them as spills to light the stove. We have an original mind here, don't forget.'

She supposed he could be right, but it was weird. 'There's
no desk, just this table. Two shallow drawers, unlocked.
One contains her cartridges, a whole box and half an opened
one. The other has a Bible.'

'Ah. Shall we start there?' He accepted it from her hand.
'Thought so.' He held it slantwise to the oil lamp. 'It had
births and deaths recorded on the first blank page, but that's
been torn out. Nothing but a vague imprint of handwritten
letters on the title-page behind it. Now, I wonder why?'

'The information inessential, so she used the page as a
spill, the way you suggested before? Or the book might
originally have belonged to another family...'

'It's a Bible, Z. People of her generation won't easily
mutilate it, even if our sacrilegious young believe it's the
ideal paper for rolling joints. No, it could be worth bringing up the impressions, seeing how far back she could trace.
The Bible itself is pretty old; look at that tooling. Perfect of
its kind.'

'Where else do we look, sir? Among the books?'

'All seven hundred or so of them. In them, among them, behind them, and under the shelves, and under the floorboards too. I'll leave you to it. I'm going myself to look over the old Brigadier's room. She seemed more careful of his relics than her own.'

Rosemary started, as it seemed logical to her, at the extreme top of the bookcases just left of the door. Which meant delay while she called the constable to inquire if he had come across a ladder. There was one, below the disused hayloft in a rear barn. The PC carried it in and wedged it in position for her just under the ceiling. 'Not too trustworthy,' was his dubious comment. 'Look at them holes there. Them's woodworm. Better you than me, miss, with my weight.'

She had completed the first wall and was a third of the way through the next when she heard Yeadings calling. 'Z, if you want any lunch, better come along now. The mobile canteen's serving hot stuff at Farlowes Wood.'

'Nothing's turned up yet,' she told him, brushing dust off her skirt before she took her seat in the Rover.

'It doesn't often happen,' Yeadings marvelled, 'that we've an identified adult body with no address book or list of phone numbers. And I don't think we'll find any, because she had no truck with phones or letters. This living as an island certainly adds to our problems. What was the name of the woman who did her shopping? She would know if Miss Pelling ever asked for stamps or stationery.'

'Mrs Lammas.'

'Ah yes. Wife of the harvest foundling.'

'Widow, it seems. He died fairly recently.'

'How? Not another classic case of lead poisoning, I hope?'

'Tetanus, actually. I don't know how he contracted it, but apparently he hadn't been immunized and they let an infected cut go too far before he was rushed to hospital. The next-door neighbours told me. Mrs Lammas is still very shocked and they warned me not to mention him to her.'

'Right. It's in the full report, I take it?'

'Yes, sir.'

'Pity we have to hold back there. We'll need to ask her quite a number of questions. How does she respond?'

'Doesn't care for the police at all, really.'

'Country people are inclined to blacken us along with gamekeepers, but that prejudice shouldn't apply round here. Apparently there weren't any restrictions on taking the odd rabbit or bird in season. Not on the dead woman's land, anyway. Incidentally I unearthed her father's shotgun upstairs, an over-and-under double-barrelled 12-bore. Not been used in decades, probably. Too heavy for a woman. Sent it to Huntingdon with the others.'

They separated for lunch, Rosemary taking her steaming plate of sloppy mince with mash and carrots to eat under the waterproof extension attached to the canteen's rear while Yeadings retired to the caravan to consult with DS Beaumont. She encountered a soaked and grumbling little group from Reading uniform branch, among whom was PC Finlay, her sometime partner on the beat. 'How goes it, then?' they demanded simultaneously.

'Makes a change,' said Finlay. 'A bit sloshy underfoot, but we've had worse downpours in town. I don't mind it out here. The smells are better than petrol fumes.'

Since Finlay appeared to be into counter-pollution, she confided to him some of the late Miss Pelling's preferences for the simple life. They agreed it was going a bit far but the general direction was right.

'And the job?'

Rosemary crossed her fingers. 'As the man said when he fell past the thirteenth-floor windows, "All right so far."'

Actually there's much the same opportunity for landing flat on your face.'

'I like a quieter life, me,' Finlay confided. 'Should've taken it up a hundred years back, been a cosy village copper.'

She wasn't deceived. If Fin didn't display open envy over her shift sideways into CID it was because her pulling out of uniform meant he was in a better position for the next set of stripes. She hoped he'd get it; it wasn't comfortable, feeling that she'd walked out on a partner.

'Right, Z!' came Yeadings's shout from the caravan. As she settled back into the Rover beside him he asked, 'Hope you avoided the canteen coffee?' And as she nodded, 'Good. I've saved myself for yours. When we've had a pot I'll leave a note for the new DI and we'll pay some more calls to the cottages.'

'Have they turned up anything new in the wood?' she inquired.

'Yes and no. You saw the highlighted passage in the prelim report from Dr Littlejohn?'

'That the woman had remained alive for some hours after being shot? Grisly, isn't it?'

'In view of that I asked SOCO to consider the shooting having taken place elsewhere. After all, people use that woodland path to get from the cottages to the bus. Mostly on weekdays, it's true, but someone could have gone through on a Saturday afternoon. In which case she would have been found earlier.'

'We got a solid no on that before. Do we have to ask the cottagers again?'

'Among other questions, yes.'

'So did SOCO come up with anything?'

'Oh yes. They've been busy picking shot out of the beech tree behind the body.' Yeadings slowed to avoid a dripping group of Friesians which were being driven from one field to its opposite, across their path.

So she *must* have been shot where she was found, Rosemary reckoned. She watched the last Friesian stiffen the base of its tail and let drop a steaming pancake just short of the Rover's offside front tyre. 'I suppose they're the kind that have to go in for an extra midday milking,' she said hurriedly to cover the incident.

'Shouldn't think so,' said Yeadings with a lazy smile. 'Not this lot. Bullocks.'

She felt the colour rising up her neck, staining her cheeks.

When he next spoke Yeadings seemed to have forgotten the bovines and was back with the dead body. 'The interesting thing is that although the shot are all of the same size there seem to be rather too many.'

'Two barrels discharged?' she asked, unsure where it led.

He answered vaguely. 'Possibly one of them deliberately aimed at the tree afterwards, to link it with the body.'

'I see.' She wasn't sure that she did entirely. But she had started to wonder if the Old Man had taken her along to act as a bimbo Dr Watson.

'And then there wasn't any seepage of blood into the ground where the body was lying. In view of there being some exit wounds from the fleshy parts and the fact that the woman lived on for some hours after the shooting, I think that we have to accept she was attacked somewhere else. All our findings to date are no more than the props of deliberate stage management.'

'But at least you know that!'

He turned his head to look at Z. Her instant rise to defence of the team's progress was so passionate, so young. He smiled. 'I know it, you know it, we know it. But we don't have to mention that we do. I want all inquiries to continue on the public assumption that the lady was shot in Far-

lowes Wood between 2.0 p.m. and 6.0 pm. on Saturday—
her likely time of death. Then it will be interesting to see who
extends an alibi to cover an earlier time and a different
place.'

'And meanwhile we go on looking for where it actually
happened.'

'We go on looking for whatever is there, expected or not.
It's a question of where to fix the frame. But the dead
woman didn't stray far afield. I think this investigation will
boil down to sifting cottagers' gossip and a minute examination of the whole Malmsmead terrain, indoor and out.'

FIVE

THE BOY LAY on his stomach, face cupped in hands, and regarded the TV screen with blistering scorn. The video cover had depicted as nasty a scene of slithery outer-space lifeforms as any artists' imagination could provide. The tape's contents were something else. Drivelling talk between this middle-aged actor with a belly hanging over his belt and this girl, a real dog. And then the usual sweaty panting and wrestling over a bed. When the window burst in and the action was supposed to start there was just this giant Dunlopillo paw waving about with the claws not even articulated. You'd get more kick out of stuffed dinosaurs at the Natural History Museum!

At the phone's insistent ringing he crawled across at carpet level, gnashing his teeth and growling to help the video along. With eyes glued to the screen and zapper at the ready he spoke his number into the receiver.

'Stu? Rory here. You doing anything?'

'Watching a video. It's putrid. What about you?'

'I had a packed lunch made up for two. Chicken and pickles and trifle. I thought you might like . . .'

'It's awful out. You wanna come here?'

'Are you on your own?' Cautious suspicion.

'Betcha. No dumbo adults, no squalling kids. Pick up some 7 Up on the way, hey?'

'Can do. *Can*, d'you get it? See you in half an hour, then.'

Stuart put the receiver back and zapped off the video. He looked round the room and wondered how on earth they could pass the time. At Welch's there had been everything;

horses, scooters, go-karts, guns. And Rory, despite all that, must be bored out of his mind. Or else he'd never have rung here.

Funny, that. There must be half a dozen other guys free this week who could offer better entertainment. Why pick on one Stuart Beaumont, sharing with him just a brief past of toggle-totting, learning knots and orienteering?

Rory had attended a private prep school while Stuart was mainstream herd. Six weeks of boarding at Stowe had widened that gap. At Saturday's 'rally' Rory hadn't shown any special interest in renewing acquaintance, so why now?

Trying to make up for yesterday morning?—Rory having shown him the door so abruptly, embarrassed by his arrival while the family wasn't properly up. Stuart didn't think it was that. Rory had been on edge then, seemed keen to keep him at a distance from his parents. Had they taken against him? Something he'd done the previous afternoon got up their noses? Or some clash between fathers when his dad came to collect him? It wouldn't be the first time people had sheered off when they knew he was Son of Filth.

But since the rally there'd been that body found. In the wood bordering on Welch's fields. Stuart recalled now the way Rory had reacted when he casually—OK, overdoing the blasé thing a bit—mentioned his dad had dropped him off on his way to investigate a murder. Sort of taut, and green round the gills. Mebbe murder really got to him. Mebbe that was why he'd jumped at the idea of coming over. He wanted more of the same. Well, Stu could supply that; lay on a few gory details, beat the pulp press at handing out the shivers.

He grinned at the prospect, rubbed his hair up into a tousled shock, undid a couple of shirt buttons, and went to check on the fridge.

'BARROW, MEDLAM, LAMMAS, Greening and Gash,' Rosemary Zyczynski reeled off from memory, as the Rover nosed
out of the Hall's drive and they glimpsed the distant cottages' rears through gaps in the lane's high hedge. Momentarily they were cut off from the gusting wind, but a forty-
degree turn with open fields falling away to either side
brought the buffeting back. Overhead, loose low cloud
raced darkly past like bonfire smoke, and a crow cawed its
protest, blown raggedly almost on to their windscreen. They
had to regain the main road before turning into Battels
Lane.

'We'll start at this end,' Yeadings decided. 'There's a
gateway I can leave the car in, if I remember it right. Can
you recite those names arse-about-face?'

'Er, Gash, Greening, Lammas, Bedlam and Marr...
Sorry. Medlam and Barrow.'

'You may well have been right the first time.' He ran the
car up on the far-side bank, avoiding the ditch, and abandoned it diagonally across a ramp of compacted earth above
a culvert. As he eased out of his seat he remarked of the
thistles richly growing beyond the five-barred gate. 'Don't
think anyone's in a rush to work that field.'

They walked on and were buffeted towards the first pair
of semis—grubby yellow-washed pebble-dash. The Gash
half had 'The Briars' hand-painted in black on a varnished
board on the low gate, but there were no roses in the tiny
front garden. Only knee-high storm-battered grass and the
remains of a frame for runner beans.

The arthritic knocker needed more force to move it than
Rosemary possessed. The Superintendent obliged, heaving
it up and forcing it back with a resounding crash. Somewhere inside the house it was answered by a thin cry of dis-
may.

With a wicked smile Yeadings moved back to stand behind the policewoman. A slow shuffling of carpet slippers was followed by a fumbling for the lock, but the bright little eyes in the weasely face peering up at them were lively enough. 'Oh, it's you again, duck,' the old man said, and showed toothless gums. 'Who's yer friend?'

Yeadings recognized it was no occasion for standing on ceremony, mildly accepting the role of the brawn sent to accompany WDC Zyczynski's brain. Old Mr Gash was willing but not particularly informative. He hadn't used the path through Farlowes Wood for over four years. 'Since me arches took bad,' as he explained. 'It's me feet and me hands, see? But I'm not deaf. No call to go knocking me house down. Another time jes' call through the letter-box like the girlie did before, and I'll hear you.'

Despite being housebound, Mr Gash did have his uses, however. His most comfortable chair was in the window of the upstairs back room, and his favourite pastime was bird-watching, for which he used an excellent if elderly pair of German field-glasses ex-First World War. 'Me old Dad got them off a Jerry,' he explained. ''Ave a go, duck.'

Rosemary focused on the landscape, adjusted the screw and murmured appreciatively. Then she handed the glasses to Yeadings. Across two acres of the remains of harvested maize, the lane to Malmsmead Hall sprang up at him. The farther side was hedged, but for a distance of some twenty feet the maize-grower had set in a triple-wired fence beyond which the lane was perfectly revealed. Gash's window-seat commanded a comprehensive view of traffic approaching the dead woman's house from the direction of the main road.

'Do you see much traffic this way?' Yeadings asked in a conversational tone.

'Nuh. Real peaceful. That's why there's still a lotta birds. Me 'obby, see?' He waved towards the walls of his room which were covered with sheets of colour photographs of British wild birds. Scrawled in beside some of them were pencilled dates on which they'd been observed. A sort of diary in reverse.

'Too many magpies, mind. What with them and the squirreys, it's a bit 'ard on the little fellers' eggs. Still, old Miss Lorely she's not above peppering 'em up proper when they gets above themselves. Helps keep 'em down, see? Magpies and jays, real varmints them are. Time was I'd give a 'and. Strung a line of squirreys' tails along me garden wall when I was a youngster. A bob a tail I used ter get in them days.'

Rosemary caught a nod from Yeadings, and asked, 'Were you bird-watching Saturday?'

'Not mornings. A'rtnoon, same as ever. Saw them gulls coming in off the river. Knew there'd be a storm then. Them ain't fools.'

'And did you see any cars or bikes come or go by the lane to Miss Lorely's?'

'Only Tom Beale's old van. Delivering the cats' meat, that'd be. 'Bout 2.15. I reckoned he'd be a mite late back for the start of the football.'

'No one else?'

'Not a soul, duck.'

'I bet you were a good shot in your day,' said Yeadings reflectively.

'Still am, you should—' Old Gash stopped, but not in time.

Yeadings smiled. 'Where d'you keep it? Somewhere safe, I hope?'

The old man scowled, hedging. 'Under the floor,' he admitted at last.

'Going to show us?'

Gash stuck out his jaw.

'We don't have to make it official, this visit.'

Rosemary watched the stubborn resistance slowly dissolve. '*You* wouldn'ta made a fuss, would yah?' he asked as he shambled past her. He knelt stiffly and folded back the worn carpet beside the wall. A loose floorboard swung up on a pivot and he reached down for a carefully shrouded package. He didn't offer it to Yeadings but unwound the oiled paper himself and exposed his treasure. Rosemary realized then what the reluctance had been about. Not a shotgun at all, but an old Lee Enfield in good condition. Relic of a later war than his old Dad's. And Gash almost certainly didn't have a licence.

Yeadings examined it without touching. 'M'm. That's not quite what we're looking for. Have you any other guns?'

'Only my old beauty 'ere.'

'Right, I'll see if I can remember to report it. Got a lot on my mind at the moment. My memory's not what it was. Who knows you've got that?'

''aven't breathed a word about it, ever.'

'What about when you use it?'

Gash almost blushed. 'Carn't, can I? They'd 'ear it next door. Just aim it, and *click*. But I still got good eyes. Jes' can't get down the woods to bag the little buggers.'

'Ammo?'

Gash sighed. 'You can take it. No use to me. It's up the far end. Can you reach it, duck?'

They watched him rewrap the rifle and lower it again under the boards. Some of the life seemed to have gone out of him.

'You remember what I came about yesterday?' Rosemary asked.

'About Miss Lorely getting shot. Yus. Else I wouldn'ta shown you me rifle. Well, she's gone now, and I'm no good. Looks like those bloody magpies and squirreys 'ave won, don't it?'

He couldn't tell them of anyone who'd want to hurt the dead woman; or anyone who'd dare, as he put it; and so they turned down his offer of tea and went away.

In the next house Mr and Mrs Greening, only a decade or so younger, were disturbed from a rug-wrapped nap on either side of the empty grate. Obliged to uncover sufficiently to converse, the woman of the house went off grumbling under her breath and came back with a small two-bar electric fire. By then her spouse, a Yorkshireman uprooted in his forties and unhappily transplanted south, had assured the visitors that yes, he used the path through Farlowes Wood most days to go to the village for his paper. He took his dog, a fat Jack Russell that was eyeing Yeadings doubtfully and looked likely to yap. On Saturday, however, as luck would have it, their daughter had driven over from Slough early and picked up the paper on her way. When he did go out, after lunch, he'd taken Freddy for a run the back way.

Pressed for the route, he showed them the gate leading from his garden into the maize field. ''Round the side and out to the back lane, then through the Hall's yard, over the waste, round a field of beet and home up our lane, Battels Lane.'

'So finally coming along the bottom of Farlowes Wood? What time would that be?'

'Three-ish.'

'And did you hear any shots fired?'

'Not then. Helluva lot a bit later. Over at Welches' the kids were letting off with air rifles. Then something heavier at the end, just before they sent that flaming balloon up.'

'Yes, we heard about that. Had some reports in about a flying saucer. No shooting after that? Or during the previous night?'

'Thought I heard poachers Sat'day night,' Mrs Greening offered, not to be outdone. 'But I must of dreamt it. There was only the one lot that woke me. Could of bin a backfire.'

'Backfire nothing! What would be making a noise like that round here? She snores,' her husband explained in quiet disgust. 'Probably did an extra loud one and woke herself up. No cars or motorbikes in this lane and the road's too far away.'

'So what time would this backfire or snore have been?' Yeadings pursued.

Greening shrugged, dissociating himself.

'How would I know,' his wife demanded, 'with the clock always kept over his side of the bed?' It was obviously a long-standing cause for complaint.

'THIS IS THE ONE we have to go cannily with?' Yeadings paused with a hand on the next garden gate. Mayfield was the only detached cottage, and had minor up-market pretensions. The straight little path to the replacement front door was constructed of pink crazy paving; the downstairs windows were framed by bright green shutters with little hearts cut out at the tops; in the tiny front garden bedding plants had been regimentally drilled in a minute central oblong, but the antirrhinums, French marigolds and asters had withered where they bloomed and not been removed. A drift of brown leaves nestled in one lower corner of the doorway, balanced on the other side by scratches and the muddy marks of a dog's paws clawing at the otherwise glossy paintwork. The windowing had evidently been recent, and had devastated someone's tidy little world.

He rang the dulcet chimes, but only the dog answered, fiercely barking from some room at the house's rear. They waited patiently and when no one came Yeadings rang again. Rosemary lifted the letter-box flap and squinted through. 'She's in, but she doesn't want us to know.'

At the third ring the dog's barking redoubled and as it drew breath they could hear a voice hissing at it to stay shut. 'Maybe we should leave her in peace,' Rosemary murmured.

'Let her know there are troubles outside her own,' the Superintendent disagreed. 'There's no better cure.'

He just might have something there, but she doubted it. In her experience grief was always capable of expanding to fit further miseries. However, the jangling of a chain being fitted, and the door opening on it sufficiently for the woman to peer out, indicated that they had at last worn down her resistance. 'What is it?'

Having no hat to raise, Yeadings made use of his thick, black eyebrows. 'Mrs Lammas? Police.' He gave her their names and mentioned the matter of the late Miss Lorely Pelling.

'I don't know anything,' the woman said, 'I've already told you people all I can,' and made to shut the door. It took the toe of the Superintendent's muddied shoe and a reminder of citizens' duties to dissuade her.

A disagreeable look settled on her face. 'I suppose you'd better come in, then.'

They followed her back down the narrow passage, Rosemary closing the door behind. Then there was some hesitation over where she should take them. The decision seemed to throw the woman. Seeing this, Yeadings pressed open the door he stood wedged against and they all went into a small, square sitting-room. Long, unlined curtains at the rear window had not been opened and in the resultant twilight the untidy room had a hopeless air. The busy-patterned wallpaper seemed recent, as were the chintz covers on the chairs, but the place was in disorder as though someone had broken in and deliberately sacked it. Three separate trays stood on furniture or floor with unfinished meals. The television screen was smashed and glass shards lay on the carpet nearby.

'Are you here alone?' Rosemary asked quietly. 'Isn't there someone who could come and stay, just for a while?'

'No one I'd care to have,' said the woman savagely. Anger, it seemed, was her only live alternative to deadly misery. Her flat, rather square face was blotched, the stringy, blonde hair standing out in tufts as though her hands had been tugging through it. Right behind her, as a mockery, hung a close-up wedding photograph. Considerably younger, it was almost unrecognizably the same face smiling out, framed in white veil, carefully made up. Perhaps the picture's glass had survived the woman's furious outburst only because of her dead husband's proud presence alongside.

'We heard about your loss,' Yeadings said simply. 'It must have been a terrible shock for you.'

The woman's face crumpled and muscles in her neck stood out in cords. 'He was—only—thirty-nine! It's so *unfair!*'

With shock Rosemary realized that the widow must be much the same age. She had taken her for ten or fifteen years older. But with her bleached hair tidied and the lines of grief removed, yes, it was a comparatively young face above the angular figure. The summer dress she wore was densely patterned with roses, and for warmth she had covered it with an over-large khaki anorak, possibly her dead husband's. Whatever pride she had once shown in home and person was gone. She clung on to her present derangement as immutably as earlier she must have devoted herself to outward pretensions.

'Although it seems we can't help *you*,' Yeadings was saying, dead level, 'I am asking you to help us. This is a terrible thing that has happened to one of your neighbours, and the sooner we know just how it happened, the better—and the safer—for everyone. You used to do the dead woman's shopping. I'm sure you must have been closer to her than most.'

Mrs Lammas stared at him as though what he said was quite incredible. The sound she made then was more snarl than laugh. '*Help?* Why should I help? What had that old witch ever done for us? What do my wonderful neighbours care what becomes of me now? It's too late! I don't know anything about the wicked old woman. I hope she burns in hell!'

Out again on the doorstep, Rosemary drew a deep breath and looked at Yeadings. 'I could have done without that,' he said sombrely.

'Do we notify Welfare?' Rosemary asked.

'Let's ask the next folks if they know who her doctor is. I don't think she's far off being sectioned.'

Mental Health Act, Rosemary supposed. No doubt Yeadings had it all off by heart, could quote the relevant section, page and paragraph.

But the next of the last pair of semis was empty. Mr and Mrs Medlam both worked, their neighbours the Barrows told them. The husband was a plumber and the wife worked in the garden-centre office. They usually got back about 6.20. As for this past weekend, the Barrows knew for a fact that they'd been away at his mother's from Friday night till late Sunday evening. As for poor Mrs L's state of health, that was best left to Mrs Medlam when she got home. They were sisters, their old dad having had the single cottage built in the garden so they'd both have homes when he'd gone, as he had done soon after.

'If anyone can get Bella Lammas sorted out it'll be her sister Madge,' Mrs Barrow said comfortably. 'Madge has her feet on the ground, no nonsense about her. Bella was always the fluffy one, though you wouldn't think it to meet her now. But she was real pretty as a girl, could have had any of the village lads she'd wanted, but it had to be Frank Lammas.'

'The foundling,' Yeadings prompted.

'That's right. Nothing wrong with him, mind. Everyone liked Frank, and nice-looking with it, but he hadn't any background, see? Nor money neither. Sort of adopted by the whole village, and handyman to everyone. Well, it wasn't till she'd got what she wanted that she saw the drawbacks. Always pushing him, she was. He had to do everything better than most, and only the best was good enough for her. Making up, really, for what she came to see as marrying beneath her. That's where she's got a lot of her silly ideas from.' Mrs Barrow folded her hands across her stomach with an air of finality as though that was as far as she was prepared to discuss the subject.

'Drove her old Dad into his grave,' her husband grumbled, removing his pipe from his mouth and glaring into its bowl. 'They lived together, the three of them, next door, but she had to have a house of her own. Madge was away then, learning book-keeping. So Old Alf spent all his savings on having the cottage built in his garden, then when he died coupla years later Madge got married and moved in where he'd been. Nice girl, Madge. Pity she went away this weekend. Sounds like Bella's had a real old tantrum on her own there. No good us offering to help, though. Looks down her nose at such as we.'

'That account of the Medlams squares with my visit with DS Beaumont, sir,' Rosemary told Yeadings. 'We found the house closed up, and a note left for the milkman.'

'Did you want to question *us* again?' Mrs Barrow invited largely. Everything about her was large and motherly, including her comfortably embracing voice. 'Sit you both down and have a cuppa tea, why don't you? Harry, pop and get another log for the fire, dear. They'll need a bit of warming up on such a dirty afternoon.'

Accompanied by the clattering of china, Mrs Barrow volunteered a fresh account of her finding of the body and the shock that it had been. 'Put me right off,' she told them. 'Too late for the eight o'clock, by the time I'd come back and phoned. And Mattins wasn't enough somehow, after what I'd seen. Poor old lady, if there was anything more I could tell you to help, I would.'

But for all the Barrows' encouragement, the two visitors had little more to show for the time spent there, except to learn that on Saturday morning, when Dr Lomax had tried calling on Mrs Lammas two doors along, she had sent him packing, blaming him and all his like at the hospital for not saving her Frank's life.

The Barrows had no firearms, and were sure that went for all the cottagers; they'd got on as well as most with Squire's daughter, poor soul; hadn't been through Farlowes Wood for a fortnight or more, Mr B having a second-hand Ford which they both went out in together, not either of them being much on for walking.

'Should do, I suppose,' said the lady of the house, comfortably patting her generous midriff, 'but country-born folks don't walk much for pleasure. It's like people who live at the seaside and never go down on the beach.' She urged them to call in whenever they felt so inclined, beamed on them and from her front window watched their departure as far as the bend in the lane.

SIX

BACK AT MALMSMEAD HALL the new DI from Bicester had arrived and was already getting into the paperwork in the little library. PC Carmichael, coming out at the sound of the Rover's tyres on the driveway, announced this with the relish of a gloomy carpenter announcing dry rot in the floorboards. A guileless expression almost masked his curiosity about this introduction of a foreigner from the far end of the Force.

'Good,' said Yeadings shortly. He looked up dubiously at the thin strip of sky exposed between eaves and spinney. 'There's going to be another downpour soon. Just time to have a look around outside before we lose the light. Ask DI Jenner to join us, will you, Carmichael?'

He was a thin man, looked bloodless and inquisitorial. Rosemary had to remind herself that she meant to give him every chance to get it right. Yeadings and he were making the usual male noises of greeting between superior and two-ranks-below.

'And this is Z,' the Superintendent said crisply. 'DI Jenner, WDC Zyczynski. You'll be working in harness on this case from now on. Let's all walk round the outbuildings.'

Rosemary fell in behind, unsure if she was meant to eavesdrop or not, but Yeadings wasn't in a chatty mood. He'd plunged his hands in raincoat pockets, tucked down his chin and was using eyes and ears to take stock in a positively textbook manner. Jenner gave a couple of sniffs and did likewise. There was nothing of note in the first empty barn they entered, apart from the cupboard which presumably was where shopping and offerings from the cottagers were left. Yeadings hooked it open with a ballpoint through the handle and they all gazed in at a bloody mess of offal in an old, lidded hand-basin.

'Tom Beale's offering for the cats,' Yeadings observed. 'What time did he call on Saturday, Z?'

'Just after 2.15, sir, according to Mr Gash.'

'And his wall clock was dead on time.'

'Had we better throw this stuff out, sir, seeing the cats have moved on?'

'You can bring it along. There's bound to be a spade somewhere. It's best buried, in case of rats. The message may have reached them that they've got the place to themselves now.'

She lifted the hand-basin out. It must rank as an antique, but judging from the rim the inside would be scoured and shining. She wondered if the RSPCA had done a thorough round-up, or if there was any half-wild stray lurking in hopes and ready to fly at her, spitting and scratching, when it got the scent of raw meat.

The adjoining building had once been a stable, and in the harness room the farming implements hung or stood all along one wall. Jenner reached for a spade and as he did so there was a scuffling in the loose hay piled in one of the stalls.

Yeadings spun on his heel and walked back. 'Hallo, who's this, then? What's your name, lad?'

He wasn't really a lad, Rosemary thought. The small face was too wizened. But he wasn't ever going to mature. His body as well as his mental development had halted before puberty. But the Super seemed to have used the right word, because the pixie head was nodding. 'Poor Peter, I be.'

His eyes shifted past the big detective to the other two, and now he was afraid. So many of them, standing over him; he was surrounded. He drew up his legs and crossed his arms across his thin chest, screwing his face against expected blows.

Yeadings drew back, nodding the other officer to withdraw. Rosemary caught the look he threw her and knelt down at the man's level, a few feet away. 'You must be the one who helps run Malmsmead. You're Miss Pelling's workman, aren't you?'

He looked at her between his fingers. His eyes said, 'What if I am?'

'It's not a very good day for working. Did you get anything done?'

His bottom lip quivered. 'Looked for Mother Cat. Cudden find 'er.'

Was Mother Cat what he called the Cat Woman? No; of course, the boss had found some kittens, one of them already dead. There'd been no sign of a female cat in milk.

'Have you looked everywhere?'

'Carnt go in the house. Mu'nt do that.'

'We've looked there already. All the cats have gone away.'

'Man came'n took 'em.' Poor Peter was trembling again, but now with anger. '*Ee* took the kitties.' He was scowling in the direction of Yeadings.

'To see they got milk. His family are taking care of them. When the kittens are bigger I expect you'll be able to see them.'

'Mother Cat's gone.'

'It seems like it. You were watching, then? You saw the cars come, and my friend here. Did you see Miss Pelling—Miss Lorely?'

He covered his face and was totally still. Wishing himself invisible, she thought. So there was something in the question that frightened him. Could he have witnessed what happened to her? Or even had something to do with it himself?

This was too crucial a moment to deal with alone. She looked towards Yeadings for instructions. He shook his head and she sat back on her heels.

'Do you live here, lad?' the big man asked kindly.

Poor Peter seemed puzzled. 'Yer?'

'At Malmsmead.'

'Nuh. Village, with me mum.'

'That's quite a walk, and it's starting to rain again. Would you like to go home in my car?'

His face betrayed the struggle within him. Perhaps he had been warned about invitations from strangers. And there were three of them.

'I sit next to 'er?'

'You can. My friend and I have work to do. Miss Zed will drive you.'

He seemed reassured. And, fortunately, shy with it. Rosemary was relieved. It wouldn't be easy driving in these country lanes with an unfamiliar car and batting off a lunatic sex attack simultaneously. The boss must have been satisfied the man was safe, because he wasn't the sort to hand out unnecessary risks.

'Come on, then. I just have to dig this cat food in first.' After all, she couldn't hand it to the DI, new to him and all.

'There's a vegetable garden behind that wall,' said Jenner unexpectedly. 'I had a look around before you came back. The soil's easier there than in the rest of the wilderness.'

They all set out in single file along a worn track. Yeadings, it seemed, was a bit of a gardener himself and stood taking in the dead woman's efforts with approval. He walked round to where fine drills had been half filled in. A wooden dibber lay on the path, slimy with mud.

He hunkered, gathering his raincoat ends in carefully. 'I rather think,' he said, 'something bigger than seed vegetables has been buried here. And recently.'

They looked where he pointed. The soil had been flattened over an area some two feet square. 'No boot marks,' Jenner appreciated. 'Must have used that board to level off.'

'Sir? This spade. Two of us have already handled it. Maybe it had dabs.' Z wasn't too happy pointing this out.

'Blade quite clean, though. Must have been used before the rains came, and rubbed off afterwards—if it is the same spade. Well, instead of speculating, we'd better take a look what's down there. If neither of you is a gardener I'll have a go myself.'

Despite the drizzle, Yeadings removed his raincoat and handed it to Jenner in exchange for the spade. He edged its blade into the soil seven or eight times to mark out the area, then started gingerly working towards the centre.

'Ah, something here. Quite near the surface.'

It was the end of some stiff material like rubberized cotton. No, plastic. Shiny green, they saw, as Jenner crouched and wiped the soil away.

'It seems to be wrapping something; smallish though. Hang on, it's coming free.'

Yeadings lifted the bundle out on to the ground, carefully unwrapped it, and Poor Peter's anguished cry came at the very moment they realized what lay there.

'*Mother Cat!*'

It was barely more than a dark lump of bloody fur. 'Run over?' Rosemary suggested, sickened.

'Oh no. These are shotgun wounds. And that's what holed this too.' Yeadings held up a corner of the green plastic apron.

'We know now why the dead woman had her arms across her chest when she was shot. She was carrying this cat, and wearing the apron too.'

POOR PETER'S DISTRESS called for a slight change of plan. In the event Jenner drove him home in his own car, with Rosemary giving what comfort she could on the back seat.

'Back off for the present,' Yeadings had advised. 'Have a word with his mother, Z. Inspector, leave it to the women, eh?'

'Do we come back here afterwards?' Jenner demanded.

'Yes. I may be gone by then, but there's plenty for you to catch up on. Z can write up her notes in the library. Later, when you've dropped her off you'd better go and check on your lodgings. Chief Inspector Atkinson will have given you the address? Right; away with you, then. Oh, and if either of you lies awake at night, give some thought to the matter of keys. Keys and the new lock the dead woman had fitted.'

When he'd singed PC Carmichael's ears for not having observed Poor Peter lurking in the grounds he rang Reading about having the garden thoroughly checked over, collected his possessions from the library and set off for relative civilization and a copy of the Yellow Pages.

There was only one locksmith advertising in Henley. Yeadings ordered a DC to go and question him; checked there was nothing new in from Beaumont, and drove home as heavy mists closed the evening in. The wind had dropped and on the car radio a weather-forecaster was hedging all his bets on what was to follow tomorrow.

WAITING IN THE CAR, Jenner was chewing at the inside of his cheeks as Rosemary reappeared in the oblong of light from the doorway. A few more murmured words with the simple man's mother and then she was getting into the car beside him, reaching for the seat-belt.

'Well?'

'Nice little woman, Mrs Howell; anxious. Peter hadn't been home since Saturday morning. He's stayed out nights before, always somewhere at Malmsmead; but in view of the killing, and the weather, she was half out of her mind. She's as close to him as anyone can get, but he doesn't communicate freely. We'll have to wait a while before we can question him.'

'That's not your decision to make. I'll see them both in the morning. Superintendent Yeadings should have tackled him on the spot, while he was soft.'

Rosemary flushed. 'Mr Yeadings—has a way with simple people.'

'That may be all right back at base, but we're the ones who have to carry the can—*and* sort out the worms.' His long face displayed a sudden tic at the extended imagery. 'Superintendents ought to ride desks and leave this sort of thing to the men.'

'And women.'

He darted a quick, chilling glance at her. 'Lib, are you? I've nothing against women, provided they pull their weight. Pity it's not a man's weight, that's all.'

She sat back and stared expressionlessly ahead at the softly flicking wipers and the rhythmic remisting of the glass. She had nothing against *outsiders*, either. But if he went on the way he'd started she would have to keep reminding herself. Sheer repetition might eventually bring total conviction.

RORY WELCH HAD BEEN as good as his word about the packed lunch; better, in fact, because he'd lifted two fours of beer from his father's cache and in the course of the afternoon they had made several trips to the fridge for a chilled can. He'd also picked up three or four video cassettes, all of them new to Stuart but, surprisingly, they'd spent most of the afternoon talking, supine on the floor, heads on cushions, their legs—minus shoes—up the wallpaper.

Rory had given him the lowdown on being a new boy at Stowe. Stuart had responded with an equally cynical account of living under the same roof as two women, one a pensioner granny. They agreed life could be pretty shitty if you weakened. They, however, were made of sterner stuff.

When mention was made of Saturday's rally Rory was quite scathing about his father's motives in throwing it. 'Still, it was that or share a Hallowe'en party with Amanda and her squeaky little playmates. She's got that tonight, so I'll be over at Alec's, while he sees they don't set light to each other with their pumpkin candles.'

'He looks after your horses?'

'And lives in a flat over the stables. Mother's horses, actually. She hunts. My father always says he's too busy.'

'But?'

'Doesn't care for riding, I suppose. Sea-sick in the saddle or something. I used to like a good gallop but I'm not mad about the beasts; not in the sloppy way girls get over their ponies.'

Privately Stuart thought Rory was lucky to get the chance of any kind of transport. It was all he could do to scrounge a lift in his father's car; his mother was always talking about buying one but it never materialized. Until he was old enough for a motorbike it was leg-power all the way.

'It was a bit thick having to be picked up at the end,' he declared loftily. 'I could've biked back.'

'And do your dad out of a noggin? No, that's the paterkins-materkins socializing bit.' Rory sounded forebear-

ingly amused. Then he sat up, chucked out his chest and
made a wide, froggy mouth, instantly reminding the other
boy of his father. A practised impersonation, it had to be;
the voice was clarety rich: 'Ask 'em back for a noggin at
seven. That'll make sure the little buggers all clear off at a
reasonable hour.'

Rory grinned and became himself again. 'Then the old-
ies hang around, wittering. Man, you should hear them.
*'Just the one quince to five Bramleys, dear. Absolute am-
brosia.'* (A piercing falsetto.) *'Told him where to get off,
what? Heh, heh!'* (Portly and self-satisfied rumble.) *'Fah,
fah too tall a hawse foh Gwegowy, dahlin'!'*—(Sex indeterminate, but definitely a chinless wonder.) *'So I pushed 'im
for another three thou—'*—(Strident and flat-vowelled,
reeking of used cars.)

'I say, that's pretty good! Do my dad.'

Rory's angelic face wrinkled. 'Can't. I never met him. He
came too early, went too soon.'

'That's him. No social graces. Same as me.'

'A copper.'

'Acting Detective-Inspector.'

'Working on this murder. It is a murder, isn't it?'

'Brother! Is it *not?*' Stuart began with relish to gild the
mortuary lilies, none the less mischievously for the growing
conviction that Rory's main motive for today's visit was to
pump him on that very subject. Well, let him pin back his
luggies. He was about to receive a load of hi-fi codswallop.

'THAT YOU, MIKE?' Nan Yeadings sang out from the
kitchen as she heard his key in the lock.

He came through, rubbing his damp hair and grinning. 'It
had better be. How's today been?'

'It had its moments.' As she transferred cake mixture to
greased tin and he peered in the basket for the kittens' pro-

gress, she gave him the rundown; her car's suspected slow puncture. Sally's new daub at art class. 'Oh yes, and the plumber turned up eventually. He's fixed the tap temporarily, but it's liable to start dripping again soon. He says the seating has gone, whatever that is.'

'Pessimism is a plumber's stock-in-trade. I'd better take a look at the suspect tyre.'

'Leave it, Mike. I pumped it back to 24. Time enough to check it just before we turn in.'

'Good girl.'

'Good nothing. I couldn't tell what time you'd get back. Was it a grim day?'

'I'll tell you when the children are bedded.'

But there was only Luke and he was already tucked up. Sally had gone off in her witch's costume to the local Hallowe'en party. If all went well she would be staying overnight.

'Seems odd, just the two of us.' He started unfastening his shirt. 'I'll snatch a shower while you get that cake in, then we can have a drink and relax.'

When he came back, in his dressing-gown, she hummed suggestively. 'I like the Noël Coward touch. No elegant cigarette-holder?'

'I'm the Green version, non-smoker. Which reminds me, our dead lady of yesterday used to shoot wildlife on her own land, but she used cardboard cartridge cases, not the stronger plastic ones.'

'Old-fashioned.'

'Not necessarily; hers were cartridges with more or less biodegradable wads. So that they can't upset any cattle or domestic animals ingesting them later.'

'Thoughtful. She liked some animals more than others, obviously.'

'Liked cats, certainly. It seems she was shot with one in her arms.'

Nan looked startled. 'But that's obscene, Mike. Maybe the light was bad and someone mistook her...'

'And left her to die slowly some hours later, from loss of blood, hypothermia, shock and possibly asphyxia from inhaling her own blood.'

Nan took the vermouth he handed her and stared at him in disbelief. 'Fiendish. Whoever it was would surely have gone close to see what he'd dropped. Then, when he realized, you mean he *turned tail?*'

'In actual fact it appears more likely that he just removed the dead cat from her grasp, then went and buried it.'

'Leaving her to bleed to death? Mike, you've really got a nut-case there.'

'Do you think so? A nut-case.' He considered this. 'Or a simpleton? I don't know.'

'It's worrying you, isn't it? You've got someone who might have done it, and you don't want...'

'There's a simple lad. An adult really, but he'll never grow up. So of course I kept thinking of Sally, how she would see it; what a male version of her might have done on discovering what he'd actually shot; maybe not want to believe anything very bad could happen to the woman, who'd been good to him, protected him; maybe making himself believe she'd get up and brush herself off and go back home. She wouldn't be the first person peppered with shot who hadn't much more than local discomfort as a result. He'd probably no experience of dead people. But the cat was different. It was in milk, maybe sickly after giving birth. A countryman, he would have seen animals sicken and die. It was limp and bloody, so he knew it was dead, and what had to be done in that case. So he just buried it.'

'Mike, I wish it was someone other than you that had to deal with this.'

'But it still might not be him. When we dug up the cat's body he was with us. I'd swear it was a shock to him, completely unexpected.'

'I suppose he could have made himself forget what he'd done.' Nan sounded doubtful.

'Is that really likely? Doesn't that take a more subtle mind?'

'What's he doing with a shotgun, anyway? Would he be allowed a certificate?'

'I had Carmichael check. He's not listed. Which is what you'd expect. But in the country people get casual, leave their guns standing in a corner before they clean them. Poor Peter could have helped himself to one, thought he'd seen a deer moving among the trees, fired. He could even have used the old lady's own gun. But if he did, he also cleaned it perfectly afterwards and returned it to her kitchen. Only—he had it drummed into him that he wasn't ever to go inside the house.'

'Someone covering up for him? The old lady herself? Could she have done all that, between being shot and dying?'

'I don't know. Anyway, I've had Hollis sent to Poor Peter's home to check his hands. I didn't want him hauled down to Division.'

'The swab tests?—to see if he'd recently fired a gun? I see. So eventually you'll know. Meanwhile, we were going to relax, remember? Let me show you some brochures.' Deliberately distracting him, Nan produced half a dozen glossy booklets from behind a cushion and waved them invitingly under his nose.

'Brochures?'

'Loo suites. For the downstairs cloakroom.'

Yeadings gave a mock groan. 'Seeing we're suddenly made of money, eh?'

'Well, we need new taps anyway. Then you know the pedestal has a hairline crack, and I've always hated that cramped little hand-basin. Nobody has white china any more. I thought if we chose a soft colour, I could match it to wallpaper and do the decoration myself.'

'Mm. What kind of soft colour were you thinking of? Pee green?'

'I hope you're not being vulgar. How about ice-blue or peach?'

Yeadings hummed and settled to study of the illustrations. When Nan came back from the oven's summons to remove the cake, she found him asleep, head sunk forward on his chest.

She eased him gently back and gathered the papers together, adding to them a final brochure from under the cushion. Time enough when Mike was keen on the idea to suggest putting in an extra shower.

SEVEN

DS BEAUMONT NOTICED that his house was in darkness as he turned into the short driveway and stopped at the closed garage doors. Time was when he'd ring ahead and Cathy would have them open for him to drive straight in. Well, that was the least of the small services he was now deprived of. He wondered where young Stuart had taken himself off to on such a filthy night.

As he let himself in, the key lodging tight in the lock so that he had to stand on his toes at chain's length struggling to get the damn thing out, the phone began ringing. It had to be trouble: nothing else came along the line these days.

'Beaumont.'

'This is Rory Welch, for Stu. Hello, sir. Just rang to thank him for having me over today. Could I have a word, please?'

'Sorry, he's out. I've not been back long enough to see if there's a note, but I'll give him your message. Anything else?'

'No-o. Funny, he never said he was going anywhere. I invited him over for the night but he wasn't having any. Ah well, see him in the Christmas hols, I expect. 'Bye sir.'

What did you have to do, Beaumont wondered, to get a son as polite as that one?—short of spending a fortune on private education. Welch senior hadn't impressed him as the ideal father; too much of a show-off. Must be the mother's influence. The right kind of mother with no silly ideas about being neglected because her husband was working his pants off to keep their heads above water. Given freedom from pressures of that sort, would even Stuart have turned out less surly?

He went upstairs, rolled back his bedroom carpet, removed a floorboard and helped himself to a can of Heineken. Not fridge-chilled but cool enough, and not plundered. He heeled his shoes off, dropped his raincoat on a chair and stretched out on the bed.

The case, he considered: a bit of a rum one. It had a funny smell. No weapon by the body, so not even intended to be taken as a suicide or accident. What were the figures for shotgun deaths? Taken over five years nationwide they'd averaged out at 63% suicide, 30% accidental and only 7% murder or manslaughter. So, unless killers were getting away with a lot of cover-ups, this was a rare one. No weapon to hand—but some covetous lunatic just might have come along and made off with it—backed up by the body's arms having been rearranged, and then some report—originating with the Old Man—that she'd been killed with a *cat* in her arms and the cat then carefully buried wrapped in the old woman's apron! Weird.

Died between 2.0 p.m. and 6.0 p.m. on Saturday, but actually shot some hours before. And not found until someone was on her way to church next morning, at a little before 8.0 a.m. It wasn't even certain she'd been shot in the wood where she was found. No blood had drained through to the ground under the body; also no one so far had come forward to say they'd been along that path during the period in question and seen anything out of the ordinary. Maybe by tomorrow the house-to-house calls through Swardley village would have turned up something or someone.

Downstairs the front doorbell gave a pathetic ping. He'd meant to check the wiring. Sometimes it made no sound at all.

In his sock soles Beaumont padded down and switched on the porch light. Stuart stood there, his arms full of packages, so he couldn't get at his key. Beaumont opened the door and moved back. No need to ask, 'What's this, then?' His nose told him. Stuart had raided the chippie.

'Brought enough for three,' the boy said casually.

'Three giants?'

'Thought you might be hungry.' Truculent voice, but the idea was sound enough.

'Put it under the grill while I get the table ready. Anything with the chips?'

'Two bits of cod. Big ones. I told them my Dad was starving me.'

Quite a feast, then. Beaumont was gratified even while something warned him this sudden initiative was too good to be quite true. Halfway through their meal he remembered Rory Welch's message and relayed it. 'Actually rang up to say thanks,' he stressed.

Stuart gave the rictus that was now his nearest to a smile. 'Bet he'd have said something different to me.'

'Oh?' Sudden suspicion. 'Why that?'

'Tried to pump me about the shooting in the wood, so I made up a wild one.'

Beaumont sighed and put down his fork. 'You realize your version'll be all over Thames Valley by the morning? Probably in the pulp press too.'

'Not as he rang me back. That was because he'd already found out it was a phoney version. I thought at the time he hadn't swallowed it all.'

'All what?'

'Well, nudity and the rape and that. Gang bang and used hypodermics. The standard orgy scene, you know.'

Beaumont stared at him round-eyed. And in CID he was called over the coals himself for being a humorist. Something in the genes, no doubt, and the boy had inherited his full share. He let the silence draw out.

'Anything the matter?' Stuart asked, and the innocence of his expression would have sat well on Rory's angelic features.

Beaumont attacked his cod again. 'Just wondering. Who he'd check with to find out the true story. This fish is good. What's for afters?'

RORY WELCH REPLACED the receiver thoughtfully. He had used the one in his mother's bedroom, knowing she had her hands full with Amanda's squeaky little friends. The house was seething with them: party games, and fireworks later if the covers hadn't let the rain in. Kids couldn't wait as long as Guy Fawkes Night these days. Gone American; but at least, marooned out here, there was no house-to-house Trick-or-Treating. And none of that disgusting effigy-burning some people still gloried in on the Fifth.

From the gallery above the hall he looked down on his sister's guests in their fancy gear. She was there in the middle, quite a credible green frog, squatting on her haunches. There were skeletons, wizards and witches, even a walking pumpkin, rats, mice and bats. Mother had on a silver evening dress: a White Witch, in case later the kids' spells got out of hand. She'd even bought some Dracula teeth for his father to sport when he would join them at supper in his white tie and tails. It might be worth coming back at that point to check if he could be persuaded to wear the things.

In the kitchen Rory picked up the plastic box of party food he was to take across to the stables. There were bottles of Coke too, but he guessed Alec would have something stronger laid on.

It would have been more fun if Stu had agreed to come for the night. Alec was all right, that is to say he was a man, but he'd no sense of humour, absolutely none. Worse, he didn't even know when Rory was taking his mickey. And all he'd ever read was the back pages of the *Standard,* for the names of tomorrow's runners. Horses he did know, but Rory didn't share his total absorption in them. Just the sound of them moving in their stalls, stamping and chumping, and the hay and ammoniac smell that crept up into Alec's rooms—that was what he most liked about them. Comfortable. There was no call to get up on their heaving backsides and go leaping over fences chasing stinky little foxes running their hearts out in fright. If vermin overran the place—as sometimes they did—he'd rather go out and shoot them cleanly.

At the thought of shooting he experienced a sudden nausea and leaned a moment against the outer wall of the house. He saw again the old woman's face staring sightlessly up at the dark tree-tops. When he put out a hand on the dressed stone edge of the brickwork it was cold, as her hand had been cold to the touch, with all the life drained away. He didn't want to think of death. Still less of killing. He didn't think he could ever go out shooting again. Maybe he'd better take up pony trekking, join the women.

Inside the stables he put down the packages and went across to scratch Doll's ears. She was his sister's now, and Amanda's outgrown Shetland was in the next stall, grown fat and lazy, only used to pull a little trap for visiting children nowadays. But Doll had originally been bought for him, bred for him; and touching her brought back something of himself that he felt he was fast losing.

He pressed his face into the animal smell of her smooth neck and seemed to listen. Then, 'She's dead, Doll,' he whispered. 'Old Lorely's gone, finished.'

The pony moved its weight restlessly, disturbing a scent of fresh hay. Then she turned and puffed on him. He

grinned sadly back, patted her bony nose and moved away.
In their farther stalls the two horses, grey gelding and roan
mare, turned inquisitively to look after him, but he didn't
address them. They were his mother's beasts and special to
her. He would as soon have climbed on their backs as tried
on one of her dresses.

Alec came out on to the top of his wooden staircase. 'You
coming up, boy? Don't you give they no fancy food, now.'

'I didn't. It's all for us. Hang on, and I'll bring it up.'
Damn Stu Beaumont, he told himself as he mounted the
steps; he could have come. He would have cheered things
up, kept a chap's mind off morbid thoughts. Why had he
first refused to stir outside, and then wasn't at home when
Rory had rung later? Had he been trying to trap him too
with that stupid made-up story about the killing, waiting for
Rory to give himself away, reveal that he knew better what
had happened? No, he couldn't have guessed, unless his detective father had discovered something. Something overlooked. Had there been anything?

Uneasily he recalled the older Superintendent who had
visited them yesterday morning, seeming so slow and quiet
but, driving in, he'd caught Rory watching from the upstairs window as the line of police made their relentless fingertip search down the grazing-field. And he'd had to close
the window, go downstairs to meet him, before ever he knew
what it was—if anything—that they'd found.

NEXT MORNING DS Beaumont lifted Rosemary Z at 7.30
and turned up early at Reading to check on progress. The
spent cartridge case and five shotguns had been bagged for
taking to Ballistics at Huntingdon. There would be further
checks on firearms certificates in the village today.

Immediate dusting locally had revealed that the plastic of
the cartridge case had no fingerprints, but definite traces of

being handled by woven fabric gloves. Microscopic photographs of these had been prepared and filed in the hope of later comparisons by the experts.

The five 12-bore guns comprised Lorely's two (the single-barrel fully choked one found in the kitchen) and an older double-barrelled over-and-under, which might once have been her father's (found locked in the approved manner in a steel cabinet upstairs); a more expensive pair belonging to Franklin Welch, one having pump-action; and a side-by-side double-barrel handed in by Alec, Welch's stableman. A report linking any of these to the cartridge case could be expected to take three or four weeks; maybe less if the boss had a friend in Ballistics at Huntingdon.

A 10.0 a.m. appointment was logged for next day when Superintendent Yeadings would issue a press release, only a single paragraph having so far appeared in some of the national dailies headlined WOMAN FOUND DEAD IN BERKSHIRE WOOD, or (in one notorious tabloid) CORPSE IN COPSE. There had been no photographs and it was hoped to keep it that way. None were available of Lorely Pelling since she became a recluse (except the local press 'Cat Woman' one), so a special guard would have to be put on the grounds of the Hall as the obvious alternative shot. While it remained at all uncertain where the woman had actually been attacked it was vital that any traces of the incident that might remain after the gale and heavy rains should not be disturbed by interlopers.

Uniform branch would again be dividing their available men between house calls to trace users of Farlowes Wood/users of shotguns, and a SOCO search of all possible areas where the shooting might have occurred. Priority was to be given to the lane and grounds within a quarter-mile radius of the Hall. Road blocks would be set up farther out to pre-

vent interference, and field-glasses issued to scan open fields
and woodland leading to the house.

One item of information Beaumont had placed on the top
of other papers in Yeadings's in-tray. It was the statement
made by a locksmith giving the date (ten days back) for replacement of the kitchen door lock for Malmsmead Hall.
Payment had been made at that time in cash, and three keys
had been supplied. With some bosses he'd have needed to
underline the final words, but not in the case of Mike
Yeadings. He was already well aware that one of those keys
had been on a new (but bloodied) string round the dead
woman's neck and a second hung on a hook inside the scullery broom cupboard. No third had so far been found. It
would be nice to discover it before someone had a chance to
drop it down a convenient drain.

The lock order had been placed a fortnight earlier by 'a
fairly young woman' who visited the shop, but no details of
her appearance could be recalled. Probably, Beaumont
thought, Mrs Lammas since that was the day she regularly
accepted a lift from her brother-in-law to shop for herself
and Miss Pelling.

'What about the new DI?' he asked Rosemary when they
had both caught up with the paperwork.

'Mr Yeadings wants me to partner him. DI Jenner had
some idea of calling on Miss Pelling's labourer again this
morning sometime, but he never suggested my meeting him
there. I think he's pretty disgusted he hasn't been given a
sergeant.'

'Which leaves me working with Silver again. And I'd just
schooled myself to put up with you.'

'It's just until Angus Mott gets back.'

'Oh, I'll survive, but I hate being buggered about, that's
all.'

'Complain too loud and you might find yourself in harness with the new man.'

Beaumont looked at her sharply. 'That bad, is it?'

'I never said so. As you mentioned, one schools oneself.'

'Um. This labourer he wants to have a go at; has Jenner set his sights on him, d'you think?'

'Possibly. It's really the boss's story, but since I was there I'll tell you how it went. As you know, there was this missing cat...'

BEAUMONT AND JENNER sat to either side as Mike Yeadings faced the press. Word had reached the radio and TV news teams, so he had to undergo the disagreeable trial by woolly microphone. He hadn't minded the all-metal jobs so much but he found the mammoth furry sausages thrust under his nose quite repellent, more even than the swivelling cameras. Accordingly he toned down the material he had on offer to its nadir of interest, hoping to be edited out, though aware that imagination would serve demands of mass circulation whenever facts were in short supply. In his opinion it would be time enough to hand out more spectacular stuff when he needed something specific in return.

In addition to the time-lag between the shooting and actual death, there was another item he suppressed for the present. When he had regained his own office and the team were reassembled he shared it with them.

'A John Longstaff telephoned in last night, having seen a paragraph in the *Evening Standard* regarding Miss Lorely Pelling's death. His number was passed through to me at home and I went out to Burnham to see him at his house. He's senior partner in a small law practice in Slough and he was holding an envelope for Miss Pelling, to be opened on her death.'

'Opened by him, or the coroner, or what?' Beaumont demanded.

'Himself. It was a hand-written will, properly witnessed and of the simplest form possible. It left her entire estate to (I quote) "my respected kinsman and kinswoman Rory Welch and Amanda Welch to be held in Trust for them by their mother Alexandra Welch jointly with a qualified legal representative chosen and appointed by the aforesaid Alexandra Welch until such time as each child shall reach the age of eighteen years."

'Unambiguously worded and unfudged by punctuation, it's legally almost perfect, except that the dotty old lady seems to have imagined a relationship that doesn't exist—unless you take it back to Adam-and-Eve level. If anyone can be traced who is fairly closely related to her by blood, then the will can be disputed and probably overthrown.

'Mr Longstaff assumes that in the event of no response being received to advertisements which he is obliged to make, Miss Pelling won't be deemed to have died intestate, because she did at least name her intended beneficiaries.'

Beaumont grunted. 'Still, she was a nutter, despite her neighbours saying she was shrewd. Was the will dated, sir?'

'Yes. Signed just a fortnight before the day of her death, the witnesses being one Norman Marsh, Veterinary Surgeon, and our old friend who delivers the cat-meat on Saturdays, Tom Beale.

'So that means Beaumont and Silver chasing that pair up for a statement, though it's highly unlikely that as witnesses they had any idea what the will contained. But the circumstances and the place of the signing could be important. Also how it came about that Longstaff got in on the act. See if either of the witnesses recommended him.

'DI Jenner will be in charge of continued examination of the grounds of Malmsmead Hall. Z, go with him. Finish checking the library. We need to turn up the third key as well as any significant papers. If Miss Pelling trusted no one to come into the house, not even her shopping lady Mrs Lammas, the key could still be hidden away there.'

'Sir,' Rosemary put in, 'should I visit the Medlams at work, or wait till tonight? In view of Mrs Lammas's mental state yesterday...'

'Ring the sister at her garden centre. She probably sorted Bella out when they got back last night. Arrange to have a helpful word at their home after work this evening. Anything else we should consider?'

Jenner nodded sharply. 'The labourer, Peter Howell. I'd like to question him again. If he wasn't allowed inside the house, as he says, how did he know the mother cat was missing?'

'Mm. I think I'll have a word with him myself, after I've called on Mrs Welch at Farlowes. I have a fancy to see how that lady reacts to the contents of Lorely Pelling's will.'

EIGHT

Normally Alexandra Welch would have risen early, gone riding alone and returned to a hot shower followed by tea-and-toast breakfast with Amanda while Franklin organized himself ready for work. But today, because both children were at home for half term, their father had taken time off and Alex had opted for a tray of breakfast in bed. While she stayed behind at Farlowes to supervise clearing up after the children's party Rory and Amanda were to be taken by car to tour Avebury, Silbury and Stonehenge, stopping off for a hotel lunch in Marlborough.

'I wish you were coming,' Rory told her when he came up to say goodbye. He was keen to go over the ancient sites because they touched on a project he was beginning at school, although hours cooped in a car in his father's company was something he usually kicked against.

'Look after Amanda,' she told him. 'It's all a bit above her head as yet. Daddy forgets sometimes how young she is. I've told him about the shop in Marlborough that sells little felt mice dressed in Beatrix Potter fashions. Remind him to buy her something there and she'll be as good as gold.'

'Stop her getting bored, right.' Rory walked over to the window and stared out in the direction of Farlowes Wood, unconsciously jingling loose change in his pocket as his father did when embarrassed. 'You'll be able to get a rest.'

'Whatever for?' She gave a nervous laugh. 'F-funny boy, there's nothing wrong with me. I'm only lazing now to keep out of the way while you're all rushing off.'

He hesitated, frowning. If he would ever have a chance to get through to her it must be now. But she was pretending everything was all right. Dare he burst out with it?—'I saw you Saturday. And I know where you'd been, because I went for the key and it wasn't there. And I saw you when you came back. God, didn't I just!'

He closed his eyes and thought the words hard but they wouldn't come out. There was too much habit of privacy built up between them, more than ever since he'd been sent away to school. It wasn't done. He wasn't expected to notice. Or if notice, must accept everything as normal adult behaviour. Maybe adult life was like that, deceptive all the way. If so, he wasn't keen. Poor Bloody Infancy, followed by Adultery: that had been one of Stu's flip jokes. But not funny at all.

He moved round to her dressing-table, fiddled with his fingertips among the discarded things lying on it. There were the diamond earrings which she'd worn with her silver dress last night. He supposed *he* had given them to her, a buying-off present because of something shitty he'd done but wouldn't openly admit to.

Keeping his head down, but eyes on the mirror, he watched her run a weary hand through her hair. The mauve shadows under her eyes were darker. Without make-up she looked fragile; as vulnerable as he knew her to be, day in day out, under the social poise. And on Saturday she'd been so much more. Terrified out of her wits.

He remembered the beginning of term. She hadn't come in the car with them then, but said goodbye at home. 'You'll be all right,' she told him. And then he'd had the courage to say, 'Will *you*? If anything goes wrong, you will write and say . . .'

And she'd smiled. 'What could go wrong?'

Well, there was no limit. The world could fall to pieces.
She could be in terrible trouble and he couldn't do a thing.
How could he go away again in two days' time when *anything* might happen? Somehow he had to hang on here a
while until he was sure . . . But his father would guess if he
faked an illness. He'd think he'd funked going back because he couldn't take it, and then there'd be hell to pay.

He made a last attempt. 'Saturday. . .' he said and left it
hanging in the air.

'Great, wasn't it? I'm so glad you enjoyed it. Don't ever
lose touch with your friends, if you can help it.' She seemed
deliberately to misunderstand.

'I meant . . . old Lorely.' This time the silence built up. He
darted a glance at her. She had her head down, her long
blonde hair curtaining her face. 'What do you think will
happen?'

'I don't know, Rory.' Her expelled breath seemed to wa-
ver. 'It doesn't bear thinking of.'

And then his father was calling from downstairs, bellow-
ing actually, because Rory was holding things up. 'I'm off,
then, Ma. *Ciao.*'

AT MALMSMEAD, just about then, they were opening up the
canvas. It was almost rotten, khaki, possibly part of an old
army tent, but it had had agricultural usage, smelled of
bonemeal. And because it had been rolled up and rammed
between the beams of the hay loft it had missed lying out in
the recent rains. On part of it blood was still stiff and choc-
olate-brown where it had wrapped a body. The stains had to
be human. DI Jenner was keen as a whippet after the rabbit.

Five minutes after the canvas was bagged and marked for
dispatch to the lab a uniform man came in to report finding
the plastic cup-wad from a cartridge ground almost into the

soil beyond the vegetable patch. The pattern of a constabulary boot overlaid it and, mud-covered, it was barely visible even at near view. Its position had been measured in relation to the house and barn. Now it had been given its own little plastic tent and awaited photography.

Rosemary Z broke off her examination of books in the library to go and view the find. Jenner's questing nose looked nipped by cold but he was as animated as she'd seen him. 'See this, Zyczynski?' he demanded. 'Shouldn't be here at all. The old woman used a different kind of cartridge.'

'With a destructible cardboard wad,' she agreed.

'You know the sort this came from? What we want now is the cartridge's outer plastic case, similar to the one found in the field next to Farlowes Wood.'

'But if it was ejected the killer would have picked it up and taken it away. This wad flew off with the shot in it, landing near his target or rebounding off it. He hadn't time to look for it, or else he thought it didn't matter because it couldn't relate to his gun. But anyone used to shooting would know better than to leave the ejected cartridge case behind.'

'We go on looking for it, all the same.'

'If the wad dropped here—'

'The target was right nearby, yes. Damn the weather, messing everything up. Any marks made by a body falling will have washed away.'

'So where did the killer stand to fire?'

They surveyed the circle round the police marker. To one side was the barn; beyond it the wood; ahead of it the vegetable patch. 'She'd been making drills for seeds,' Rosemary said. 'I think something interrupted her and she left the dibber lying at the point she'd reached. Was it the killer's arrival?'

Jenner narrowed his eyes. 'According to the idiot, she was carrying the cat, remember. It had gone missing. Feline post-parturition insanity, like some women get. Abandoned its young and went on the loose. Maybe the old woman heard it crying in the wood and went to gather it in, getting scratched in the process. Was bringing it back, facing this way, then suddenly—bang!'

They turned and looked behind, towards the house.

'Judging from the spread of shot, a range of fifteen metres using an open barrel or twenty with a fully choked one, according to Firearms,' Rosemary recalled.

'Right, then. If that theory is correct, it means the killer stood somewhere by the doorway to the scullery. He could have just come out of the house.'

'Which she didn't allow anyone inside.'

Jenner half-closed his eyes. 'Who's going to keep to her petty rules when he's already decided to kill her? Suppose—yes, just suppose our man (or woman, since you insist on equality) has already done something far, far worse and the old woman has caught him out and means to expose him. He has to stop her at all costs. He watches her go after the cat, and while she's gone he acts, darts into the house; seizes the gun standing ready in its corner—' He stopped, hand dramatically to brow.

'Wrong kind of cartridge?' Z supplied.

'So he'd brought one with him. Always had some in his pocket, or else had premeditated the killing.'

'In which case he'd have brought his own gun along.'

'Didn't want to be seen out shooting when he'd murder in mind.'

Rosemary looked doubtful. 'There are a lot of options there.'

A thin smile answered her. 'So we go and ask him just how he did it. I don't think he'll hold out for long, do you?'

He could mean only one person, surely. The case was prejudged. 'You do mean Poor Peter?'

'Peter Howell himself. Who else? You can come with me and deal with the mother. Do you use shorthand?'

For this case he was supposed to be her Guv, but she had to stand her ground over this. 'The Super said he'd see the Howells.'

'That was before we had the evidence to nick our man. And Yeadings is going to the Welches first. If we're nippy we'll be home and dry before he gets past the gentry's sherry.'

He hurried to the car, leaving her to warn the constable on duty that they were off before rejoining him. For the second time in twenty-four hours Jenner pulled into Swardley village, and as they passed the Falcon three men came out, one loaded with photographic equipment.

'Press,' Rosemary warned.

Instead of keeping his head well down Jenner slowed and looked back. They were staring after the car and as it stopped one ran forward, bending to rap on the girl's window.

'Wind it down,' the DI ordered.

Rosemary received a warm blast of beery breath as the man called eagerly across her, 'Any progress, squire?'

Jenner was at his most superior, the smile at its thinnest. 'You could say that.'

'Arrest imminent? That sort of thing?'

'I should hang around a little longer if I were you.' The words could mean anything, but the emphasis was clear.

'You're not one of our local CID, sir, are you?'

'Specially drafted in for the job,' Jenner told him significantly. Rosemary sat stiffly back and gritted her teeth.

'Could I have your name, sir?'

He hesitated only a second, then the dizzy prospect of fame was too great a temptation. 'Albert Jenner, Detective-Inspector.' He nodded to Rosemary and she wound the window back up, almost catching the little man's pencil.

As they drew up at the cottage door she tried again. 'Sir, with respect, I do think we ought to let the Super know first.'

'WDC Zyczynski, "with respect" is invariably the opening before a piece of rank insolence. Just this once I shall forget you said it. I have considerable experience in a sphere you're an utter beginner in. So you can please me best by staying shut and doing as you're told.'

IN THE QUIET that followed the children's departure Alexandra Welch discovered her lethargy remained. She came in from waving the car off, examined her face and thin shoulders in the hall's long mirror, retied her bathrobe and ruefully admitted that in other circumstances it would have been a day for self-indulgence. Yet not enjoyably. Rather more an occasion of wallowing unprofitably in woes and regrets.

It was a pattern increasingly familiar to her whenever she'd been with the children and they'd gone off, leaving her behind. It didn't happen often, but she suspected it was deliberate on Franklin's part, arranging outings in which he claimed she'd have no interest or when she had standing appointments. Was it meant to illustrate how close to Rory and Amanda he was, and how well they all got on without her? She couldn't say why she allowed it to happen. A family outing, so wasn't it the natural thing for all of them to be together over half-term?

In two days' time Rory would return to Stowe, then there'd be nothing but little stilted notes from him until almost Christmas. Amanda would be home each night and at weekends, but Franklin drove her to school every morning and if he couldn't pick her up himself sent a car from work, so there was no ferrying duty for Alex like other mothers had. Almost imperceptibly Amanda was growing coolly apart, as if forced into the same mould that Alex herself had once been subject to, separated from her own globe-trotting parents by a screen of servants. It was an unspeakably lonely way to live when you needed warmth and closeness, a secure sense of family.

Alex supposed that had really been her own reason for marrying: to make up for what she had never known. Family to her parents had meant something quite different; nothing cosy, but pride in a name and in an unbroken line of torch-carriers for king and country. A double pride, because cousin had married cousin, the budding ambassador mating with army at one remove. Eminently suited, Sir Douglas and the Honourable Jennifer Trewin had accepted a shared duty that offered no natural place for the small child who, almost distractingly, appeared at a time of international crisis. Duty had demanded their almost continuous absence abroad, and Alex had been taught that duty required certain observances from her too, notably to cause no embarrassments, to live up to expectations, and not to confide in anyone lest she be indiscreet.

That had left her with horses to make friends of, but by early adolescence it was not quite enough.

She remembered now the parties she had been expected to attend when at last her mother took stock of her marriageable age: formal façades that had covered up quite grotesquely uninhibited lustings. She had found the whole business distasteful. Things were ordered more properly in the stud. She must marry as expected of her, yes, and produce an extension to the family line, but where were the suitable partners? In her parents' absence England had changed, swung into the 'sixties and spaced out into the 'seventies. Family, the Trewins had to admit, now embraced second, third and even fourth wives, single-parent

families, abortion waiting-lists that included some of the
greatest names in the land. After her miserable Season they
were quite relieved when Alex opted for helping a onetime
school acquaintance run a combined livery stables and rid-
ing-school in Surrey.

There for the first time she discovered, among the begin-
ners, timid children who had some need of her. She knew
then she wanted children of her own. And there, by chance,
she met in a country pub a gauche and quite clever young
man with red hair who also seemed to need to belong.
Franklin Welch, already pushing his way upwards from ob-
scurity.

And she'd not the experience at that time to see that what
she found most acceptable in him was the skin he was
learning to slough off, the consciousness of his own social
ineptness. She recognized him as vulnerable, as she felt
herself to be, and she longed to devote herself to his protection. She wasn't to know that with financial success he
would outgrow his need for her, ride roughshod over his
marriage vows and look elsewhere for what he came to see
as lacking in their sexual relationship.

Alex shivered, though the hall was warm. She stood in an
oblong of sunlight that fell across the red brick floor from
the inner glass doors. Outside, the heavy oak ones stood
open to the terrace, and beyond it she glimpsed a corner of
the grazing-field. Today the horses were loose out there with
the two ponies, all waiting to be exercised. And she had no
energy, was wasted by the weekend's events and the useless
snatches of sleep that had bedevilled her nights between.

Because—as Rory had to remind her—because of Saturday. Strange that 'old Lorely' was what he should remember Saturday by and not his friends being here for their
reunion. For him it wasn't until Sunday that the horror must
have started.

A shadow suddenly cut off the sunlight. Hunched with crossed arms, she looked up and saw the bulk of a man's figure black against the glass doors. He must be looking in, catching her before she had dressed; a slut not properly up, at past ten in the morning. She hadn't heard a car's engine, so he would have left it at the drive's end. She supposed that was what policemen liked to do: creep up and catch you with your defences down.

She wouldn't give him the satisfaction of seeing her dart away. Not waiting for him to ring and the maid to come, Alex went swiftly forward to the encounter. She pulled the door open. 'Superintendent, how c-can I help you?' Sudden anger was the best specific for fear.

He smiled, bushy eyebrows rising towards black hairline. 'By pardoning my socks perhaps? I'm afraid the mud on my boots is past excuse.'

'Of course. Come in.' She watched while he worked on the iron heel-grip by the outer door and planted the wellies neatly side by side in the porch.

Too aware now of her inadequate dress, Alex stood waiting and shivered again. 'I'm sure you'd like coffee,' she said quickly. 'I know I would.'

He accepted and let her guide him to the same sunny room in which he had met the whole family two days before.

The far inner wall was draped entirely with black and had silver stars glued on. In front of it was a raised daïs as though some performance had been held there. While Alex went to alert the kitchen he went over and examined the dark velvet curtains which had been unhooked and folded over the top of open step ladders.

Alex came back in sweater and jeans, her hair tousled and her colour high. 'I'm waiting for the men to come and clear the platform away,' she explained quickly. 'My daughter gave a party last night for Hallowe'en. We had a conjuror.'

'Did she enjoy it?' he asked unexpectedly.

'She certainly seemed to. Yes, I'm sure she did.' Alex motioned him to a chair in the window recess.

'My daughter went to a neighbour's,' Yeadings said thoughtfully, 'as a witch. She loves dressing up, but I don't think she was quite ready for the conjuror. She had nightmares afterwards. His actions didn't relate to reality as she tried to understand it. She's just a little older than your Amanda, but has Down's Syndrome.'

Alex looked startled. 'Did—did her mother go with her?'

'No, and that was our mistake. Sally was to spend the night there afterwards. I think we were rushing things too much. If Nan or I had been there to say it was all a sort of joke she might not have been so frightened. It's partly our fault. Maybe we've worked too hard at explaining factually how one thing leads to another.'

'Then along comes a stranger and stands her w-world on its head.'

'Worse; he wasn't a stranger. Just a friend's Dad with a .book on parlour tricks. Now she's afraid anyone can turn into a wizard and make magic.'

A girl in a patterned blue overall came in carrying a tray with the coffee things. Yeadings allowed his hostess to pour without interruption, then as he took his cup he sighed gently. 'Perhaps it's because of the time of year, but there's talk in the village of your late neighbour having been a witch.'

'Because she lived alone and was considered eccentric?'

'Kept cats too. The Grimalkin familiar and so on. But she'd such a lot, I don't suppose she had names for them all.'

'Oh, but she did…I mean, I suppose, she had. We'd hear her sometimes calling them in from the wood.'

'Really?' His tone was conversational, lightly amused. 'What names did she give them, then?'

Alex cast about her wildly. 'Sable was one, I think. Dorabella. Faustus.' She broke off. 'No special associations there, are there?'

'Rather musical and literary, I'd say. Did you know her well?'

'No, hardly at all. My husband and she had a disagreement over some boundaries when we first came. He preferred us to leave her well alone. She didn't encourage familiarity in any case, you see.'

'Friendless,' Yeadings murmured, as if to himself. 'A proud lady, perhaps, who tried to be independent.'

Alexandra seemed to sense criticism. 'There was no question of cold-shouldering her. It's more that as neighbours we all value our privacy. Some of the cottagers could tell you more about her, I'm sure. Gash used to work for her father, so did Mrs Medlam's and Mrs Lammas's father, now dead. Mrs Lammas shopped for her, of course, and various people went to her for honey or candles.'

'And herbal remedies.'

'Well, perhaps. Maybe that's behind the gossip that she was a witch, but I don't think anyone was really afraid of her. One just watched one's Ps and Qs, because she had quite a fierce manner when you happened on her without warning.'

'And where was that likely to happen?'

Alex Welch gave a vague gesture. 'About the fields and lanes.'

'And sometimes in Farlowes Wood, it seems. Did you ever meet her there?'

'We don't use that footpath. There's no need to. Our own d-driveway is a quicker route to the village.'

The Superintendent nodded, but noted that she hadn't quite answered his question. He let a short silence build up but the woman offered no more. 'I'm rather disappointed,' he confessed. 'I'd hoped that you could give me quite a lot of help about the lady.'

'I'm sorry, Mr Yeadings, but there it is. We had no connection with Miss Pelling.'

'Not even enough to venture an opinion on whether she was of sound mind?'

'I've certainly no evidence that she was anything else.' For the first time Mrs Welch's voice had asperity in it, even indignation. There was no sign of a stutter.

'But surely—just a little odd, wouldn't you agree?'

'I'm no judge, Superintendent. And n-neither are malicious-minded villagers.'

'So can you suggest any reason, Mrs Welch, why she should name your two children as the only beneficiaries in her will?'

The woman started up, wild-eyed. 'No! No, of course not! Unless—p-perhaps she'd seen them from a d-distance. Maybe she'd secretly always wanted children of her own— No, that's nonsense, of course!'

'Or know of any reason why she should imagine she had some family relationship with them?'

'No!' This time the word was no more than a whisper. 'She didn't—I mean, maybe the villagers are right. She could have been more odd than we g-guessed. Really, she m-must have been quite out of her m-mind to pretend anything like that.'

NINE

MRS HOWELL FACED JENNER and the girl defiantly, holding on to the knob and filling the space of the partly-opened door. 'No, you can't,' she said again doggedly. She was a submissive person by nature, continually undervalued by her neighbours because of Poor Peter's state from birth. But hers was all the protection he had and she was ready now to see this lot off before they tried to lay a hand on his innocent head.

'It won't take long, Mrs Howell. We just need a word—'

'I've told you: no! Doctor's been and he's guv un some pills. So he's sleeping, like. You wudden make no sense of un anyway, even if he cud keep his eyes open. Doctor said it shudden of bin, that other lot comen last night and doing all that to un.'

'What lot?' Jenner asked suspiciously. 'Have you let the press in?'

'Them police. Wiping un over with them swab things. Not jes' his hands, mind, but his chin and his eyebrows and even up his nose holes. And then combing his hair with that bit of tissue paper in, like he's got nits!'

'Yeadings,' Jenner breathed. 'He's on to him, had him checked out for having discharged a firearm. Mrs Howell, had your son washed himself before the police came?'

'Cleaned hisself for his tea, nach'ly. Jes' his hands.'

'Ah.' The sigh denoted satisfaction. 'Well, we'll doubtless have enough to go on there. You're sure he didn't take a bath?'

'Not on Mondays, he wudden. Lot of nonsense all this is anyways. My Peter never had no gun, don't like the nasty things. No more do I. Next thing you'll be saying he's a poacher. Well, I tell you now, it wuz Miss Lorely useta give un a rabbit or pheasant for the pot, as she'd every right to do. My Peter never took aught he shuddenta, and that's God's truth.'

Rosemary looked sideways at Jenner as he sucked his lean cheeks in, then she ventured gently. 'Mrs Howell, tell Peter we'd like to come and see him when he's had a good rest, will you? He's had a bad time these last two or three days, but I expect he'll be telling you all about it when he's able.'

'Went on a lot about a cat,' the woman admitted, sounding troubled. 'I'd heard it wuz Miss Lorely'd got killed, but seems it wuz jes' folk's exaggeratings. Still, it upset un. He's very fond of dumb beasts.'

'What you heard was right,' Jenner said shortly. 'The cat was with Miss Pelling at the time, so we need to talk to your son before he gets further confused by discussing it with anyone else. Do you understand? We'll be back this afternoon, with a warrant if necessary.'

'You can save your trouble. He'll still be asleep,' the woman threw after them, and closed the door with firmness. The knocker rose a little and thumped back derisively.

'You drive,' Jenner mumbled. He was fishing in an inner pocket for another of the white tablets he kept crunching between his teeth. Antacid, Rosemary supposed. He probably had mouth ulcers, constantly biting the inside of his cheeks and sucking them in on the teeth. A pity Poor Peter's doctor wasn't prescribing for him. A Jenner tranquillized might do the case a power of good.

'Where to?' she demanded, switching on.

'Back to the Hall.' He sat muttering about the time things took the so-called experts to get their act together. 'Three or four weeks for the ballistics report, two or three for the swabs to be analysed. Meanwhile the villains have it all their own way. If we don't get confessions right off we haven't a chance.'

Rosemary might have pointed out that to prove the case in court the physical evidence had to be faultless. If the investigator was half as careful as the scientists (and lucky too), then by logic he might reach the same conclusion in much the same time. But with a few more 'induced' confessions the police might as well pack up and join the dole queue. She wasn't in the job to stand over prisoners with a zapper in her hand. However, she didn't trust her voice to keep out the contempt she felt, and so she stayed silent.

Back at Malmsmead Jenner followed her into the little library. 'Have you much more to do here?'

'A wall and a half. Mr Yeadings wants me to examine every book and check what's behind.'

'A job for life. Was the ladder in here when you came?'

'No, it's from outside.'

'Stands to reason you'll find nothing in the upper rows. A woman of near eighty wasn't that spry to go climbing up there when she'd something to hide. You should just go for the books within easy reach.'

'She was exceptionally secretive, and there's nothing like a safe anywhere in the house. The third key's still not turned up, and she must have had papers of some sort. You can't be sure what lengths she'd go to to keep things secure.'

'Well, I'm telling you, time's running out. Leave the bit you've got to. Start again by the bed and work outwards. Much more logical.'

There was something in what he said, and if it was meant to make her less sure of her own judgment, it did that. He had seniority, and no one could have so sharp a nose without having honed it on some considerable grindstones.

She followed his orders, pushed the ladder into a corner, pulled the divan into the centre of the room and started taking out the books that had been behind it. Jenner went back to the kitchen and made himself coffee.

ALEXANDRA WELCH saw the Superintendent to the door where he thanked her, climbed back into his muddied boots and clomped off by way of the stables and rear driveway, presumably heading again for the Hall. She had told him little, and yet she had the feeling he could make something out of it. He had a disturbing way of going silent, so that from sheer nerves you felt compelled to rush in and say something, almost anything, to keep him from thinking about you.

Going back over their conversation she could see no deliberate pattern in it. He'd responded with normal social interest to what she'd told him of Amanda's party, and that had led to him telling her about his little girl. He hadn't been expecting sympathy, but spoke as a parent, inured by time to the irreversible fact of Down's Syndrome, now coping with some fresh aspect, a confrontation with conjuring.

From that, while she'd poured their coffee, he'd gone on to general magic, and then the specific suspicions of witchcraft supposedly held in the village regarding old Lorely. Suspicions which were unfounded and malicious.

She hoped she hadn't rebutted them too angrily. Yeadings had let his eyes rest gently on her, consideringly, and then inquired about her own relations with the dead woman.

Of course, that was what he had come about. All the previous lead-in had been to set her at her ease, for the truth to emerge more freely. And she thought she had handled it well, schooled for so long at negative deceptions. But she had had no warning of the bombshell he was so calmly about to drop.

Not that the fact in itself was a bombshell, but simply that the policeman should somehow have got to learn about it: Lorely's interest in the children. The relationship.

Alex had responded with the only explanation she could think of then: that Lorely was a prey to the fantasies of a childless old maid, had persuaded herself of what she wished to believe. She was ashamed of betraying the tough old lady who, if anyone, had gone through life with her feet firmly on the ground, even dug greenly into it. Anyway, in desperation, Alex had lied in her teeth. But she wasn't certain she'd convinced the big, watchful man quietly sitting opposite in his sock soles.

ALMOST AN HOUR LATER, when Rosemary had come on little of note, Superintendent Yeadings walked in unannounced. 'I've just been hearing from the DI that he's cracked the case,' he commented drily. His eyebrows twitched. 'Thought I'd find you here. Nearly finished?'

She explained that she was now using a different scheme. Radiating from the bed space, she had only three rows left to examine at the top on the short wall.

'And nothing's turned up?'

'Only the fact that the dead woman had catholic tastes. The books within reach of the bed were all well thumbed and dust-free. Kipling, Shaw, Voltaire in the original, Geoffrey Household, Pope, Ibsen, all mixed together. And this, sir, quite close at the back.'

She put a hand behind a corner book and drew out a small oval frame of some polished dark wood. In the centre was a double portrait finely done in oils. It showed a smiling man in military uniform seated with a small, fair-haired child on one knee. The other leg, relaxed, pointed forward,

the impeccable cavalry boot posed on the stuffed head of a
tiger-skin rug.

'Wasn't she lovely, sir? If that is the dead woman as a
child.'

She was indeed. Small wonder that she'd been given the
name of an enchantress. And whose choice would that have
been? he wondered. The Brigadier—at that time a mere
major—or his long-dead wife?

'Need the ladder moved?' Yeadings inquired.

'Just a couple of feet, then I'm finished. Thanks.'

And in the provoking way that Sod has regulated affairs,
wasn't it behind the very next row, the thing they'd been
waiting for all along? A fat box-file with yellowing papers
at the bottom and a number of fresher documents tucked
under the old-fashioned spring. And hidden, as Rosemary
had imagined it might be, right up near the ceiling where
anyone bothering less would never have looked.

THE PORTRAIT HELD HIM in thrall. There was no reason why
he should retain it, but Yeadings had a purpose for it. He
slid it, plastic-wrapped, into the side pocket of his car, and
when he reached home that evening placed it on the desk of
the room he used as an office. He left it shut away there as
he went through the routine family evening, helped bath
Luke, read Sally to sleep, observed that the cloakroom taps
had both begun to drip again. He went to bed when Nan
did, exhausted, only to wake at a little before 2.0 a.m.,
knowing that for him the night's rest was over.

His mind seethed. Angry with himself, he felt he'd got
some assumption basically wrong. Yet what had he at all?
So little. The dead woman was an enigma.

The woman. She was what frustrated him. Never mind
the killer; it was she who had left him no clues. While he
trudged around her onetime neighbours picking up their

unconsidered attitudes, second-hand opinions, the essential Lorely continued to elude him. Who was she? What was she *about*, with her fierce reclusiveness, her avoidance of all human contact?

He reached out for paper and began to write her name. The single word, scratched irritably with a fine fibre-tip, stared back spider-like, black on white. Scowling, he started to thicken the letters, discovered the 'r' was out of kilter, had missed its loop. Looked like an 'n'. The word he stared at was 'Lonely'.

Lonely Lorely. The daunting, half-scarecrow recluse. But also the exquisite child of the painting. Once *Lovely* Lorely, surely adored by her father, the gently smiling military man, kind to his tenants—like his daughter, proud and undemanding.

So—she was lonely. But hadn't she chosen to be?—refusing to be groomed for marriage, to be made into a commodity (as she saw it). Already as a girl in India she had chosen the hermit path. Then came return to England.

No, correction: loss of India. She had been born there, knew little of the 'homeland'. It had been no return, but a voyage into an alien culture. Nothing familiar had remained for her then except her father. She accompanied *his* return, began to recognize his resumption of a past she had no part in.

Accepted it—for his sake? Loved him? Nursed him devotedly in his last years, people said. (People said—nothing from her directly on this.) Devotedly, or desperately?

Lorely Pelling, come out wherever you are! Dammit, woman, I've almost got to you. Don't slip away now.

Yeadings rose from his chair, began wandering absently about the room, his hands occasionally lifting and replacing objects as if pressing them into cooperation with his own nervous energy. Two o'clock in the morning was an hour that should never be. He knew that the man who paced here while the rest of the world slept was an abnormal him, without the daytime rationale. A nocturnal with wild thoughts and imaginings.

Wild. He stopped in his tracks, remembering. Z had mentioned the books most in use, close to hand as Lorely lay in bed. Kipling was one. Naturally so, with the Indian childhood and the father's army background. She would have known the *Just So Stories* almost by heart, and the ironic soldier's verses. And most certainly—*The Cat That Walked By Himself.*

They had that book somewhere in the house. Nan had been reading it to Sally just a few weeks ago. *Wild!* That was the key-word his subconscious had been dangling before him, possibly what had stirred the restlessness in him, brought him awake.

He sat down by the desk on which the oval-framed painting stood, and closed his eyes, waiting for the context to settle. And in just a few seconds it came, complete.

The Cat. He walked by himself, and all places were alike to him... He went back through the Wet Wild Woods, waving his wild tail, and walking by his wild lone. But he—never—told—anybody.

'Lorely Pelling,' Yeadings murmured aloud. 'Witch of the Woods, you were just such a wild one yourself.'

And she too had never told anyone anything, until that piece of witnessed paper lodged with an unknown solicitor in Slough. Did that contain her confession? Had she been a wild one in that far off, respectable society of the British Raj? Mocking at marriage, had she flouted propriety and taken a lover, borne a child? Was that what lay behind the return to England, her father's avoidance of society, eventually her own hermit existence?

If so, what became of that child?

Yeadings picked up the oval frame and stared at the little girl in it. He knew now why she had looked vaguely familiar. He had even thought, seeing the picture for the first time, that all blonde little girls of that age looked alike. All normal little girls.

Amanda Welch had the same wide eyes, broad forehead, golden hair as this child. Her tidy plaits had disguised how curly and thick it would lie on her shoulders when loosed.

Was it quite beyond sober, daytime belief that she was Lorely's granddaughter? If so, it accounted for her mother's defensive anger at the slurs on the dead woman. Accounted too for the sense Yeadings received of her concealed emotion when he mentioned the terms of the will. Alex Welch certainly knew more than she was admitting. But if—a big if—she had been an adopted child herself, why should revealing it matter?

Lorely Pelling, Wild Cat-Woman, offer another clue. Don't slip away now.

But despite the sense of her shadow momentarily within reach he felt the essence escaping. He looked again at the blank sheet of paper with a single word twice inked in. *Lonely. Lorely.* That was the reasonable alternative to his imaginative leap: the fantasies of frustration, balanced against the existence of a secret love-child. At least the second option could be checked on, but for the present he must leave it there. If he closed his mind down, refused to impose thought on it, maybe the rest of Lorely would come to him of itself.

Do nothing, then. That is to say, mentally.

But he couldn't return to bed. Sleep was impossible with so much adrenalin active; too much of his old Welsh granny aroused. This was a moment to employ his hands and let the brain go idle. Only, if he went out at 2.0 a.m. with a lantern to dig over the border he'd get a name for madness with any insomniac neighbours who might look out. Some other job, then, unlikely to disturb the household.

He tightened the cord of his dressing-gown, looked out his box of tools and went quietly along to the downstairs cloakroom to wrestle again with the taps. Accompanying him went the insubstantial Lorely, old, lonely and not a little grotesque, but carrying with her—a ghost within a ghost—the beautiful child of the miniature in oils.

TEN

'So DI JENNER'S setting up a case against the local—' Beaumont began, stopping short of 'idiot' when he realized the Superintendent had cause to resent the term.

'The simple lad, yes.' Yeadings surveyed him calmly. 'Based on the fact he was thereabouts and unaccounted for. Jenner's had a wheelbarrow from the Hall barn bagged and sent to Forensic Science. The SOCO picked up a mass of muddy dabs from the handles overlaid by marks from fabric gloves—same as the cartridge case from Farlowes grazing-field. They're hardly likely to find blood anywhere on it if it stood out in any of that rain. And even if they do, it'll tell us nothing about who it was that trundled the old lady from A to B.'

'But you accept she was shot in the Hall's grounds?'

'Near the vegetable plot she'd been working on, after retrieving the missing mother-cat and in the process of carrying it back to do its bit for the kittens. The cat's body caught a good blast of shot, as did the heavy-duty apron the woman was wearing. They were wrapped up together and buried in soft ground near the seed drills. Miss Pelling's body was concealed and later dumped in Farlowes Wood with a new scene set up, probably in an attempt to lay blame for the killing on whatever wild shots the lads had let off in the higher field beyond.'

'And she survived for some hours after being shot. Any chance she could have buried the cat herself?'

'I asked Dr Littlejohn that. He thinks it's most unlikely. She certainly couldn't have reached Farlowes Wood under her own steam. As for the route, there's a well-used track worn from the rear of the hall, round two fields and into Battels Lane which borders the wood. There's also a rear driveway from that lane to Farlowes Farm about fifty yards farther on.'

'You think there was more come-and-go between the two households than Welch implied?'

Yeadings rasped a hand across his chin and grunted. 'Let me try out a wild notion on you. Tell me it's daft if you like.' And he sketched briefly his night-time theory of a blood relationship between Lorely and 'Farmer' Welch's wife.

'How do dates and ages fit?' Beaumont asked cautiously.

'Roughly possible, I think, but it needs checking at Public Records. I'd say Mrs Welch was fortyish. Do we know exactly when the Pellings took up residence at the Hall?'

Beaumont grimaced. 'Does it matter? Lorely could have had the child either in India or back here.'

'M'm, of course Malmsmead's been in the Pelling family three generations at least. But the Welches came here from away. They're townees. We need to know what brought them. Was it some connection with Swardley or pure chance?'

'I might know the person to ask,' Beaumont offered. 'Welch's old mum has a cottage in the village. Stuart pointed it out to me; said Rory used to visit his granny there at weekends before he went away to school. It was a condition of his getting pocket-money out of Welch. An old dear living on her own, she'd likely be pleased to reminisce. Maybe Z could go along.'

MRS WELCH SENIOR was a vague-eyed person with an ominous tremor and a querulous voice. She assumed at first that Rosemary was an applicant for the vacant job of home help. The girl was installed on a chair in the kitchen before she got across that she was a minor police inquirer looking into village life. Even then her lack of uniform allowed the old lady's cogs to slip a tooth or two. By the time she had transferred her caller to the cluttered sitting-room she was marvelling how women were taking over men's jobs. 'A reporter, just fancy. No wonder,' she added tetchily, 'that there's no one left to come and keep house.'

Gently but firmly Rosemary declined the pressure on her to change her career. 'I'm not at all domesticated,' she excused herself. 'Quite clumsy, actually. I'd break all your pretty china.'

May Welch looked fondly at the crowded surfaces of small tables and whatnots. To her these treasures were all quite beautiful, the seaside souvenirs along with son Franklin's more recent gifts of Meissen and Limoges. There were besides some grotesque pottery mugs, majolica items and a garish pair of plaster Alsatians.

'You must have lived here a long time to gather such a collection,' Rosemary suggested.

'A long time, yes.' Rather sadly. Perhaps dates were a little beyond her now.

'Were you born in Swardley?'

'Oh no!' You could hear the contempt quite plainly. 'We're from Middlesex. My parents had ever such a nice house in Uxbridge. On the north side, of course.' Clearly any other part was less illustrious.

'And you went to school there?'

Schooling, it seemed, was something to be passed over quickly. 'My husband—my late husband, that is—Ronald, he worked as storeman at a big electronics place in Hayes. He was killed on his motorbike one frosty morning. They were ever so nice about it. Franklin was only a little tot then, but I got a pension, and they said when he grew up he could ask them for a job.'

'So did he?'

Mrs Welch gazed at her with empty, faded blue eyes. 'Did he what?'

'Did Franklin ask them for a job when he left school?'

'I suppose so, after college. He was ever so clever, like his dad. He won a scholarship, and then a grant to go for his degree. In the north somewhere. Bradford or Birmingham.

'After Ronald died I was mostly living with my mother between jobs. She helped with little Franklin. Then I lived in Amersham. When I left that job I moved here. It's a nice cottage, but so far away from everything. Nothing much to do, you see. Except church. I remember the village from when I was nanny for a while in a big house that's been pulled down since. They were Americans, nice people, but my husband didn't like me away five days a week. Said we didn't need the extra money anyway.' She sounded disgruntled.

'Swardley's not the same now. People have no respect any more. Some really nasty things go on these days.'

'So why did you choose Swardley to live? Did your son suggest it? Or perhaps his wife?'

'Oh, I was here long before he married, and when Franklin did so well—he has his own firm now, you know—he bought a house down in Surrey. Then he met Alexandra. She's from ever such a nice family. Her mother was a Hon. And her father a baronet. Not that my son wasn't good enough for them. He's very clever with all those electronics. He worked hard to make his money. Then he bought up his old company and he makes lots of parts you can't get anywhere else.'

The enthusiasm and the rambling explanation seemed to have tired her. The tremor had passed up her arm and now her head was shaking. Rosemary tried one last time. 'But why come to Swardley?'

Mrs Welch looked vaguely back, a wisp of pinkly tinted white hair wagging independently of her body's jerking. 'Well, they came to be near me, didn't they? I should think anyone could see that! Franklin bought Farlowes for Alexandra when little Amanda was a baby. To get her away from those awful smelly stables.'

'I HONESTLY BELIEVE,' Rosemary reported back, 'that she doesn't remember exactly when or why she came to Swardley herself. She recalls incidents here and there, but nothing consecutive. No dates. The Welches moving in next to Lorely Pelling, even buying the home farm which was once the late Brigadier's, must have been chance. It came free at the time when they wanted somewhere more upmarket, not too far from the old lady—the only grandparent the children had left. In all her ramblings old Mrs Welch never mentioned the Pellings or any connection they might have with her daughter-in-law.'

'Well, the Public Records Office will have the final say, but it does look as though the Welches came in order to be near Franklin's mother and not Alexandra's,' Yeadings allowed. 'With such a distinguished family as the Trewins it shouldn't be difficult to discover whether Alexandra was their own daughter or a discreet adoption. I think DI Jenner might profit from a half-day in London following that up.'

'What's happening about the Pelling will?' Beaumont inquired.

'I assume it's being played down for the present. The Slough solicitor—Longstaff, is it?—made an appointment to see Mrs Welch in the afternoon following my visit. He hadn't cared for my breaking the news to her, but in view of the police interest he eventually agreed I should sound the lady out before he saw her.'

'Assuming his client could have been murdered for her money?'

'He already had misgivings about holding the sealed will without having spoken to the testatrix, but the vet, Norman Marsh—who was a witness and had suggested the solicitor—thought to ring him and explain the circumstances. Longstaff had confidence in the man, so he agreed to respect Miss Pelling's wish for privacy.'

'Did the old girl actually have anything to leave?' Beaumont asked doubtfully.

'Oh yes. There's Malmsmead, neglected but unmortgaged, fifty-seven remaining acres of reasonable arable land bordering an area designated for building, and—'

'This is the punch-line coming?'

'A fortune in antique furniture and Old Masters.' Yeadings grinned at the puzzled expression of the other two. 'You recall the box-file Z unearthed yesterday? Among other things of note it had some interesting receipts in it. Apparently, for safe-keeping and to escape the hassle of renewing insurance, Miss Pelling loaned twenty-three named canvases and two van-loads of George III and French Empire furniture to the National Trust. Presumably they're now dispersed throughout the UK, gracing stately homes handed over by less shrewd or less fortunate families.'

'Dollar Almighty!' swore Beaumont.

'And the Welches don't need money anyway,' Rosemary marvelled.

'So it looks. But you can't tell with these mushrooming family firms. There will have to be a discreet inquiry into the financial standing of Miraprax Electronics. If the company is rocky we must consider that the Welches do have motive.'

'Except that the will's faulty,' Beaumont reminded him. 'Wouldn't they have to admit blood relationship?'

'Suppose they never knew the wording of the will,' Rosemary suggested.

'Exactly. But to add another option,' Yeadings said sardonically, piling on the snags, 'we can't assume they'd any knowledge of the will in the first place!'

There came a sharp rap on the Superintendent's door and Jenner's pinched face looked in. 'Am I late?' he demanded accusingly.

'Even a minute or two early,' Yeadings said easily. 'Good thing. I want you to go up to London and chase a few facts up. Have a look at this list and tell me if you see any difficulties.'

He turned to the others. 'Beaumont, have a word with your boy. Find out all you can about the Welch lad—hobbies, career intentions if any, attitudes to current issues. See him in the round, eh?'

Beaumont looked doubtful. 'That's all?'

'For the moment. Z, I want you to trot along and gossip with the cottagers again. Make sure old Gash's field-glasses haven't picked up something we've all missed. Have a proper go at the Widow Lammas and find out why she's so steamed up against the dead woman. She was willing to go shopping for her, and she's hardly the sort to do favours for a mortal enemy. Then wander up to Welch's stables at Farlowes. Pet the horses and draw out the stable-man, Alec Benson. We've not much on him except that he owns a shotgun. He may have noticed movement in the wood when he was clearing up after the boy's reunion on Saturday. Even if he saw someone innocently walking through, that could lead to fixing a time when the body hadn't yet been dumped there.'

'Yessir.'

'That leaves me to look through the reports again and have a few more words with Firearms down at the range.'

He watched them dismiss, then turned his attention to the green file he took from his second drawer down. For a little over two hours he worked steadily through papers that were already familiar, hoping that some phrase would leap out at him with new significance. But he went unrewarded. At 11.45 his watch bleeped him. He reached for his jacket, smoothed his hair, and went downstairs jingling his car keys. 'If I'm needed, leave a message on the answering machine at my house,' he instructed DCI Atkinson.

Outside, the sun was fitfully appearing at breaks in the low cloud cover. It could brighten, Yeadings thought, heading for home to pick up Nan and the children.

They took on calories at McDonalds, to Nan's muted disapproval and Sally's huge delight. Luke sat in his high chair, making a mess of a homemade sandwich and a yoghurt. When all exterior traces of lunch had been removed they went *en famille* to choose the new toilet suite for the downstairs cloakroom.

Since the builder's yard supplied a wealth of interest and distraction it was past three when they left. Yeadings saw the others into a taxi and drove straight to Maidenhead before the instruction session should end and the Firearms team disperse. Sergeant Philimore was expecting him and had the range set up for the experiments. They had all been done before, but Yeadings had a fancy to see the action for himself after reviewing the still photographs of the death scene.

'Terminal Ballistics,' Philimore introduced the subject.

Terminal indeed for Lorely Pelling, Yeadings thought.

'What happens at the end of a projectile's path,' the comfortable Lancashire voice offered as sub-title. 'Right then, sir, you want to see the effect of 15-metre range, firing from an open barrel, and 20-metre range with a fully choked barrel. Using 6-shot "Western" cartridges. Will you put your ear-muffs on, sir, please. We all need to, indoors.'

A marksman stepped to the 15-metre marker, and the instructor said, 'When you're ready, Constable.' The target hung like a plastic-covered mattress at the gallery's end, shining creamy-peach in this light—much the colour of the suite just chosen for the loo, Yeadings noted.

The man with the shotgun levelled it, aimed and fired, ejected the cartridge case, moved back to the next marker and exchanged guns. He placed the second hail of shot at the far side of the target, level with the first. All three men moved forward to examine the results.

'Of course, you never get identical patterns,' Philimore warned.

'I appreciate that. Both of these are similar to the spread we found in the dead woman. What I'm not happy about is the second Farlowes discharge, into the beech tree. I brought a copy of the shot pattern. You've seen this, I understand?'

'He stood much closer that time,' Philimore gave as his opinion.

'So why did he? He knew the range she was killed at if it was the same man who shot her. He was trying to change the background of the crime. From this photo it looks as if he roughly blocked off an area to represent the woman's torso on the tree, and then repeated the shot without the body being there.'

'Trying to produce a frame to fit the body.'

'Exactly. So why change the range?'

'There could have been some intervening object in the wood—a tree, say.'

'We checked on that. There was undergrowth up to waist-height, but unrestricted passage for the shot at that level for at least 20 metres.'

'So perhaps he didn't know the range she'd been shot at.'

'Which would mean it wasn't the killer who did the covering up. On the other hand—' Yeadings ran a hand through his hair—'could it be the killer both times, but ignorant of—er, terminal ballistics?'

Philimore stroked his chin. 'I—was wondering. Maybe it was a different gun. Look at the photo of the tree, sir. The shot's too bunched, right? There's a chunk of wood punched clean away. Because the stuff's concentrated, and it's still only small stuff, 6-shot.'

'Which means he stood too close. We know that. But *why* did he?'

'Suppose he was expecting it to spray out wider?'

'Why should he?'

'We-ell, I've come across some funny villains, real wallies at the job. There was a case some years back: a fellow got hold of a sawn-off shotgun, knew nothing about it. Didn't try it out because he never really intended using it. But he loaded it for the job—a warehouse hold-up. Got overexcited and discharged it when the watchman dived behind his desk. Blew the poor devil's shoulder right off.

'He was in a terrible state afterwards—the villain, I mean. He'd thought that because the gun was shortened the shot would spray out like firework, pink the man enough to hold him off, and no more. A lot of people make the same assumption, that the shorter the barrel the wider the spread. There's some truth in it, but it's only minimal. The sawn-off type's less accurate to use, but the shot pattern's not all that different from a full-length gun.'

'This introduces a whole new element,' Yeadings said softly. 'I get the point. Our man, either the killer or another, uses a second gun on the tree. This time it's a sawn-off model and he knows nothing of its performance. So he supposes, wrongly, that the shot pattern will be more widely spread, and he allows for it by shooting from closer range, thereby producing the more concentrated pattern.'

'Complicated, but it could be that way.'

'New question: *why* a sawn-off?'

'All he could lay hands on at the time.'

'And the thing's illegal. So he's a villain already, or—more likely—he knows a villain and borrows the gun in ignorance of its performance.'

'I'd go along with that, sir. Easily portable; you could hide one under your jacket even in daylight.'

'Which leaves us looking for a villain in the neighbourhood of Farlowes Wood and Swardley Village who'd have reason to own a sawn-off shotgun. We'll have to turn up records.'

'There is another possibility,' Philimore reminded him. 'You get gun-buffs who collect the things secretly, keep them hidden.

'Oh Lord,' said Yeadings, 'you do indeed.' He had a brief vision then of old Gash reaching under the floorboards for his treasured Lee Enfield.

ELEVEN

YEADINGS REGARDED HIMSELF sombrely in the shaving mirror. The case, he felt, had entered the doldrums and it showed in his face. There was often a becalmed period like this when he was less aware of the suspects or even the victims than of the team beavering away. And beavering without significant result.

True, facts were being turned up—like the peculiar will; the furniture on loan to the National Trust; the apron-wrapped dead cat—but none of this had so far led anywhere markedly useful.

He missed talking things over with Angus Mott, each sounding out the other's reactions. Jenner was a poor substitute, too keen to fix the crime to a pre-judged target, so personally involved. He was personally involved himself, Yeadings had to admit; but in the opposite direction, using the same information to exonerate Peter Howell rather than tie him down. He could have admitted as much to Mott, who would have understood. But Jenner was ignorant of his connection with the simple-minded; his prejudice on their behalf, because of Sally.

It was true that Poor Peter could have done it. Having no gun himself, he could have used Lorely's and cleaned it afterwards with the devotion to routine detail to which the simple-minded were so easily trained. But if the plastic cup-wad in the garden and the cartridge case found in the field above Farlowes Wood came from the cartridge used to kill Lorely Pelling, Peter couldn't have taken that from the Hall. Lorely's were of a different make. So who would have supplied him? Jenner was assuming that Peter had his own cartridges for poaching purposes, but he'd no firearms certificate and no one so far questioned had ever seen Peter carrying a gun.

Could that be because there was possibly a sawn-off shotgun in the case, as Philimore of Firearms had suggested? Peter using the old lady's own gun to kill her (because it was handy at the time) and later going for the sawn-off one, which he kept hidden, for the mock-up in Farlowes Wood? The planning seemed too complicated for someone of Peter's capability. Would he have thought of throwing the ejected case into the grazing-field, to make it seem the boys could have shot her by accident?

Yeadings recalled the man's miserable state when they had found him. Wretched, because cold and hungry and wet, he hadn't found the mother cat he'd been sent to look for on the Saturday. It wasn't until they had stood over him, seeming menacing, that he'd shown fear. Z had calmed him and they'd gone to bury the unused cat-meat, discovering the animal's grave in the vegetable plot. That was when the real terror had seized him, and he'd seemed to lose his wits entirely. The sight of the dead cat and the bloodied apron had been too much. Because of suddenly remembered guilt? Or was it pure shock?

Yeadings sighed, patted his chin with aftershave, slung his damp towel in the laundry basket and went down to breakfast. He had the kitchen to himself and he continued brooding. The team were all tackling the case at different levels: himself too personally; Jenner inquisitorially; Z still learning the job and seeing it as taking orders, overcompensating for her dislike of Jenner by being too ready to accept her intuitive assessments as wrong if told she was out of step. Perhaps for once it was Beaumont proving himself the best straightforward jack, working doggedly through the recognized stages of inquiry, even if he was merely using the certainties of the job to block out his present domestic miseries.

Dammit, Yeadings thought; I can't see the wood for the trees, or the crime for the team. Start at the beginning, then. With the gun. Or guns. Trot along this morning and have a word with old Gash.

There was a downpour as he drove out towards Swardley, turning off before the village into Battels Lane. The row of cottages, two sets of semis with the newer bungalow in between, looked more dismal under a wash of grey. An unmarked police car in Medlams' short drive reminded him that with Jenner in London, Rosemary Z was tackling the locals on her own. He drove past Gash's and the next two, to pull in behind the other car, the Rover's rear just clearing the gateway.

There was no answer to his knock. He waited, water dripping from an upper window-sill to supplement the driving rain on his shoulders. The Medlams, he remembered then, both worked. He went over to the timber garage and peered through the window. Their car was away. Z must be in one of the neighbouring cottages.

A curtain twitched at an upper window of the Barrows' end cottage, but no face showed, so he turned in the opposite direction and walked up the path of the widowed Mrs Lammas.

As he did so the front door opened abruptly and Mrs Medlam stood there. 'Superintendent? Your police young lady's here. Were you looking for her?'

She appeared flustered and a little breathless. Behind her he heard another female voice winding upwards in a hysterical spiral. 'Anything I can do to help?' he asked.

'Oh, I don't know. She's right upset. My sister, I mean. Your young lady's been trying to get her to take doctor's advice, but she's half out of her mind. Still, she's always been—difficult. I stayed home today to keep an eye on her, but I don't know why I bothered. She won't listen.'

'Maybe she wants us to listen to her. Can I come in?' He followed her into the disordered living-room.

Rosemary sat on the settee with her back towards him. She had her head down and her hands clasped on her knees, waiting. The other woman stood at the far end of the room, arms outstretched and palms flat against the wall, like some defiant victim of a firing-squad. As her eyes fell on Yeadings the words trailed off into silence and she gazed at him open-mouthed.

Yeadings raised the sodden tweed hat he'd rammed over his ears to keep off the rain. ''Morning, ma'am. Another filthy day. I came to see if there's anything I can do to help.' Water ran from the hem of his Burberry on to the carpet. 'Afraid I'm rather wet, though.'

'Here, I'll take your things,' Mrs Medlam offered.

'And maybe we could all have a pot of tea?' Rosemary murmured.

As her sister disappeared Mrs Lammas seemed to relax a little. 'Won't you sit down and tell us about it?' Yeadings invited, indicating the settee. There was a pause and then somnambulantly the woman started moving across. When she was seated by Rosemary he removed a tray with a bowl of soggy cereal from a nearby armchair and drew it up opposite.

'She thinks I'm mad,' said Mrs Lammas.

'Perhaps she doesn't understand.'

'She doesn't care! She says shut up and don't make a fuss. Well, it's not right. She says—it's all round the village—the old girl left everything to those Welch kids at Farlowes. She wouldn'ta done that. They're nothing to her. It shoulda come to me. Frank's money, like she promised.'

'Frank was your husband, is that right? What exactly did she say, Mrs Lammas?'

'She said she knew her own, even if no one else did. And she'd see right was done by them. She promised.'

'Her own? Who did she mean by that?'

'Well, Frank, of course! He was a Pelling, even if it was on the wrong side of the blanket. You'd only to look at his face.' She pointed unsteadily to the black and white wedding photograph on the wall.

'You mean that your husband was related in some way—'

'Left in the church porch, wasn't he? On August 1st, Lammas Day. Just a day or two old, he'd be. And you can't get away from that. And all that summer *she* was away. Travelling, they said. Come back in October for her birthday. Forty-one, she was then. And by then the baby was fostered because nobody ever claimed him. Grew up belonging to the village, he did. Well, everyone respected Squire. The Pellings were gentry, see, and he didn't seem to guess. But Lady Muck—we weren't any of us good enough for her! Never could be bothered with us, no more than she could with her poor little fatherless baby. 'Twasn't till I was ten or so that I understood what folks were saying behind her back. Not that it mattered by then. Everyone got along well with Frank. He was a lovely lad. There was nobody could hold a candle to my Frank.'

'Did he ever claim her as his mother?'

Mrs Lammas was struck silent by the question. She plucked at the frilled collar of her grubby pink blouse. 'Used to laugh about it,' she conceded at last. 'Said he popped up overnight, like a mushroom. And whoever asked what a mushroom's folks were?'

'Did anyone find out where Miss Pelling was that summer?'

'Not then. And afterwards it was too late.' Mrs Lammas spoke resentfully. 'Vicar would surely've said something, but we never did hear what. The baker adopted him along with his own three but, like I said, Frank belonged to all the village. Everybody helped out, Squire included. And by the time we got married Squire was dead, but he'd left money in trust for the reception and a hundred pounds besides. But we got nothing from her. Too proud, is my opinion. Didn't want her shame known. She was a sly one, that Miss Lorely.'

Yeadings got up and went slowly over to the wedding photograph. The young groom was smiling proudly. He had an open, ingenuous face. Something about the spacing of the eyes and the slant of the cheekbones was familiar. The dead woman's face had worn no smile, and the child in the miniature in oils had been solemn, but there was something in common. The soldier father had it too; the bone structure of the upper face. Nothing conclusive, but Mrs Lammas, determined to see a likeness, had found it.

Yeadings went back to his chair. 'You used to see Miss Pelling quite regularly, I believe?' he asked gently.

'She avoided me, like she did everyone. When I went for the list, or to take the shopping, she'd go off into the woods. I could feel her there sometimes watching me. She'd gone wild, she had. Like her cats. Nasty vicious creatures. Still, I caught her once or twice.' Mrs Lammas added the last with smug satisfaction.

'And then you spoke together?'

'I told her things. About the village. About Frank. Things she ought to know.'

'And what did she say?'

'Not a lot. Said she could live without Swardley, just as she always had, and Swardley could do the same without her. Then I said some folks had responsibilities they hadn't owned up to.'

'And that's when she mentioned knowing her own and that she'd see right was done by them?'

'That's when, right enough.'

'And you understood that she meant your husband, and yourself subsequently as his widow.'

'Who else?'

Yeadings merely shook his head: it could have meant anything. Mrs Lammas took it as sympathy.

'So what'm I to do, sir? How can I make my claim now she's gone?'

'We'll have to find out,' he temporized. Grateful for the interruption, he stood to take the tray of tea-things from Mrs Medlam as she came in eyeing her sister with suspicion.

'There's ways of finding out, with blood, isn't there?' Mrs Lammas persisted. 'My poor man, they took blood enough from him in the end. It must be written down somewhere.'

And Lorely Pelling's body still in cold store, Yeadings reflected. The path. lab could go some way to settling whether the two blood groups were compatible. A pity there was no idea who the missing father had been.

Yeadings sighed. 'Ladies, thank you for your tea, but I mustn't stay longer. I have to call on your neighbour Mr Gash.'

Rosemary rose as if to leave with him. 'Sir—'

'You stay and enjoy your tea, Z. I'll see you later.'

'But, sir, it's about Mr Gash. I called on him first myself. And he wasn't in. That's what I went to ask Mrs Lammas about. Whether he'd gone into hospital or something.'

'There's been no cars past,' Mrs Medlam said definitely. 'He'll be lying low, pretending he's not there. He never goes out at all. He can't walk.'

'In that case I'll try again,' said Yeadings. 'And in case we have to break in, maybe you'd better come along, Z.'

They left Mrs Lammas glumly slumped on the settee. The earlier hysteria had all been used up. She seemed exhausted by pouring out her suspicions of her dead Frank's origins. Grief had again taken over from her fury at Lorely's heartless denial of her son.

When they reached the gate, Rosemary touched the Superintendent's arm. 'Sir, I didn't want to say it in front of them because they seemed so sure, but Mr Gash isn't in the house. The back door was unlocked and I went right through, upstairs and down.'

'So it would seem he's more mobile than he gives everyone to believe. That could put a new complexion on things.'

They splashed through puddles and stood by the front door knocking. When no one came, Yeadings said, 'Stay here. I'll go in by the back.'

Rosemary waited, peering occasionally through the stiffly opening letter-box. She heard the Superintendent's movements about the rooms and on the stairs. Eventually he rejoined her outside. 'There's neither hide nor hair of him. And his field-glasses aren't there.'

'How about the rifle?'

'Safe where it should be, thank God. But I think we'd better brave the wet and have a look in the fields. He can't have gone far unless someone gave him a lift at the lane end. Just walk to the junction and see if there's anyone about. Since he must have left by the back door I'll try and get through to the maize field. Give a shout if you need me.'

Rosemary pulled the hood tighter on her anorak. Already the sodden tweed of her skirt clung chillingly to her thighs. She plunged on towards the main road and heard the swearing of brambles against Yeadings's raincoat as he thrust a way bodily through the hedge. Barely three or four minutes later she heard him whistle and came running back.

'There's a gap behind Gash's shed,' he called. 'Use that. Come and help me lift him.'

Gash was lying prone in the open field among the smashed stalks of the decaying maize. His hands and chest were daubed with mud where he'd struggled unsuccessfully to get upright, but at least his face lay clear of the water-filled ruts. An old brown overcoat inadequately covered his striped pyjamas. He'd lost a slipper. Everything was soaked through.

'He's breathing, just,' said Yeadings. 'Seems to have collapsed. Let's get him to the road and I'll drive him to hospital. Both together, now, li-ift.'

Back in the lane she supported Gash's thin frame as Yeadings ran for his car, then helped him load the man in. 'Get home and change,' the Superintendent ordered.

She nodded, but had to go back among the maize stalks for the field-glasses which she'd stumbled over on their way out. Then there was the back door to secure. In a kitchen drawer she found a key that fitted, locked up and brought the key away. Wherever Gash was taken they'd find night-clothes and toilet things for him. Anything more he needed could be fetched from the cottage later.

She squelched her way back to her issue car and eased herself wetly in. Then sat, staring ahead as the wipers cleared the windscreen and the car warmed slightly.

All the time she was with Mrs Lammas, she reflected, that poor old man had been lying in the rain, helpless, losing body heat. She shouldn't have been satisfied with searching the house. She should have tried the fields behind. If he died of exposure it would be her fault. Because she was a fool, suspecting him of God knows what duplicity just because he kept a gun under his floorboards as a memento. If the Boss hadn't come along and insisted on looking himself...

She tilted the driving mirror to check that she didn't look as if she'd been crying. 'Bath,' she said firmly. A good hot soak and some dry clothes, then she'd find out where Yeadings had taken him and go sit with Gash till he came awake. Because he had to get over it. He just had to.

YEADINGS RANG THROUGH to Pathology from the desk at Casualty. Gash was being seen to in one of the curtained cubicles. It was an age since the Superintendent had smelled these smells and heard those disturbing sounds, amplified by the outsider's fear which such scenes of emergency evoked. It took him back to his raw days in the Met, when he used to look in at the Westminster to catch Nan's eye, Sister on Casualty, two years before he dared ask her to marry him.

The set-up still disturbed him, such density of suffering and such suddenness of crisis. At least when he was called to a murder case the victim was past all this. He knew he hadn't the sort of courage repeatedly to fight incursive death.

Littlejohn wasn't in the building, although expected for a post-mortem. The mortuary attendant had had the case notes typed up and would put them out for Yeadings to look at.

'No immediate hurry. I have to dry off first.' He used the medical staff cloakroom, stripped off his outer clothing, laying jacket, shirt and trousers across a hot radiator, watching the legs steam while he towelled his face and shoulders. When he dressed again the things were still damp, but temporarily warm. The wool mixture cloth gave off an intimate doggy odour.

When he reached the mortuary Littlejohn was already at work on his new corpse. 'Motorcycle artist,' he complained. 'First one I ever did was a neighbour's only son. Now every time a biker turns up, for me it's the same one over again. Bloody waste.'

'I've a couple more questions about the late Miss Lorely Pelling,' Yeadings distracted him.

'Thought you might have. Fire away.'

Yeadings briefly told him Mrs Lammas's tale of the Swardley foundling. 'So I'd appreciate your opinion on the blood groups.'

'She was O + ,' Littlejohn answered, still probing. 'Same as almost half the population of the UK. Get Phil to look up Frank Lammas's file. It's probably not gone through to Admin. yet.'

The attendant went for the papers, came back and held them under the doctor's bifocals. 'Got him trained not to hand anything over to non-medicals,' Littlejohn commented with grim humour. 'Police are the worst for helping themselves. Well, well, it seems Lammas too was O, Rhesus Positive. Not that it's conclusive, of course. Merely not *ex*clusive.'

He mopped his forehead. 'Is someone trying to prove a case of *Droit de Seigneur* in the feminine form?'

Yeadings grunted. 'There might be another—or alternative—offspring of the dead woman. Or else the village is a hotbed of uninformed malicious gossip. But I may have more trouble getting the information on a living person. Have to try maternity records for that one, I guess.'

'M'm. The dead are more cooperative, you'll agree. Look, Mike, let me save you further hassle, with a single small fact. It's in the full report on your dead woman, but a detail easily overlooked in the plethora of medical verbiage.'

He pulled down his mask and grinned, showing long, yellowing teeth. 'Rest easy. Miss Pelling was *virgo intacta*. So, short of blasphemy, I must admit she can't ever have had a child.'

TWELVE

RORY WELCH THRASHED restlessly in his duvet, then came urgently awake in the half-light, knowing something was very wrong. He could hear his own heart padding like the creature that had pursued him in his dream, something immense and hairy—bear or Yeti. Horrible, anyway.

What he heard now distantly was the clunk of the stable door, and Blanco's dancing hooves clopping on the cobbles. Ma was up and going off riding—after a night at least as troubled as his own.

He had slept deeply at first, but he knew nobody was ever totally asleep. The part that keeps watch and prowls about in search of the stuff for dreams had gone eavesdropping downstairs. It came back and tapped him persistently until he woke.

Not that they were shouting. Not at that point. Ma had been pleading in a low, too-controlled voice. The Old Man's overrode it, harsh and without any of the classy bray he put on when he knew there were listeners. The words—nothing distinct. Just that deadly, mounting rumble, so that to break through she had to raise her pitch, sharpen.

Then the Old Man more emphatic, separating each word from the last, as if some deliberate physical act took place between—twisting her wrist?—brutally squeezing those fine bones with his stubby fingers?

Her voice tremulous, rising to a stifled shriek.

The man's anger bursting out then in a vituperative flood. The sound of two doors slammed in quick succession. Silence, then a car starting up, a roar of acceleration, a savage scattering of gravel as it turned under Rory's window, the headlights sweeping the farther wall and ceiling with an elongated window-pattern . . .

He had stolen out on the landing to listen. Watching her leave the library. Not instantly. There had been a terrible delay while nothing happened, no sound. He had even thought of going down in case . . . But it was unthinkable to walk in on her before . . . She was so . . . apart, so very private.

At last she came out, and he slid again behind his door as she slowly mounted the stairs, paused a moment on the far side of the panels almost as if she guessed he was there, holding his breath so as not to be discovered spying. Finally she passed on, switched off the lights, regained her own room, softly closed the door.

Later, when he finally slept he was out on the landing again, watching her come up in slow motion, with a wind making her clothing stream and billow. He stood his ground and she came up close, continued sightlessly, passing right through him as though he never existed. And then followed the flight dreams and pursuit by the Yeti-bear thing.

And now, properly awake, he had to face it.

How had she felt this morning as she saddled Blanco and rode off? Still shaken? Outraged? Frightened? Not desperate, surely. Whatever, she shouldn't be left alone.

Rory reached for jeans and sweater. In the jumble of his cupboard he couldn't locate his hard hat. His jodhpur boots were too tight now. He flung them aside and slipped into his trainers.

Outside it struck cold. The wind had dropped and the rain turned to a fine suspension of mist. It blurred the outlines of trees and buildings. He'd never find which way she'd gone.

Light slanted from the stable block. He could hear Alec moving about inside, shifting things, the clink of harness rings. He went in and saw he had the roan mare saddled. The man turned and looked at the boy, expressionless. 'I thought to go after her,' he said.

'No. I'll go.'

Alec hesitated, rasping a hand across his stubbled chin. 'You're no rider.'

'All the same, I'll go.'

'Better put this on, then.' The man pulled a leather jacket from a hook on the wall. It was too large, but had a fleecy lining, was warm at least. Rory took the reins and backed the roan out. In the yard he stepped up and swung into the saddle.

'Goes off towards the river most mornings. You're not like to catch her up in this mist, though.'

'Maybe not.' It sounded cool, despite the knot inside him.

It wasn't the real world. More like some Victorian monochrome. Grey ghosts of trees, hedges, gates, looming suddenly and oozing moisture. Over towards the road, through the skeletal spinney, came the peering eyes of car headlights, disappearing at Cutts Corner and replaced by twin red spots. He resisted the pull as the roan threw her head, resenting his unfamiliar touch. With shortened rein he nudged her into Battels Lane.

He knew it was impossible to find anyone in this mist. It was stupid to have come. When he reined in there was no sound but the dripping of moisture and a distant hum of traffic from the main road. The mare snickered, not that she scented another horse, but petulantly, demanding movement.

'Presently,' he told her.

It seemed likely Ma would have given up her gallop; even possible she'd turned off down towards the Hall. It must be on her mind all the time now, as it was with him. He should have checked whether the key was gone from its hook in the kitchen cupboard.

Indistinctly he made out the darker frame of a gate, with a sea of mist behind it. He dismounted and, with the reins over one arm, opened the way into the field. Along the side of this and through the waste beyond, he would reach the rear of Malmsmead. He went on foot, leading the mare and leaving the gate open.

There were no lights showing in the house, so it wasn't policed at night. He thought that in cases like this—violent death—there'd be a seal put on the doors. He wondered if his mother knew that, but she'd hardly be inside there in the dark. And there was no sign of Blanco.

He looped the reins on a shutter hook by the scullery window and sat on the sill. His mind was as clouded as the saturated air around, full of shadowy threats and unbelievable shapes. Old Lorely dead, he reminded himself. Killed with a shotgun. That was horror enough, but the suspicion... And this latest row between his parents, so openly vicious, maybe final.

The one sure thing in all this was that he couldn't walk away and leave things as they were. It was impossible to cut himself off, continue with the second half of term, switch his mind over to Maths and Latin, the dorm, the other guys's ragging.

The mare tossed her head and he stood up stiffly, scratched her nose, the flat bone above the eyes. 'OK, we'll move.'

She wasn't as good a jumper as Blanco, he knew. Had this habit of refusing at the last. Well, she'd be no bolder in this mist, and that should save her.

He mounted, his trainers slithering in the wet stirrups, pressed his heels in her flanks and turned her back towards the fields. She cantered easily, but he had to urge her into the gallop, set her across the steaming turf, crouched over the saddle and headed for where he guessed the hedge would be highest.

THE SPEED WITH WHICH news travelled in Swardley village was quite something. DC Silver, arriving early at the Incident Caravan, had picked it up with some hot rolls from the baker, son and successor to the good man who had included the foundling Frank Lammas in his brood.

One of the Farlowes Farm hunters had come home with an empty saddle, and their groom had organized a party to go looking for the rider. It had been the Welch son, found easily enough because there'd been a field with an open gate on the far side of Battels Lane. They'd come on him hanging in a hedge, his feet just short of the choked ditch, where the beast must have thrown him. Reports on his condition varied from a few minor bruises to a broken neck.

Silver phoned Superintendent Yeadings at home for instructions whether to take action.

Yeadings in turn phoned Farlowes Farm. A concerned housemaid told him that the Master was away and Madam had gone with Master Rory in the ambulance, taking Amanda along. He ascertained that they were bound for the same upgraded Cottage Hospital that Gash had been taken to. There seemed nothing for it but to return there himself and put in a morning of sick-visiting.

He found WDC Z clasping a polystyrene beaker of coffee in Casualty waiting-area. She had obviously spent the night in her clothes. 'Still here, then?' he greeted her, and brought her up to date on the news.

'I saw Rory brought in,' she told him, 'so I hung on, hoping to pick something up. Mr Gash came awake and I had a few words with him, though he's in a bad way. A weak chest, Sister says. They've moved him to Intensive Therapy.'

'What was he doing in the maize field?'

'He kept on about herons. A pair of them flew in. As far as I could make out, they must have settled on his own roof. Because he couldn't see them there he tried going outside, limped too far and his energy gave out. Then came the downpour.'

'The perils of geriatric bird-watching. Poor old chap. I'm glad no one else was responsible. Let's hope it's the same for young Rory Welch.'

Rosemary looked her question.

'The mare was a reluctant jumper, so Alec Benson told me when I questioned him. But she went hell-for-leather at the hedge before she refused it. I've got men down there looking for footmarks in the mud, in case some vicious beggar gave the mare a hard slap. There were cuts on her flanks, but she may have done that on her wild dash home. How's the boy, do you know?'

'Still unconscious. His mother's sitting with him. The little sister's somewhere around. We played *I spy* until she felt she'd entertained me enough.'

'I'll see if I can find her.'

The little girl was kneeling on a chair in the Sister's office, peering out of the window into the mist. She looked over her shoulder as Yeadings came in, then back at the glass. He came up close behind and intoned softly,

' '''No sun—no moon!
No morn—no noon,
No dawn—no dusk—no proper time of day. . .
No shade, no shine, no butterflies, no bees,
No fruits, no flowers, no leaves, no birds—
November!'' '

She faced him solemnly. 'I don't know that one. It's lovely.'

'Written by a man called Thomas Hood. He lived about the time your house was built.'

'Is it in a book?'

'In most anthologies, yes. I'd write it out for you, but I've forgotten the middle. It's better you should read the whole poem yourself.'

She stared at him and her lower lip began to tremble. 'Is Rory going to be all right?'

'I hope so. Shall I go and find out?'

'Yes, please.' She stood up, remembering the manners she had been taught, hands behind her back, prep-school pupil politely answering a question.

'Is he usually a rough rider?'

'Oh no. He doesn't ride any more since he got too big for my pony. Mummy thinks he just followed her out because of the mist.'

'Yes, it's what Alec thought too. That was kind of him.'

'Only—'

'Only what?'

'He wouldn't have jumped Minnie.' Amanda wasn't going to say any more. Already she was unsure whether she'd gone too far.

'He'll tell us about it when he wakes up, I expect.' Yeadings smiled and nodded, walked unhurriedly away. A nurse directed him to the upper corridor where Rory had been put in a single room.

Alexandra Welch got up as he came in. She was still in breeches and boots. 'Superintendent, more trouble, I'm afraid. Since Sunday nothing has gone right at all.'

'Since Saturday,' he corrected her. 'Miss Pelling was shot on Saturday, found Sunday.'

'Yes, of course.'

'How's Rory?'

'He came to, but they put him out again after the X-rays. He couldn't remember what happened, but they say that's often the case at first. They think his skull's all right. No more than bruising, but one shoulder—the muscles seem to be torn.'

'Shall I relieve you here while you tell your daughter? She's imagining all sorts of possibilities.'

'Amanda! Oh yes, thank you.'

He held the door open for her, then took her place at the bedside. The boy's face was waxen except for swollen bruising on one cheek and an oblique strip of dressing across the brow.

He kept watch for a few minutes, then got up and prowled round the small room.

'Tea, Superintendent?' asked a nurse brightly, popping her head in.

When she had gone to fetch it he went across to a tall locker and looked inside. Most of Rory's clothes were soiled and in a blue plastic sack on its floor, but a scuffed brown leather jacket was on a hanger. It smelled of horse. He went through the deep pockets and found food for thought there. Then he replaced the jacket and closed the door on it. When Alex Welch returned with Amanda the Superintendent appeared to be comfortably dozing, the empty cup and saucer by his feet. He jerked awake and stood up.

'I'm taking Amanda home now,' Mrs Welch told him. 'Rory will probably sleep on for some hours and then they'll ring me. I'll need to bring him some fresh clothes.'

'Has his father been informed?'

She darted a startled glance at him. 'I rang the office earlier. He hadn't come in. They were to tell him when he did.'

'He had already left the house, then, when the accident happened?'

'He—yes. That is, he was away overnight.' She wished the man didn't look at her as if he understood. Nothing in his face had actually changed but she felt his mind keeping pace with her own discomfiture.

'No doubt he'll drop by when he gets the message.'

'Unless—he may be away on business.' The more she covered for Franklin the wilder she sounded to herself. Yeadings would take her for a neurotic fool.

She turned away abruptly. 'I'd better take Rory's clothes away. He'll need different things in here.'

'Leave them, please. I'll have to let Forensic Science see them. Just in case there was a second person involved. My men are examining the field where it happened. Normal precautions, you know.'

She didn't know, and she didn't quite believe him. 'But it was an accident, Superintendent. P-police don't do this every time someone falls off a horse. God, I should know!'

'These aren't quite normal circumstances at present. And in view of where it happened—on Malmsmead Hall land— we must check all possibilities.'

She stared back at him, her lower lip trembling. 'You don't really think anyone would— No! He simply followed me out because he was worried about the mist.'

'Yes, I agree he was probably worried. He wasn't that keen on riding as a rule, was he?'

'No, but he's—unusually protective.'

Yeadings continued regarding her levelly and she didn't need to hear the question he asked himself: What need was there for such protection?

What he actually said was, 'I find that curious, you being such an accomplished rider. Rather like a non-swimmer jumping in to save a cross-Channel champion.'

'Oh, how do you know what goes on in the mind of a child—of an adolescent? You must understand how it is.'

He understood all right. Her apparent bafflement, and his own. Last night Sally had cried out three times in her sleep, each time in fear about water. Psychoanalysts might interpret that as a general state of insecurity, but he knew he'd been the specific cause. He blamed himself because days ago he'd left her down in the cloakroom when the hand-basin overflowed. She'd tried to turn the tap off but it hadn't responded. For her, magic gone wrong. For him a few minutes' neglect that might take an age before her security was restored.

He opened the locker door, took out the blue plastic sack of clothes and the leather hip-length coat. 'A bit on the big side for your son, isn't it?' he asked.

Mrs Welch barely gave it a glance. 'It's an old thing of my husband's.'

He held the door for her to pass through and they walked together along the corridor, Amanda trailing behind. 'I have to see a neighbour of yours now,' he said. 'Did you know Mr Gash had been brought in?'

'No; is he very ill?' She sounded genuinely concerned.

Yeadings told her what seemed to have happened.

'How awful. He should have someone to share the cottage with him. He has no family left.'

'Do you know him well?'

'As well as he'll allow.' Alex smiled wryly. 'He's proud and independent. I only get to see him when I take my turn with Meals on Wheels. Please give him my warm good wishes. Next time I come to see Rory I'll look in on him.'

Yeadings watched her go down the stairs, straight-backed and slim in her riding clothes. At the end of the first flight Amanda looked over her shoulder and waggled her fingers. He smiled back.

'Ullo,' Mr Gash greeted him as he leaned over his inert form. He had pulled the transparent plastic mask from his face. 'Got me wired up, they 'ave.'

'Take it easy,' Yeadings warned, 'or they'll throw me out. I've only been allowed five minutes.'

'S'enough. Wanted to—see yuh. Been thinking. Better you take—me old you-know-what. Safer that way, me being here—and the cottage—empty.'

He was panting horribly. The Superintendent stood up again, patted his naked shoulder. 'I came to suggest it. Glad you feel that way, Mr Gash. Much wiser, I'm sure.'

'You'll do it? *Today?*' His voice rasped, he started to cough, and Yeadings gently fitted the oxygen mask back over his nose and mouth.

He nodded. 'Consider it done. Concentrate on getting fit now. I'll call in again.'

WDC ROSEMARY ZYCZYNSKI was waiting for him at the main entrance. He shrugged on his overcoat while she relieved him of Rory's things. They emerged together into noonday mist only slightly less dense than it had been at dawn. It was definitely turning colder.

'Frost on the way,' declared Yeadings, sniffing the air. 'We're to pick up Gash's rifle, then I think we'd better try for a statement from Poor Peter Howell. I rather feel DI Jenner's struck a medal to pin on him and it's not an Order of Merit. So let's clear him off our list if we can.'

'Leaving whom?' asked Z primly.

'*Whom,*' Yeadings echoed roundly. 'Now there's a pearl of state education. I like it. More than I like the question. Anyone and no one, that's who. But I'm damned if I'll have it pinned on an incompetent for lack of the right villain. Here, you drive. I want a quiet think.'

Rosemary still had the key to Gash's cottage. When they reached it she held it up. 'Shall I—?'

Yeadings nodded, sat back and closed his eyes. She returned in a few minutes, locked something weighty in the car's boot along with Rory's clothes, and came round again in the front.

Yeadings was now in the driving seat. 'I'm leaving you to tackle the Howells,' he told her, letting in the clutch. 'You know what we need to cover.'

He was as good as his word, hanging back at the door, wandering after her into the cottage in an untypically vague and bumbling manner so that Mrs Howell seemed to overlook his presence once he'd planted himself on a chair in a corner of the living-room.

It was perhaps her experience that men laboured outside the house and ate or snored indoors, but women got on with what had to be done and saw to it that they kept the peace. She was about that function now, firm in the defence of her small, inadequate son, and ready to take offence on his behalf if the police young lady showed any sign of being less understanding than she had been so far.

Gently and slowly Rosemary went through the past few days with Poor Peter. Saturday, the day of his employer's death, was meant to be his free day, but that morning Peter had walked down to Malmsmead Hall through Farlowes Wood, meeting no one on the way once he'd left the village. He was hoping Miss Lorely would show him the kittens. He'd looked out through the thinning trees at one point and seen two men fixing targets in the grazing-field above the west side of the wood. One of them was Farmer Welch and t'other the ostler, Alec.

'You said *Farmer* Welch. But he doesn't farm, does he?'

'Lives at the home farm, doan' he?' Into Peter's eyes crept a look of sly cunning. 'Wanted to be Squire, 'e did.

Thought 'e cud buy it, but she wudden let un. Everybody knows. Us all doan' call un Squire, but *Farmer*, see?'

Peter grinned and rubbed his knuckles, bobbing his shaggy head. 'Diddun' like Miss Lorely. She got in 'is way, like.'

'And did she like him?'

This was more difficult for Peter. He looked across at his mother, brows puckered.

'Miss Lorely wuz a lady,' said Mrs Howell with firm finality, meaning apparently that whatever Squire's daughter had privately felt would be properly covered over. She smoothed the front of her skirt with flat palms, then stood straight with her hands loosely clasped. Something of her stance prompted Rosemary's next question. 'Did you know the Pelling family well, Mrs Howell.'

'I wuz in service with them in the Old Squire's time, as kitchen-maid. The Brigadier's father, that wuz. That's when they still 'ad staff at the Hall, miss.'

'I see. That would be before the Brigadier and his daughter came back from India?'

'I left service that same year as Old Squire died and they came 'ome, miss. Expecting Peter 'ere, I wuz, miss. And my man wuz carpenter in the village, working on the new vestry.'

They seemed to have wandered from the crime. Rosemary looked anxiously in the Superintendent's direction, but he had his eyes closed again. Stage by stage she went through the day of the shooting with Peter, unable to fix the hours accurately because he wore no watch, measured time only by meals and the spaces between.

Miss Lorely had said that Mother Cat was out all night. He had milked the goats and left the milk in the butane gas cooler. Then gone right down to the river, calling the cat. No, he hadn't seen Miss Lorely a second time. She wasn't about, but he'd thought she could be out back, sowing the spring carrots, because she'd started the drills. But then she'd gone off somewhere, leaving a cover spread over the ground.

'What kind of cover?'

This flummoxed him and again he appealed to his mother. She asked several questions to get it from him, then explained. 'Sounds like a tarpaulin or summat such.'

'Canvas, maybe? Like a ground-sheet or part of a tent?'

'Cud be,' Peter answered for himself.

Yeadings opened his eyes and nodded almost imperceptibly. Rosemary accepted the hint and pursued the matter. 'Where exactly was it?'

It had been spread over things she'd have left on the vegetable patch. Not flat, no. Lumpy, like. No, he hadn't looked underneath.

If he'd looked, Rosemary wondered, could he have saved the woman, slowly dying there, bleeding and in shock?

'Then what did you do?'

'Meat came for the cats, and I put it in the cold safe.'

'Inside the barn?'

'You saw ut there.'

'Yes. Did you feed some to the cats?'

He shook his head. '*Her* allus done that. Indoors. I duzzen's go indoors.'

'So who did feed them that day? We found some meat still in some bowls on Sunday.'

'Well, *her!*' He didn't appreciate yet that by then she'd been incapable or dead.

But someone had done it, using perhaps the last of some existing stock inside the house. She felt a shiver of fear as she thought of the killer leaving the woman to agonize for hours but burying her dead cat, filling the food bowls of the others. What kind of twisted mentality did it take? It was hard to concentrate again on the line of questioning.

'If you never went inside the house, who did?'

'Jus' Miss Lorely.'

'Surely at times somebody came—'

'She never let no one in.'

Perhaps she had been afraid of tramps and burglars, being on her own. Or didn't want anything known of the empty places where pictures and furniture had once been? Yet somehow they'd been spirited away. She couldn't have done it on her own.

'Did any large vans—lorries—come to the Hall?'

He shook his head.

Well, if she'd arranged for the secret transport of her treasures it would be for some time when Peter wasn't expected; a time when the younger cottagers in Battels Lane would be at work and the old ones dozing. Only the spry-eyed Mr Gash might have observed the tops of tall vehicles surmounting the hedgerows across the maize field from his bedroom window. That would be a question to keep for another visit to him.

'You weren't needed for work on a Saturday, but you stayed on, all night too. Why was that?'

'Mother Cat haddun' come back.'

'How could you tell without going inside to look?'

'Miss Lorely said she'd put the old red jug in the window when Mother Cat came home. So's I'd know. I'm not stoopid.'

'No, Peter, you're not.'

'She guv me messages that way, and I remembered.'

'So you stayed on to look for Mother Cat some more. What about your own mother? Wouldn't she be worried?'

This troubled him. He flicked a sideways glance at Mrs Howell and looked truculent.

'I knew where un wuz,' she said loyally. 'There's places enough there to keep warm and dry in. He had his coat along.'

Rosemary frowned. 'That night, in the barn, did you hear any sounds outside—anything unusual, I mean?'

'Slep' through,' he admitted.

'You didn't hear a shot, some way off?'

He looked puzzled. 'Boys shooting. At Farlowes.'

'That was in the afternoon. I meant after dark.'

He started to deny it, then stopped, confused. When she thought he was on the point of admitting something he shook his head. Perhaps he had heard a shot, either earlier or during the night, but it would hardly have registered. He knew that people round here were often potting at wild creatures, with no notice taken. And the hours of a clock had little significance for Peter.

She looked at him now. There were dark rings round his eyes which seemed to be sinking backwards in his skull.

'I think,' said the Superintendent, appearing to wake up in his corner, 'that's probably enough for now. We'll leave you in peace.'

So Rosemary thanked Peter, smiled at Mrs Howell and followed her to the front door, with Yeadings still in her wake.

THIRTEEN

UNAWARE THAT THE OBJECT of his interest was at that moment unconscious, suspended in a scuffed leather jacket from a thorn hedge, DS Beaumont had squinted at his son across their breakfast cornflakes and decided the time was ripe to wheedle some background information about Rory.

'Any special plans for today?' he opened.

Stuart continued spooning up the milky debris from his bowl. He grunted. 'Survive, I guess.'

'Dizzy ambition,' his father commented sourly. 'I thought you might like to stand young Welch a modest lunch.'

'Wow.' It couldn't have been delivered more flatly.

That's what you get, Beaumont regretted, for being a joker and raising the next generation in your image. 'Last day of half-term, officially,' he drove it home.

'Then back to Mumsie Darling. Not to mention Grandmumsie,' Stuart mocked. 'Fab!'

'So why not make the most—?'

'Rory's last day too. His folks will have set up something big. Nuclear submarine trip or family free-fall. His dad drives him back to Stowe tonight.'

'How does he like it? Boarding-school, I mean.'

Stuart sniffed. 'It's just the next thing. Tote that barge; lift that bale; go to school; sink a little Pepsi; do the Christmas thing; go to school; come back—'

'There never were treadmills before your generation, of course.'

'Who's complaining, man? We just hang in there, is all.'

Beaumont overlooked the mid-Atlantic world-weariness.
Like youth, it was something to grow out of—he hoped.
'Has he any idea what he wants to do later?'

'Yeah. Actually he has. Something with animals. You
know something? You can break into Medicine with lower
A-Levels then to study Vet. It takes at least three Science A's
with A Grades, and even then you need to be a vet's kid or
a breeder's.'

'Will he get there?'

'Rory? Sure. He's cool.'

'Struck me he plays his cards close to his chest.'

'Same thing. Cool, man. *Aw, shit!*' This last was because
the phone suddenly cut through, making him spill a casually balanced coffee mug over his freshly washed jeans.

His father leaned back and reached for the receiver on the
kitchen wall. 'Beaumont.'

As he listened the pert Pinocchio expression came back.
'You do? Well, how about... Hang on a bit... No, I'm
bloody not. You said five days and this is the— Hold it! You
can tell him yourself.'

He scowled and handed the receiver across to Stuart. The
cord was reluctant to stretch and the boy had to stand,
leaning over the table.

'Hi. Wait a minute, can you?' Stuart put a hand over the
mouthpiece, heaved on the cord and loped round the table
making febrile falsetto noises at his father with appropriate
grimaces. Arrived beside the rest of the instrument, he set
his shoulders against the wall and slowly slid down to floor
level.

'Hi, Mum. I'm back. What's the trouble?... You at
work?... What?' He listened, expressionless, then nodded. 'OK, no sweat. Did you ask the Old Man?... Yeah, if
I have to.'

He rested the receiver against one thigh. 'She says can you stand me another few days. Something about going to Colchester for an interview. Sounds like they've sacked her from Hailey's and Gran can't stand my undiluted company.'

'Give it to me.' Beaumont took the phone, watched his son rise, dust off his backside with something more like satisfaction than he'd evinced to date, and saunter from the kitchen.

'Cathy, it's me. Listen, I'm more tied up by this new case than I care to be. He'll have to go back to the old school from here or stay on with your mother. That's if they'll put up with all this dithering about... Well, it's up to you. I don't see why you can't...' He listened a while, his face hardening into wooden resentment. Finally, 'Listen, if you want it this way, you fix it.' He shoved the receiver back on its hook. 'Bloody women.'

Stuart reappeared suspiciously on cue. 'Well, Dad?'

'I guess so. We're stuck with each other for another week.'

He watched the boy slide back into his place across the table, bland and seraphic. 'Right. You were grilling me, remember? About Rory. What else do you want to know about him?'

In the end he thought he'd got good value for the time spent. Of course, it was only one person's opinion, but Stuart was shrewd for his age, sufficiently detached from his contemporaries for his observations to be valid.

Beaumont wasn't altogether happy about this general attitude. He would have given a lot to see the boy enthuse over something, throw himself unreservedly in, admire just one other human being out loud. Otherwise he'd grow up bloody lonely. Like me, the DS admitted. Still, for reasons of his own—probably as payment for the extended leave his mother had granted him to stay on here— Stuart had seen fit to cough up the information required.

Could he actually prefer this shell of an existence, even find some pleasure in his father's sporadic company? Beaumont didn't permit himself an answer, but he had to recognize that for himself the past five days had provided some quite acceptable moments.

Well, back to the job. There was always that, and plenty of it. With Rory Welch documented, he had now completed the Welch family dossier. For access to that unbeatable source of knowledge—the local newspaper morgue—Beaumont had fixed a meeting with its compiler.

Stanley Elkins himself had an unusual history, which was an inversion of the familiar provincial-scribbler-to-Fleet-Street success story. He had joined the staff of the *Daily Post* as a keen-eyed youngster straight from the North London Poly, settled rapidly into the hot-news pattern and by middle-age had graduated to be regular contributor to a much-quoted comment column. At that point a badly shattered leg, his main memento of an M1 car crash, interrupted his lifestyle. Temporarily invalided into the care of a female country cousin in Sussex, he met Molly Bassett, a visiting ex-schoolfriend comfortably widowed in the Thames Valley. Barely a fortnight after abandoning his crutches he had also thrown off the *Daily Post* and confirmed bachelorhood, following Molly to her cottage at Hambleden with the avowed intent of saving his failing liver and precarious sex-life.

He thrived on the change but, unable to escape a lifelong need to scratch and scribble, had accepted the vacant editorship of a family-owned local newspaper, winning, over subsequent years, the reputation of a personified British Library. Gregarious and ferret-minded, in no time he knew everyone and almost everything in the area. His proudest boast was to have created the definitive newspaper 'morgue' of local personalities so scrupulously updated that whoever dropped dead without notice could be instantly resurrected in print for the next bi-weekly edition.

So, naturally, it was to Stanley Elkins, supremely erudite in local social topography, that DS Beaumont had gone for information on 'Farmer' Welch and his wife.

Behind the comfortably misted windows of the Oaken Cask's coffee lounge the two men had exchanged their stock-in-trade, Elkins volubly and in the knowledge that Beaumont would be equally helpful when the present investigation bore fruit.

'So you're on to "Farmer" Welch, are you?' the editor chuckled. 'He wanted his complaint published anonymously, but I guessed you'd not be long finding out who it was wanted Miss Pelling and her cats cleared out. Now, who on my staff spilled the beans?'

Beaumont looked wise and tapped his nose. 'You know all about protecting one's sources. I'll be equally discreet about you. So how about dishing the dirt?'

Franklin Welch, born October 1947, was seemingly a self-made man, if such existed. In his case it meant that his father—who might otherwise have cushioned his early years by scrimping to provide private education and later pulled career strings—had walked out of the matrimonial home in a rage one frosty morning and wrapped his Norton round a lamp standard on his way to work, declared DOA at Hillingdon Casualty shortly after the boy saw light of day.

His mother, a onetime nanny, had—despite indifferent health—supported the pair of them with various domestic jobs; nursemaid, cook, housekeeper. She had gone back to live at her mother's and the old lady had looked after the child until her death. Shortly after that, May Welch's successful application for the post of Warden at a sheltered housing project near Amersham enabled her farmed-out son to become resident with her.

As a growing lad Franklin had been coopted as handyman, messenger, window-cleaner and sous-carpenter, learned early to utilize what practical gifts he had, won first a scholarship to Dr Challoner's Grammar School and later an Exhibition to Imperial College, London. From then on, by dint of hard work, good luck and imaginative exploitation of a patent, he had risen to be Chief Engineer of a rapidly developing factory making electronic components. It was after acquiring a major shareholding that he took the wraps off a new process for detecting fatigue in metal structures. It hit the market during a scandal over a collapsed span bridge and met with a diamonds-from-coaldust reception. Almost overnight Welch became MD-Chairman and a man with an indisputable future.

While Franklin Welch exemplified success hard-wrested from modest origins, his wife Alexandra represented—if not exactly blue blood—the established county background he now had pretensions to merge into. She was the product of a long line of couplings between equine-featured landed ladies and the mainly chinless budding diplomats available as escorts during the London Seasons. In appearance Alex Trewin had avoided both physical extremes, having a fine-boned, gently undistinguished face, a tall, slender body and the remnants of a childhood stutter when upset. There were two children of her union with Welch; a boy who must now be turned thirteen and a girl about three years younger.

'Yes, I've met 'em,' Beaumont admitted. 'My boy knew young Rory through the Scouts.'

'Not at school with him, though?'

'Different systems. Rory Welch has just started boarding at Stowe. His father gave him a half-term party—sorry, *rally*—so he'd not lose touch with the local yokels. My boy was invited.'

'Pretty glitzy affair, so I heard.' (Understandably it would have reached Elkins's ears.)

'Flaming success,' he continued with a smile. 'Especially the finale—dispatching a hot-air balloon.'

'That came from Welch's? Is that certain?'

'I had it from an eye-witness.'

Beaumont grunted. 'I heard about it, of course, but nothing of the sort happened while I was there.'

'The invitations were for 11.0 a.m. to 7.0 p.m., as I recall. Parents welcome from six.'

'I was the first to arrive, didn't stay. Had a passenger waiting in the car.'

Elkins must have known about that too, because he hummed between closed lips and then asked, 'How's Cathy these days?'

To the press nothing was sacred, Beaumont reflected gloomily—especially marriages falling apart.

RORY TRIED TO EASE himself into a new position on the narrow bed. His shoulder was ablaze with pain. As he moved, new dragging pinpricks responded in neck and wrists and scalp where the thorn hedge had torn him.

He seemed to have been awake for hours. Although it was daylight outside he felt himself owed sleep. He missed his little radio-clock with its green digital display flicking the seconds away. Here in hospital time didn't exist; there was just a yawning present, full of pain. And a dim, artificial light constantly spying on him.

They had told him to ring if he wanted a pain-killing tablet, but he kept putting it off, surviving a little longer on his own. Now it was getting to him, making him want to lash out. When the little brown nurse looked through the port-hole glass of the swing door he scowled back.

She came through. 'Like a hot drink?'

'Cocoa?'

'Drinking chocolate. And I'll bring you something to help you sleep.'

Then, absurdly, he seemed to drift off for a while and when she returned it was a bother to drink the stuff.

Sleep finally came, not deep at first but like stifling bands constricting him. He fought back and they seemed elastic, giving a little, then tightening back with each breath, finally slackening again into a sloppy treacle that stickily covered his limbs so that he couldn't separate them.

Couldn't run. Couldn't reach out for the ball. Never play rugger again, he thought. Not that he was a games buff, but he didn't want to seem different from the rest, a freak.

And then he fell away into space, back in time, and it was last Saturday again, although different, misty and with things confusedly in the wrong order. He was helping Alec fix up the targets, but it was in the kitchen, surrounded by the go-karts and trays of caterer's food.

And behind all the activity he was waiting for something, apprehensive, knowing it would signal the start of the horror action. When it came there would be no escaping the follow-through.

But at the distant gunshot, everyone turned silently to stare, and one after the other they pointed stiffly at him. He tried to run, but his legs were sticky with the treacle. All he could manage was a strange slow-motion loping, like a moon man.

Then, although he had scarcely moved he was in old Lorely's garden and alone again, opening out the heavy canvas to cover her bleeding body. And from somewhere behind came a huge shadow. His father was there, holding up the

key and shaking it in a fury. Rory tried to reach out to take
it away but the man put it into his mouth and now it was a
silver whistle.

The sound was piercing. It went through him like a pain,
it *was* pain. The canvas fell from his hands and he felt himself falling forward. On to the bleeding body.

And it wasn't old Lorely any more, but his mother.

Then he knew the full horror—that he was the one who
had killed her!

ALEX GRIPPED the steering-wheel tightly, frowning as she
cleared the town traffic to emerge again into the misted
green alleys of the Berkshire countryside. *Rory was going to
be all right*. She must concentrate on that one positive fact.

The past week had been so horrific that she felt sub-
merged in disasters. And then the last twelve hours! Franklin—the memory came harshly back in its entirety—so
crudely furious. He reappeared now before her, red and
bloated. His face and neck, his hands, even his eyes had
taken on the fierce colour of his hair. And beside this pulsating vision of his redness she felt herself quite drained,
blanched like limp celery, bloodless.

Ridiculous idea—laughable, except that it was so hide-
ously frightening. So final—because in a flash it had come
through to her, his contempt, his concept of her as the outsider, the menace, the one who threatened his security, his
good name, his—yes, *his*—family! As if they weren't hers
at all and she'd no say in what happened to them.

Yet he didn't begin to understand children; couldn't meet
them on their level but condescended from the great height
of his supposed importance. So puffed up with appearances, with presenting an impressive image. Hollow inside,
for all his success and the money he'd made. God, what had

happened to the man she'd once loved? He'd been eaten alive by this self-sufficient monster!

She felt her body's shuddering transfer to the movement of the car, until it juddered as if it had some major engine fault. She slowed, gritted her teeth, pulled in to the side of the road and stopped by the green verge, hunched over the wheel.

'Mummy?' From her seat in the back Amanda leaned over. 'Mummy!'

'I'm all right, d-darling. Just g-give me a minute.'

But she wasn't all right. Nothing was.

Amanda gave her the minute. Then: 'Is Daddy coming back?'

Alex moaned softly. She answered too quickly. 'What do you mean? He's been away before.'

There was no response. Well, it hadn't deserved one. When had she begun to deceive the children? 'Amanda, I— Yes, of course he'll be back. As soon as he hears of Rory's accident.'

Only it wasn't an accident. Rory had deliberately set the mare at the hedge, knowing she'd refuse and throw him. Meaning to hurt himself. Not more than that! Dear God, he hadn't meant to kill himself.

It shocked her. Even the lesser thing—it was so un-Rory; the risk he'd taken, for himself and the mare.

When Franklin heard, wrongly as ever he'd simply assume his son had chickened out of going back to school. He'd lay into him with all the scorn of parental pride under attack.

And the truth was so different. Like Amanda, Rory must have overheard the raised voices last night and his father's angry departure.

How much did he actually *know?* Perhaps just intui-
tively that things were very wrong. So he'd made up his
mind to be on hand when the final calamity struck.

'*Mummy!*' Amanda sounded alarmed now.

'Darling.' Impulsively Alex twisted in her seat, reaching
back for the little girl's hand. 'I'm so sorry. This has been a
horrid half-term for you. What would you like to do today? Shall we go somewhere special? Tell me what you'd
like best.'

'I don't know. It's so drippy.' She thought a moment.
'Could we make toast by the fire, and you read me a book?'

'An indoors day. Yes, of course. And I could c-cut out
that material for your Teddy's t-trousers.'

'Pyjamas. I wish—'

'Go on.'

'Wouldn't it be nice if we had a kitten?'

Alex looked at Amanda. The words had come out like a
confession, as if the child was ashamed of her need for
something soft and responsive. Something more than a
stuffed bear. Because people were so distant and unrelent-
ing?

Alex's heart ached for her daughter, kept apart by so
much more than the physical restraint of their seat-belts.
God, I do try, she told herself; but it's not enough.

'I think,' she said slowly, 'we might ask that big policeman for one of Lorely's kittens. He told me he didn't need
them both. I thought at the time he might be hinting. Shall
we do that?'

FOURTEEN

WHEN DS BEAUMONT entered the Superintendent's office for the morning conference he caught him shutting a fat book away in his desk's second drawer.

'Dictionary,' Yeadings excused himself, catching Beaumont's eye. 'Since medical evidence proves Miss Pelling had no offspring, I wondered if she'd taken "akin" in the broad sense of having interests in common.'

'What does the dictionary give?'

'M'm. Holds out for a family relationship. The loosest meaning is "having common ancestry". I guess that Miss Pelling's Indian governess never sharpened her interest in semantics. If her will had simply stated "my young friends..." it would have presented no challenge. As it is, Longstaff has an anomaly to swallow. Lucky that Miss Pelling actually named the Welch children.'

'At least we've scotched the Lammas claim that the foundling of Swardley was Lorely's bastard son. Scandalous feudal minds some of these villagers have.'

'Mebbe, but when you're looking for physical likeness it's not hard to spot it, wherever.'

'Anyway, were the Welch kids even the Pelling woman's "young friends" in your opinion?'

'What do you think?'

'Being kids, nothing would have kept them off Malmsmead land if they'd a mind to it. So when they met up, either they'd have hit it off with the old girl or they'd have got up her nose. The little girl's too polite, to my mind, to go upsetting hermits. Rory?—he'd a lot in common with the old woman: fond of animals, approved of shooting game and vermin, a bit of a Green, according to Stuart. Does that make them "akin"?'

Yeadings considered. 'Somebody fed those cats Saturday night. There were scraps left next morning in bowls indoors. That implies someone was present who cared for animals and who knew, or suspected, that Lorely wasn't going to turn up. Peter Howell just might have taken pity on them and dared to go in if he knew the old lady was dead, but I don't think it was him. Pilchard tins had been opened. Peter knew Tom Beale had delivered the raw meat; he'd have used that. Can we fit young Welch into the part?'

'There'd been no break-in. He'd have to have a key, if only to lock himself out. It's not a self-lock on the door, and all windows were tight fastened.'

'We know there was a third key provided by the locksmith. Miss Pelling wore her own on a cord round her neck. The second was in the house. She'd have no need to leave a spare under a pot, unless—'

'Unless she expected callers. But if there was one person allowed in, then he or she could have held the key.'

'Again the question is—could it be the Welch boy? And if so, did he know the reason for old Lorely not being able to feed the cats herself on Saturday night?'

Beaumont grunted, digging his hands deep in his anorak pockets. 'Whoever you're writing in as the kind feeder of cats could well be the one who considerately buried the dead one. Which must have meant removing it from the dead woman's arms. Who could that be but the killer?'

As he spoke there was a rapping on the door and Jenner looked in followed by WDC Zyczynski. Either the keen air or embarrassment had brought unaccustomed bright colour to the DI's hollowed cheeks. 'Sorry we're late, sir. Car trouble.'

It was obvious that he seethed with irritation, but he swung on Beaumont with quivering intensity, having overheard his last words.

'Who is "the killer" you've settled for?'

Yeadings nodded him to a chair. 'We were playing with an idea. Not a nice one, if we end by charging a thirteen-year-old boy.'

'Young Welch?' The whippet features sharpened even more. 'I heard he tried to kill himself. Is that true?'

'He had a spill from one of his mother's horses, charging a fence in yesterday's mist. We don't have all the details yet. I'll be having a word with him today,' Yeadings offered cautiously.

'All for nothing,' Jenner was quick to claim. 'Killing the old woman, I mean, since we've proved she wasn't his granny after all.' He seemed to have overlooked that the will specifically named the children and the claim could stand on that.

'If he ever thought she was,' Rosemary murmured.

The look Jenner treated her to was one he normally reserved for squeamish social workers. This entire team, it struck him, showed more concern for cocooning the suspects than was healthy.

'Has his father been traced yet?' Beaumont inquired innocently. Welch's sudden departure was another detail Jenner would probably have missed, being in London chasing Lorely's non-existent heirs.

'Has he gone missing, then?'

Nobody seemed eager to enlighten the DI. Yeadings swung his chair back towards the desk and looked through some papers. 'Neither his wife nor his office seemed to know where he was the previous night and yesterday,' he offered over his shoulder. 'Some business trip, or perhaps a woman.

Did you get any hint of a girlfriend from your newspaper friend, Beaumont?'

The DS ran a hand through his hair. 'Not directly. He did say something at the end about Alexandra Welch being wasted on a slob like that.'

'And you didn't invite him to enlarge on it?'

The truth was that whenever the marital aspect entered their conversation Beaumont had felt himself too vulnerable and had sheered off the topic. Which was stupid, but at that time there hadn't been any prospect of Welch disappearing into the blue.

'Just a minute,' he said. 'If Welch was away the night before Rory's accident, how did he know he needn't come back to drive him to school? He'd arranged to do it yesterday evening. Maybe he wasn't entirely incommunicado. Or else something's happened to him.'

Yeadings looked hard at him, then lifted a phone from his desk and asked for an outside line. With his other hand he ringed one of the telephone numbers on a pad beside him. Almost immediately after dialling he was speaking to Mrs Welch, reassuring her it was only him. Had she heard from the hospital yet that morning? Well, he was sure the news would be good when it came. He was hoping still for a word with her husband.

They waited, watching the Superintendent's impassive face. The woman's voice quickened. She entered on explanations, but the words didn't come through.

'Are you satisfied,' he asked evenly, 'that there's no cause for concern about your husband's not being in touch?'

There followed a short silence, then the woman was speaking again, in a lower voice, with pauses between. It went on for some minutes, with Yeadings making understanding noises.

Finally he apologized for raising the matter by telephone and announced that he would be calling on her during the morning. He replaced the receiver.

'M'm,' he told the others, 'apparently this has happened before. They had "a rather heated argument" Thursday night and Welch went off without any explanation. Mrs Welch believes he has a bolt-hole somewhere. Last time he was away from home for three days but turned up at work on the second. If he does so this time his secretary will tell him of Rory's accident. I don't want the boy questioned in any depth before his father's informed.'

'Do you think,' Rosemary suggested, 'that Rory knew about the quarrel and deliberately hurt himself to get his parents back together?'

'Possible.' Yeadings looked at Beaumont. 'Or to avoid going back to boarding-school? How would that fit in with your son's opinion of him?'

'Or,' said Jenner, warming to the chase and rushing in, 'to distract attention from the murder, while placing himself where he'd still get updated news of the investigation.'

Beaumont shook his head. 'Stuart's only useful opinion is that Rory's "real cool", whatever that adds up to in this case. I dunno. Kids of that age are a bit beyond me.'

'I'd like to summarize, with the Welch boy in centre frame,' Jenner interposed quickly.

'Go ahead. Objections and comments at the end,' Yeadings allowed.

'Right, then. Miss Pelling was killed in her own garden, carrying back the cat she'd sent Peter Howell away to find. Something or someone had disturbed her while she was making drills for sowing seeds. Because of the constricted layout there, she must have been shot by someone standing almost at the back door of her house. We've still no identification for which gun was used, but there was a choice, including the dead woman's own.'

Jenner looked brightly at Yeadings. 'All right so far?'

He received a nod and continued. 'We know she didn't die instantly but some hours later. Yet she might have looked dead to anyone inexperienced. The cat, however, was well peppered and dead enough to warrant burying, wrapped in the apron the woman wore for gardening. We're agreed she still had it on when she was shot?'

'The apron's holes corresponded with entry of shot on her body.'

'So our kind cat-lover had to remove it from the woman's body. A streak of coolness there, you'll agree? Or was he still so furious with his victim that it was a pleasurable form of desecration?'

This time as he paused there was no movement from his listeners. 'To remove the cat and the apron it was necessary to leave the unconscious woman with her arms outflung. There was no attempt to tidy the supposed body, but a canvas was brought from an outhouse and laid over to hide it from casual view. As she'd fallen back over the seed bed her labourer later assumed the cover was for protection of new sowings against birds or expected rain.'

'Howell in the clear, then?' Beaumont marvelled just audibly.

Jenner bit at the inside of one cheek. 'I'm concentrating on a scenario with *the boy* as killer. My point is this: he was cool, but he was in a hurry. Fetched spade and canvas, dug a shallow grave for the small body, hid the big one temporarily. Now why was he in such a hurry?'

'At any moment Peter Howell could have come back from his futile attempt to find the cat.'

'He probably hadn't seen Howell, and it was Saturday, remember: Howell's free day. Howell had only turned up because of his obsession about finding the cat. The fact the killer didn't move the body means he felt pretty sure no one would be entering that part of the garden before he could get back and provide a better cover-up.'

Jenner's pale eyes gleamed. 'And he was in a hurry because he had specific jobs to do that morning, so he could well be missed. All this was before 11.0 a.m., the moment his guests were to arrive. The fact that no fuss was made about his brief disappearance is because his father assumed he was helping the hired man Alec, and Alec thought he was doing something for his father. The recorded comings and goings at Farlowes Farm are much too sketchy for that period. I know; conditions were unusual and everyone was rushing to get things ready in time. But if I were a betting man I'd have money on there being a stretch—say twenty minutes to half an hour—when no one had any idea where Master Rory had got to!'

'Which could be true for any of the Welch family, the servants, or the catering firm brought in for the occasion.'

'And we can't eliminate the cottagers, for that matter. They all knew in advance about the do at Farlowes Farm, so they could think no one from that direction would have time to come poking about down at the Hall.'

'Let Jenner go on,' Yeadings reminded the others. 'Comments at the end.'

'Right. Part two of the drama: With the slowly dying woman covered over by the canvas, the "real cool" Rory Welch had to sit out the rest of the day until after dark. There would still be clearing up to do after the last of the guests had left. He would have to wait for midnight or later to feel sure his parents were asleep. Then, having acquired his father's keys to the cabinet, he chose a gun and, wearing fabric gloves he'd taken from Farlowes kitchen, he returned to the Hall, borrowed Miss Pelling's wheelbarrow to trundle the body (by now certainly dead) up to Farlowes Wood, blanked off a part of the beech tree and discharged the shotgun into it, leaving the body spread-eagled at a suitable distance in front of it. It's my guess he would have retrieved the spent cartridge case and hurled it up-field from the edge of the wood, hoping it would appear that a stray cartridge from the boys' shooting would be blamed for an ''accidental'' death. It was his bad luck he didn't throw it any farther than the point the targets had been set up, but even there it caused a useful complication. Any arguments against?'

'Your scenario doesn't allow for the sawn-off shotgun which Firearms had me sold on,' Yeadings said ruefully. 'But I'll admit we've no proof there was one. It would have been convenient, that's all. Anyone want to suggest the Welches had access to a sawn-off?'

'The fabric gloves,' Beaumont offered. 'We haven't found any thrown away at the Hall or in the compost heap. If it was the boy he'd have got rid of them *after* returning the wheelbarrow and gun. Maybe he took them home. We'll have to look there; also ask if a pair went missing from the Welches' kitchen.'

Jenner sniffed. 'Proof of premeditation in that case. Boys of his age don't go around with cleaning-gloves in their pockets. He'd have helped himself to them for a purpose, the purpose for which they were actually used. That's more than cool: sheer cold-blooded.'

'How about motive?' Rosemary asked tentatively after a silence. 'If Rory's so cool, what got to him so that he had to let fly at an old lady with a shotgun? It just doesn't seem likely to me. I know there's the will, but we can't even be sure he knew about it.'

'The cat?' Jenner suggested suddenly. 'What happened to it after exhumation?'

'It would be tagged and refrigerated,' Beaumont said with distaste. 'In case we ever need it as an exhibit in court.'

'Was it examined? Do we have the report? Suppose the boy had been caught out deliberately hurting it and the old lady threatened to make a public scandal of it?'

'It could blow his chances later of getting a vacancy in Vet,' Beaumont admitted. 'Any record of trouble the RSPCA—'

'Wants to train as a vet?' Jenner jumped on it. 'Vivisection: why not? Kids can be ruthless. He'd probably taken it apart. Unhealthy interest in its mammary organs. If it died after being opened, that'd be his real reason for burying the animal. Didn't anyone examine it properly at the time?'

'My doing,' Yeadings admitted. 'It was just a mess of muddy, bloodstained fur after being in the wet ground. It was removed from the apron and both bagged separately. Has anyone seen a post-mortem report on it?'

No one had. He reached for the phone again and asked to be connected with the science lab.

There was a short pause while the relevant expert was called. They had taken a look at the animal, but an inrush of more urgent work had so far prevented any internal examination. The notes on the exhibit merely read, 'Female cat, recently produced litter; gunshot pellets in body. Neck and shoulder badly torn by wire such as snare.'

'Thank you,' Yeadings said heavily. He turned to the others. 'No signs of surgical interference. It seems the cat didn't go home because she was caught in a snare. She might even have been dead before the shooting.'

'A snare?' Rosemary echoed. 'I shouldn't have thought Rory...'

'There's a further detail I hadn't yet told you,' Yeadings said. 'I found three snares in the right-hand pocket of the jacket Rory was wearing when he was thrown by the mare. And in the left-hand, two unused "Western" 6-shot cartridges.'

FIFTEEN

YEADINGS WAS STILL briefing the team when the phone call came from the hospital. As he took it his face grew longer. 'Thank you,' he said at its end. 'One of my men will be with you shortly.'

He turned to the others. 'The boy has done a runner. His mother left him some clothes yesterday to wear around the ward and they've gone too. He was in bed after breakfast, when the doctor saw him. At 9.35 his father arrived from work in a fine old state, discovered his son had scarpered and simply blew up. Now he's gone haring off home to make trouble there.

'Beaumont, I want you and Silver to cover the hospital end, get a description of the clothes, interview everyone involved and make sure Rory's not hiding in the building. Z and I will go and see the mother. Jenner, take over here, will you? Advise mobile units as required, and keep in touch with me by radio. I don't like this at all. The boy may only have gone home, or he may simply be avoiding a row with his father, but we have to remember he could have intended something much more serious when he set that mare at the hedge.'

'Do you really think he might kill himself?' Rosemary asked as she buckled on her seat-belt.

'If he was crazy enough to kill a defenceless old woman, there's no knowing what he might yet do. What I'm hoping is that he's run home, but I don't care to think what sort of reception he'll get from his father when they meet up.'

He bounced the Rover down the curving driveway to the farmhouse and drew up with a spray of gravel. There was scarcely any interval between Rosemary's touching the bell and the door opening on a scared-looking maid. She must have recognized the Superintendent because she moved back and let him go straight through the hall to the sunny room he had been in before. The door was open and the two voices were still shouting against each other as he strode in.

'Mrs Welch,' Yeadings demanded, 'are you all right?'

The struggling figures froze, then moved apart. The woman's arms fell to her sides. She attempted to speak but her husband cut through what she might have said. 'Superintendent, what the devil do you mean by bursting into my house like this?'

'Mrs Welch?' More gently this time. The woman was in shock.

'I—y-you heard about Rory? He's gone.'

'Probably on his way here at this moment. Did he have any money with him?'

'Just five p-pounds, for m-magazines and things.'

'Perhaps you would give my assistant a description of the clothes you took in for him. Mr Welch, a word, sir, if you please.'

He moved away from the woman and after a moment's tense refusal Welch followed him. 'Please tell me exactly what happened when you arrived at the hospital.'

The high colour was starting to drain from the man's face. His teeth were so tightly clenched that Yeadings thought he would never be able to speak. 'Shall we sit down, sir?'

Angrily Welch gestured towards a group of chairs round a low table.

'I didn't know,' he started breathlessly, 'that there'd been an accident. I was away. When I got to work this morning—'

'Take your time, sir.' He watched the spasmodic movement of the man's knuckles as he sat, balling his fists on his
knees. When the fingers at last stiffly opened, Yeadings
helped him out. 'That was when your wife's message was
given you.'

'Yes. Just that Rory had been riding and had a fall. I
thought—' The man's mouth tightened.

'Yes, Mr Welch, what did you think?'

'I—It doesn't matter what I thought. I went straight to the
hospital to see him.'

'You thought perhaps it wasn't entirely an accident. Is
that it? Because Rory had been due to return to school that
evening. You had intended taking him yourself, but in fact
you weren't here to do so.'

'I was called away. My wife is perfectly capable of driving the boy herself.'

'And as it happened, that wasn't necessary. Your son was
injured and in hospital, which you thought was a ploy to
delay his return to school. Yes, do go on. You arrived at the
hospital and asked to see your son.'

'She hadn't said which ward he'd be in. The woman at
Admissions—was difficult.'

Yeadings might have pointed out that visiting wasn't allowed in the mornings, and a display of bad temper
wouldn't have endeared him to hospital staff, but he had no
intention of helping the man out. He waited.

Welch stopped, gave himself time to take stock and prepare his next statement. He had obviously stormed in and
been generally offensive. His version of the incident would
certainly be at odds with the ones Beaumont was getting
from the hospital.

'She did eventually tell me where he was, and I went up.
When I got there—he'd been given a private room; no doubt
you knew that—when I got there, his bed was empty. Not a

nurse anywhere to be found. They'd all followed the doctor off somewhere. Some little ward-maid or pan-washer told me where I'd find the Hospital Manager and I went to see him.'

'Which was when Rory's disappearance was first notified.'

'Yes. Deplorably slack, the whole place.'

'Then what?'

'Once it seemed certain he wasn't on the premises— though God knows how any of that lot could be sure of anything—I got back in the car and came here.'

'And?'

This was where Yeadings himself had come in. Welch paused to find a fit explanation for the scene the Superintendent had interrupted.

'I asked my wife just what had been going on.'

'And what had?'

Suddenly Welch rose from his chair, furious. 'This is preposterous! What do you mean by questioning me like this, as if I were a common criminal? You should be out looking for my son. He's a missing person, for God's sake!'

'Mr Welch, I understand your distress. Because of it I am overlooking the tone of your remarks.' Yeadings spoke coldly, without any evidence of the understanding he'd claimed. 'Just as you don't find it necessary to stick on the stamps for your own business letters, I too have men to do the chasing around. That is what they are now doing, first concentrating on routes between the hospital and here. Later, if necessary, the search will be extended to any places you or your wife think Rory might be likely to go to. So perhaps you would give your mind to that and we can all work together.'

The man began to shake. Yeadings nodded him to the chair again. Rosemary came across and put her notebook in the Superintendent's hand, with Alex Welch's description of Rory's clothing uppermost. When Yeadings spoke it was to fill the gap while Welch mastered his emotion. For a moment he had seemed about to burst into tears.

'Strictly speaking, Rory isn't yet a missing person, but we are concerned because he is a minor and it seems he is inadequately clothed. The things Mrs Welch provided were suitable for wear in a heated hospital room, but not outdoors in this frost. Let's hope the boy had the sense to borrow an overcoat from a staff cloakroom.'

Welch glared back at him. 'My son is not a thief.' Meant as defiance, it merely sounded lame.

'If you will excuse me, I should like a word now with your wife. WDC Zyczynski here will take down the address we can now contact you at.'

'No!' Welch gazed at him incredulously. Although he protested he stayed sprawled in the chair, his mottled face sunk between hunched shoulders. '*This* is my address.'

He levered himself upright and looked round at his wife in expectation of support. Alex Welch looked swiftly away and moved behind him.

'I'm going up to my room,' he said unsteadily. 'When Rory gets back, I expect to be informed.'

There was an uncomfortable silence while the man left the room. Yeadings walked across to the broad window where he had first seen Alex Welch seated in silhouette, the Sunday papers scattered about her and her fine hands busy with the coffee things. He waited there, his back to the room, and stared out at the frosted view. In bright sunlight every leaf of the dark ivy framing the window was outlined with a fine diamanté thread. From the gravel drive a light mist rose steadily. He looked up at the innocent sky, the pale autumn blue which in his mind was always linked with heartbreak.

On just such a pure, crisp day he had broken the news to Nan that her longed-for first baby was not perfect.

This woman behind him was a mother too, might have to face some even more horrific truth about her son. He wanted to be out of this situation, miles away and having nothing more to do with the job. Sometimes it was all too much. Hunting of any kind was a blood sport. And right now he'd no stomach for it.

'Superintendent?' Alex Welch was just behind him. 'Tell me how I can help.'

Rosemary came quietly across and sat down with her pencil and notebook ready. She looked steadily at Yeadings, then turned to the woman. 'Mrs Welch, can you give us a list of places where Rory might have gone if he doesn't come directly home?' she asked, and for the moment Yeadings was reprieved.

RORY SAT HUDDLED at the edge of the water. Already the grass under him had lost its stiffness. He could feel the damp penetrating his cotton shorts. Because of the overheated hospital Ma had brought in sports clothes. The Lacoste T-shirt had been all right indoors, but once he was outside the chill had really started to reach him. Still, why think of the cold now, when soon it wouldn't matter? The cold would help.

The bus conductor who took his money had given him a funny look. Lucky he'd thought to get change buying a paper at the hospital; offering a fiver could have made the conductor turn him off the bus.

He looked across the grey expanse of the gravel pits. He had swum it once two years back for a dare, and against a ban by his father. He could do it again, except for his shoulder and the frost. He had only to wade in and start swimming. It was making the first move that was hardest.

Maybe he should take off his clothes. But he had a sudden vision of being pulled out, and nakedness under all those censorious eyes was quite different from the freedom it had been before. He saw his mother's eyes, the pain in them. He couldn't shame her that much more.

Just his shoes, then. He unlaced his trainers to take them off; something he didn't always bother with. Then he emptied his pockets and put the change inside his shoes, silver in the left and copper in the right. He unslung the felt-tipped pen from round his neck and he was that much more ready.

He stared at the fat plastic pen lying beside the neatly placed shoes, and knew he should leave a note. But he'd no paper. Anything white, then. He dug again in his pockets and there was only the lining. That would do. He stood up to drop his shorts, tore one pocket out. Then he pulled his shorts back up, sat down again and spread the material over one thigh, ready to write.

Write what?

Who would be reading it? Apart from his family there'd be the police—that dark, slow-moving Superintendent, and Stu's father with the perky face. Whatever he wrote, it would have to mean something different for all of them. So keep it short. Enigmatic, that was the word. Then it could mean whatever the reader wanted it to mean. Only, what did he need to say?

Sorry. Yes. God, that was true. He was sorry all the way through him. It was the most total thing he had ever known. Sorry about everything. Mostly about old Lorely. He'd admired her. She stood for so much he privately wanted, and it seemed impossible that she had to die like that.

He smoothed out the material and wrote her name. 'Sorry Lorely.' It was a message to her, but the others would read it as something else. A confession maybe.

Two words weren't enough for all he felt. He wanted to reach out and say something that mattered. Some explanation of himself.

He shuddered. It wasn't with cold. He didn't seem to feel that so much now. He bent over the torn pocket and wrote again. 'I don't know why.'

Finally he signed it, lifted the shoes and put the cloth underneath them, so that if a wind sprang up it wouldn't blow away.

And then there was nothing left but to stand up and go forward, wading in, with the terrible ice-pain piercing his knees, his thighs. As he stumbled he fell forward and the water struck his belly like an axe. He plunged downwards and touched gravel, then surfaced and the cold was less dire.

From habit his limbs were striking out, but the left arm in its strapping was useless. He lay on his other side and scissored with his legs. The farther he went the harder it was to breathe holding the position.

How long? He started to count his strokes and then found he couldn't remember where he'd reached.

And now he knew his body didn't want to die. There was no alternative, and yet it tried to fight back on its own, wouldn't let him kill it. Desperate, like a small animal struggling in a trap. The lower part of his body not yet stunned out of pain.

The far bank was as distant as ever. He could barely see it. Hardly make a movement. There was only water now and his own dead weight. No choice left. Just death. Or perhaps God, if all that religion was true.

Momentarily he seemed to see Him then, an old man, bearded, and furiously angry, shouting, waving his fists just above him. He'd never thought of God like that—in such a rage. And so *scruffy!*

SIXTEEN

DI JENNER WAS AT Reading Control and in his element. The opportunity of a murder inquiry, with secondment to a division of the force where major crimes were no small beer, had seemed heaven-sent, particularly since it gave relief from some of the more abrasive relationships that had built up round him in Bicester.

Superintendent Yeadings had at first bugged him with his insistence on swanning round the case himself, but he'd been allowed freedom to circulate and familiarize himself with the persons involved. Now, to be at the centre of a sensitive man-hunt, or rather boy-hunt, gave him something approaching euphoria.

The case had been solved in under a week; he was in charge of bringing in the killer. The entire operation must benefit him career-wise.

He toyed with the idea that when promotion to DCI came through he might put in for a permanent transfer to E Division. It should be possible to jockey Yeadings back to his rightful desk. He'd have sufficient seniority himself to keep Beaumont in his place. Maybe he'd even get Z swapped for a male DC.

The only snag he envisaged was Doris and her smothering family. Even the prospect of being closer to London would be brushed aside. She'd been raised a market-town girl and a market-town old woman she would die, secure among her cronies and female relatives at whatever cost to his own advancement.

Down in this Berks-Bucks corner there were equally rural places she might settle into, but it was distance from her roots that she would object to. Anyway her objections would be overruled. It was Reading he wanted to be posted to, Reading where the nitty-gritty crime was, where statistics were mounting, and with them unlimited opportunity for making one's mark. Like this case.

He looked down the list, neatly ticked where checks had been made and no Rory Welch unearthed. There'd be no harm perhaps in radioing Mr Yeadings to keep him up to date. He tapped the shoulder of one of the constables wearing a mike, nodded to him to vacate his place, and took over. Rosemary, who was listening for the car radio, went out to take the message. She noted it down and came back to Yeadings.

The Superintendent shook his head at the boy's mother. 'It seems he's not anywhere on the Malmsmead property, and he hasn't gone to his grandmother in Swardley village. They've run a check on the homes of all the boys who were here last Saturday, without result. A negative from the taxi rank close by the hospital, but no news yet from the bus garage. Nearby shops have been visited: no result. Can you suggest anywhere else he might go to be quiet and think? Somewhere warm for preference.'

'A public library? There aren't many museums, unless he took a train to London. He'd enough money for that.'

If he'd headed for London he could be anywhere by now. Even travelling round and round the Inner Circle, Yeadings thought sourly. That was a temporary solution which might well occur to a boy on the run. Did he think he could go hobo, join others who spent their nights in cardboard boxes?

He wrote a message for Jenner and gave it to the WDC to transmit. It was time to acquaint the Met with details of the

Thames Valley runaway. After that there were graver options: a search of isolated railway tracks, high bridges, lavatories where an unwatched lad could swallow crushed pills; finally they'd have to drag ponds and notorious stretches of river.

He looked across to Alex Welch and he saw that, anxious as she was, she hadn't yet accepted that final option. But without occupation she might. 'You have a key to Malmsmead Hall,' he said with certainty. 'Shall we go and search it again together?'

She didn't deny it or question him; merely went to fetch the key, drew on a coat and warm boots and stood waiting. They walked down by the farm's back drive, crossed Battels Lane and went into a field by the gate Rory had used on horseback.

There was none of the mist left from that earlier day. In the clear air the thorn-and-oak hedge sparkled with rime, a sudden break and torn branches showing where the boy had been catapulted in and later released. Alex turned up the collar of her coat and trudged by, face averted.

She used her key on the Hall's back door and when it closed again behind them Yeadings caught himself listening. In the scullery a tap slowly dripped with a soft *putt-putt*. There was a pervading scent of wood ash from the range, mixed with the dry bitterness of the bunched herbs and the lingering smell of cats and tinned fish.

'You knew her quite well, didn't you?' he prompted.

'Lorely? Yes. We used to come down here quite often. Rory and I mostly, on our own—Amanda wasn't quite so sure. She's a very proper child.'

Earlier he had asked where the girl was and he'd been told she had gone to a friend's for the day. Alex had felt unable to keep up appearances in front of her.

He forced his mind back to the dead woman. 'Would you say you were friends?'

Alex turned and looked at him directly. 'I was very fond of her. I admired her and I felt . . .' She was groping for the right words and seemed to give up.

'Sorry for her?'

'No. You couldn't feel that. She was too proud, and strong-minded. Not pity. Sympathy. I felt sorry *about* her. She deserved to have had so much more.'

'But she didn't want more than she had, surely?'

'That's right. But—companionship. She was good to be with, very wise. Not clever, the way people value cleverness these days. But she'd seen a lot and she thought about things. And although she was old and what Rory affection- ately called fuddy-duddy, her ideas worked for her. She was one of the few contented people I know. What I'm most sorry about—ashamed—is that we weren't more open about our friendship.'

She had spoken with a passionate conviction he hadn't heard from her before. And not once had she stuttered. 'It had to be kept secret, this association?'

'I—my husband disapproved of her. He forbade the chil- dren to go anywhere near the Hall grounds. He told Amanda Lorely was a witch, and at one time she half be- lieved it.'

'As some of the villagers do.'

'Perhaps. Stupid of them in that case.'

'So your grief at her death had to be concealed too.' He made it a statement, and she didn't respond. He wondered how much of the anger between Rory's parents had been fired by this concealment and the need for it.

Alex shivered again. 'Rory isn't here. I'd know if he was,' she said abruptly.

'Then we'll go back, if you'd rather.'

They walked in silence back along the scullery passage and Alex locked the door after them. 'I haven't been down here since...' She stopped and looked towards the corner of the outhouse where part of the kitchen garden showed. 'That's where...?'

'Yes. We think she was shot from about here.' He wondered who had told her Lorely hadn't died in Farlowes Wood. How many people now knew of the murder scene the police had fitted together? Perhaps it was common knowledge.

When they reached Farlowes again she turned and offered him her hand. 'Thank you, Mr Yeadings. I know the police are doing everything they can.'

He was being politely dismissed, but before she closed the door on him some memory broke her mask of detachment.

'Oh, I almost forgot. Amanda asked me. C-could she have one of the kittens, do you think? If you're giving one away?'

'Of course. Sally has already chosen her favourite, so it'll be the all-black one.'

'Thank you once more. She'll be so pleased.' With a stiff smile she closed him out again. Perhaps she already regretted the admissions she'd made.

Yeadings went back to the car where Z was sitting. She looked up as he got in beside her. 'A bus conductor's just taken his tea-break at Uxbridge terminus. He thinks a boy of Rory's description got on near the hospital and off at the turn-round. That's on the Met's ground. DI Jenner had already notified them. They're questioning staff at the Underground station there. It's the west end of the Piccadilly and Metropolitan lines.'

BEAUMONT HAD PHONED in his report from the hospital. He hunted in his pockets for more change and, finding none, asked the operator for his own home number, gave his name and demanded reversed charges. There was a pause while the connection was made and then Stuart came on, sounding puzzled.

'Hi Dad, what's wrong?'

'Just checking you're there. Can you stay on twenty minutes till I get across?'

'Heck, I was going over to Rod's. I promised we'd pig out together at McDonalds.'

'This is urgent. I'll fill you in when I get there. I need your opinion on something.'

He could picture Stuart's grimace: distaste, apprehension, a touch of churlishness to cover his embarrassment at a flattering need. 'It'll cost you,' the boy warned pertly.

'So it'll cost me. But be there. *Ciao.*'

THE GARAGE DOOR was open and Stuart was waiting on the front step. He seemed suddenly taller. Beaumont realized he most often saw him seated or lounging. Now he stood alerted, scowling to hide some inner emotion. 'Is it Mum?' he demanded.

'No, something else. Let's go inside.'

'I made some tea.' It was offered brusquely.

'Good idea. The fact is Rory Welch has us all by the ears. He's done a runner.'

'Aw, shit, you don't think I'd help you find him?'

'Not if he was running from trouble, no. I don't suppose you would, even if you could. But it seems he's running *into* trouble. Possibly panicked. It could be the worst.'

'*Rory?*'

'Your Mr Cool himself. This is the real chill. You knew he'd taken a header from a horse and been injured? Well, that was just the beginning.' And Beaumont, seated across the kitchen table from his son, quickly sketched the latest events.

'Now, before you jump to any conclusions,' Beaumont warned, 'let me explain I'm not accepting the obvious myself. He's running, and it looks as though he's running scared. But there could be another explanation.'

'Crossing the fox's scent,' Stuart suggested.

'Diverting attention, maybe, but he does have some connection with the Pelling murder. The sooner his part is sorted out, the sooner we can see what else the situation holds. Now listen, I'm telling you something now that no one outside a few CID knows. Rory's hacking jacket had some objects in a pocket which might have significance in the case. I want you to think before you answer, and then say what use you think he'd have put them to.'

'That's committing myself.'

'Dammit, he could be topping himself right now!'

'All right, but I don't have to answer. You tell me: what did he have in his pocket?'

Beaumont sat back and spoke quietly. 'Snares.'

A flicker of surprise showed on the boy's face, then his reaction was sarcastic. 'Snares, like in snare drums, man?'

'In his *pockets,* idiot.'

'Well, don't ask me to believe he was into trapping wild animals that way. He might have set up a Guinness-Clock sort of machine to catch them so he could photograph them, but he'd never deliberately hurt them.'

'So how do you account for the snares?'

'He took them off someone else, or found them set and removed them.'

'Possible, I guess.'

'Yeah. Or he picked up someone else's coat in a hurry. That often happens at school.'

'Not so likely. There's no one else his size at Farlowes. His sister's hacking jacket would be too small; everyone else's too large.'

'His mother's might fit, except for her boobs.'

Irritated, Beaumont fetched him a cuff. 'Don't use that word.'

Stuart rubbed his ear ruefully. 'Whatever you call 'em, the meaning's the same. Anyway, which way did it button?'

'I don't know, haven't seen it.' Yes, it had gone direct to the experts. He'd give them a bell and ask for a full description. It shouldn't take great lab-hours to look for a maker's label and size tag.

IT WAS TOUCH AND GO at first. If the tramp hadn't been such a dedicated scrounger of old newspapers and no respecter of hasps on site-works' huts, the results might have been more tragic. As it was, his rage on seeing what the little idiot was up to had given him the energy to drag the unconscious body the short distance to the bank and wrap it round in tabloid scandals.

'Mad, that's what you are!' he shouted as he shook the lolling shape. ''Ere, wake up. Doan' yer go sliding off, now I got meself all wet. That's right, mate. Jes' 'ang on a jiffy while I whistles up the transport. 'Old on, can't yer? Nod yer bleedin' 'ead, if yer understands, right? Five minnits. Jes' start countin'. Think of sumfink. Think 'ard.' For all that, the boy had lost consciousness again by the time Harry was back with the reject trolley from the old gravel workings.

It was quite by chance that the old tramp had been standing swigging his meths by the hut's broken window overlooking the lake when the boy started taking off his shoes for all the world as if he was going for a paddle. And then the little fool had waded in, started struggling to cross the widest part.

Only he couldn't go straight. With one shoulder bandaged, he'd only one arm to dog-paddle. So he rolled, veered lopsided, lunging round in a circle. Bleeding little idiot meant to drown. He was going round, ever lower in the water, ever more feeble, as Harry reached the bank.

When he'd shouted and waved his fists the boy seemed at first to see him although his eyes were half closed, and when he drifted near enough, Harry waded out and heaved him back. Only a little bugger he was, but weighty, waterlogged. Couldn't have hoped to get him to the nearest house if he hadn't had the old trolley.

Two hours later he was still dining off the story in Uxbridge police canteen, stuffing his whiskery cheeks with corned beef and pickle sandwiches, and a mug of scotched-up coffee alongside. 'Cor,' he marvelled from time to time. 'What gets inter them, eh? Ev'ybody's got somfink to live for, 'aven't they?'

Well, old Harry probably would have from now on, Beaumont thought. Rory's parents weren't going to stop short at saying thank-you and shaking the old codger's hand. Whether Rory himself would be all that grateful remained to be seen.

When the call had come through for Beaumont to get to Uxbridge, being then the nearest, Stuart had refused to believe what had happened.

'He couldn't have. You've got it all wrong. Not Rory! Bloody hell, let *me* see him! He'll tell me straight.'

And for some reason Beaumont had accepted it, that the boys were franker with each other than across the generation gap. Quite contrary to proper practice, he'd let Stuart go along. He was sitting opposite now, watching old Harry stuff himself, impatient because Rory had already been sent off to Ascot.

Why Ascot, for Heaven's sake, he'd asked, and been told it was for the chance of treatment in a hyperbaric oxygen unit. They had a uniform constable sitting outside the door there, ready for when he came round enough to talk.

Meanwhile, Beaumont held the note scrawled on the pocket lining, which Harry (long practised in picking up whatever lay about) had collected with the shoes and tucked into his newspaper parcel. It wasn't quite a suicide note and it didn't admit the killing of Lorely Pelling. It was simply the outpouring of ultimate despair. What had driven Rory to such lengths could only be guessed at.

The unit in which Rory was being temporarily looked after had a separate entrance on the ground floor. There was some doubt about allowing Stuart in, but Beaumont had a word with the Sister in charge and she finally agreed while keeping a chilly eye on him for signs of irresponsible behaviour. It annoyed Beaumont, who hadn't introduced him as anything but the patient's nearest friend. Now, looking at his son with an outsider's eyes, he had to admit that he wasn't impressive. It was mostly due to his gear, sloppy to eccentric, but there was also a quirkiness to the face that wouldn't inspire confidence among establishment types.

He hoped appearances were deceptive in this case, as indeed they'd been with Rory—such a steady, dependable-seeming lad, and then he went and did all this! Maybe Sister was right to look askance at anything under years of discretion, wherever that might fall.

As it happened, Stuart's behaviour was beyond reproach. He retreated to a chair against the wall, slid on to it and tucked his discarded anorak on the floor underneath. Then he settled gravely to watch and listen to the tubular glass coffin Rory had been arranged inside. It reminded him of a horizontal version of those modern external lifts, sleek and sophisticated ways of entering stores and multi-storey hotels. But the stillness of its single occupant was frightening, recalling pictures he'd seen of iron lungs from the age when poliomyelitis had been rife and that was the only permanent way to keep a body breathing. Sufferers had spent years in the things, a lifetime sometimes. He didn't think Rory would be able to stand more than a short time on oxygen at pressure. He stared at the attachments.

'It's wired for sound,' he observed aloud.

The Sister looked across at him. 'We need to talk with the patient inside when he's conscious.'

'What if he's not?'

Unexpectedly she smiled. 'Then too we talk to them sometimes.'

'Because the subconscious part of the brain can hear,' he appreciated. 'Suppose I—'

'You'd have to be very careful what you said. We don't allow just anyone. . .'

'I know the sort of music Rory likes,' Stuart offered. 'Suppose I brought some tapes in, real quiet ones, d'you think they'd let me play them to him?'

'It might help him coming round. I'll ask the staff on Intensive Care for you, if you like. He'll be going up there shortly.'

'Thanks.' Stuart blinked. 'It's awful, isn't it? Maybe he'll not want to come back.' He sounded then like a very small boy, Beaumont thought.

'We don't know what he meant to do in the first place,' the woman said kindly. 'But I've nursed a few cases like this, when they've been very close to going, and they're usually quite happy to wake up still with us.'

SEVENTEEN

As FRANKLIN WELCH had demanded, news that Rory had been found was taken to him immediately. Alex heard directly from the Superintendent, with Rosemary standing by, and she reached out almost clutching him as she demanded, 'He'll live, won't he? Now they've got him . . .'

'You may depend on it, everything possible will be done.'

'I must see him. Where is he?'

'*He* won't be able to see *you* just yet, Mrs Welch. He's unconscious. Take a little time to get used to it, then I'll have one of my men drive you over. Your husband will also wish to be informed. Will you do that or shall I?'

She put a hand over her eyes and shook her head. Yeadings took it that she had opted out. Well, he'd welcome seeing the way Welch took the news.

Welch was in his dressing-room. Yeadings had a brief glimpse of him crouched forward in a brocaded chair, head in hands, before the man heard his soft approach over the bedroom carpet and struggled upright. His eyes appeared smaller, shrunk back into their hollows. Half a mangled cigar was still smouldering in an ashtray beside an empty tumbler. He faced the Superintendent belligerently. 'So what's the fool boy done now?'

Yeadings waited, and the expected shamed grimace followed, but still there was no apprehension.

'What did you think he might do, sir?'

'Something bloody embarrassing that would force me to take him away from the school. God, what I'd have given at his age to have the chances he's been given, and all he thinks about is his own present comfort. As if there isn't enough...'

Again Yeadings waited. Enough to worry him? Was that what the man meant? Hadn't it occurred to him that Rory might be so deep in trouble of his own that death looked the only way out? Was Welch so unimaginative? Or had he some way of knowing that Rory couldn't have been involved in the murder case now under investigation?

'We have news of your son. He was seen to wade into the old gravel pits near Iver. A note has been found with his shoes.'

Now at last the man was shaken. 'Rory? *Drowned?*'

'That must be what he had in mind. Fortunately the witness, a locally-known tramp, went in and pulled him out. The boy's trouble at present is hypothermia plus any further damage to the shoulder muscles torn in his riding accident.'

Welch had risen to stand dishevelled and baffled in front of him. '*My boy tried to kill himself?* Is that what you want me to believe?' He bunched his fists and a wild light came into his eyes. 'Where's that sodding tramp? He chucked him in, didn't he? I'll kill the—'

Yeadings fixed him with an icy stare. 'Consider, Mr Welch, why the boy left hospital and made for the pits. The fact that he's alive now, and has any chance of pulling through, is entirely due to one Harry Carter, gentleman of the road, as he calls himself.'

Welch put a hand over his face and started shaking. Yeadings picked up the glass. 'Where do I get this refilled?' He looked round and saw the unstoppered decanter on a tallboy.

He took the brandy across to Welch who had sunk back in his chair and was muttering between clenched teeth; a man at the end of his tether. The sight was nothing new to the policeman. He'd worked on criminals to bring them to such a state and it always left him with bile in his throat. The very familiarity of the situation strengthened the niggling doubt he'd thrust away when it first occurred. Welch as Lorely Pelling's killer. Why not?

First of all—*why?* Because he so detested the woman that he wouldn't allow his family to associate with her. And this went so far that he even mounted a campaign against her cats, making it seem a question of hygiene, and calling in the local press to make a public scandal of the way she chose to live.

And he was a violent man. Yeadings had witnessed his outburst against his wife and now against the unknown tramp. Suppose he'd discovered that despite his ban his wife and children had made a friend of the isolated old woman he despised. So, learning this, if he'd come across her—no; gone to seek her on her own ground—with a shotgun in his hands...

Yeadings walked across to the window and stood there stolidly, hands loosely clasped behind his back. When the man had quietened somewhat he said conversationally over his shoulder, 'The lad was wearing only light sports clothes. If he'd kept the leather jacket on it would have weighed him down earlier. I assume it was an old one of yours, sir. Tan-coloured, from Russell and Laing, Jermyn Street.'

Welch lifted his head, his lip curled at the policeman's introduction of small talk. 'Sounds like one I chucked out. An old shooting jacket. Made me look like a beater.'

And that would have mattered to the parvenu sports-man. The real gentry knew to dress down for a shoot. 'So you passed it to your son.'

'No. Alex, for rough riding.' He was sounding testy now at being sidetracked from the main concern. 'So where is Rory?'

At last he had asked. Yeadings told him shortly, and warned that he shouldn't yet expect any response. He had left the hospital's phone number on a pad by the hall telephone, and Mrs Welch had gone over to Ascot to stand by.

LEAVING WELCH to deal with this new situation as he chose, Yeadings rejoined Rosemary Z in the Rover. 'Let's get back to base and pick each other's brains,' he said. 'I want to try setting up a case against Franklin Welch. Your job is to knock it down. We'll get Jenner in on this too, and Beaumont when he gets back.'

They met in the Superintendent's office after a hastily snatched meal and he assembled the facts so far known. 'Our first consideration is means. Welch had two shotguns in good working order and he was familiar with their use. Both are at present with Ballistics. Considering Huntingdon's past track record, we couldn't normally hope they'd match any of the five guns to the cartridge case from the field above the wood for at least another fortnight. However, if we seem to have half a case against any of the shotgun certificate-holders I'll go up to Ballistics in person and politely apply boot to backside, which could hurry things on.

'Even if we get a positive on that, don't forget we can't prove the cartridge case came from the shot that killed Lorely Pelling. All we have is a strong suspicion because it showed signs of having been handled with fabric gloves similar to those that handled the plastic apron, and the pilchard tins retrieved from a waste sack in the Hall kitchen. Parts of the underside of the wheelbarrow also have smudges which may eventually be identified as glove marks. They're still being worked on. Transporting the body, probably by then in a rigid state, couldn't have been easy on a single-wheeled vehicle. There would certainly be points at which the thing threatened to overturn or actually did so. It's just our bad luck that the heavy rains following discovery of the body led to all tracks from Malmsmead Hall's rear to Farlowes Wood being washed out and subsequently tramped over.

'The gloves. DC Silver has hung about the kitchen at Farlowes Farm—'

'Hung about the kitchen-maid,' Beaumont muttered.

'—and traced two pairs of fabric gloves of the kind used for cleaning silver plate, windows and so on. One pair was still sealed in its plastic wrapping. The other had only recently been soiled and never washed. Silver asked for the loan of a less tidy pair for some adjustment to his motorbike and was told that the old pair had disappeared, but the maid had used them early Saturday when bringing in replenishments for the log-basket in the living-room. She hadn't thrown them away herself, but assumed that Madam had considered them past laundering. A search of the domestic rubbish has failed to turn them up, but there was a bonfire of caterer's wrappings on the Sunday morning after the boys' rally. Anyone passing by—and this includes Welch senior—could have thrown on a pair of cotton gloves once the fire was well alight.

'Means of transport for the body—yes, Welch had as good access to the wheelbarrow as anyone. He could presume there must be one on the property, and had only to look.'

'At risk of being seen searching by Peter Howell, who was there chasing the missing cat,' Jenner reminded him.

'That depends on timing. We have two separate visits to consider; one in the morning for the shooting, the other after dark for dumping the body elsewhere. The first could have coincided with Peter's search taking him down to the river, and the other when Peter was asleep in the old stable.

The killer was fortunate enough not to disturb him, which he might have done if he'd gone anywhere near to get the wheelbarrow. It's not beyond the bounds of possibility that old Lorely had been using it herself and it was already standing out in the open with her gardening things.

'This has brought us to the question of opportunity. Welch was pretty busy Saturday morning, but he's more the organizer than the worker. He could have so ordered others' jobs that everyone was satisfactorily occupied, leaving him the chance to fade away at a time of his own choosing.'

'Which must have been well before 11.0 a.m. when the kids were due to arrive,' Beaumont put in. 'Say before 10.30, to be on the safe side. After all, he wouldn't have gone down to see the old woman—even just to bawl her out—wearing the upmarket casual things he had on for the kids' do.'

'Unless he covered them up with the old leather hunting jacket he'd officially handed over to his wife for wearing round the stables. We'd need to know where that was normally kept.'

'Walking about openly with a shotgun at that hour?' Jenner queried. He still favoured pinning the murder on the man's son.

'Why not? The household all knew the guns would be in use later that day. If he was observed slipping away down the rear driveway he could always find some excuse for having unlocked one from the cabinet to check on it. Remember that the jacket had loose cartridges of the required type in its pockets. And snares to boot. Anyone mean enough to stir up a local hygiene scandal against the old lady over her cats could have been malicious enough to try trapping them.'

'Is Welch all that unsavoury?' Beaumont asked.

'What do you say, Z? You've seen him in action today when his ire's roused.'

Rosemary hesitated before answering. 'He did seem almost out of his mind about what he saw as Rory's attempt to avoid school. And he must have reached open warfare with his wife some time back. According to village gossip, he's a womanizer, treats his wife offhandedly, even disparagingly. He sets more store by his mother. As I see it, they have a mutual admiration arrangement. She's no Brain of Britain, and maybe that's why she looks up to him so. He needs her, to keep his self-regard fuelled.

'I think that despite his professional success, like many a self-made man he's basically insecure. His wife's social background is less of a challenge to him now than a reproof, because for all his bluffing he knows he's a phoney, and independent Miss Pelling—elderly and apparently not well-off—was a positive irritant. This need to be accepted as "Squire" went deep with him, and the late Squire's daughter was all that stood in the way of buying his way in. It could have been the last straw when he discovered his wife and children had broken his ban on fraternizing with the old lady. Yes, I can see him wanting to make someone suffer for it.' Granting all this, Rosemary still sounded doubtful.

'But . . .' Yeadings prompted.

'Well, are we seeing this as a killing in the heat of the moment, or as premeditated murder? It seems that you want it both ways. He goes out ready armed to finish her off, or else he goes in a rage to have it out with her, loses his cool and lets fly—possibly with the old lady's own gun when she finds the snared cat and cuts up rough.'

'It could be either way. We'll know better when we have some results from fingerprinting the unused cartridges in the jacket pocket. Not that that will prove anything, unless Welch was actually seen entering Malmsmead grounds at the time in question and wearing the discarded leather jacket.'

'Which Rory also put on to take his Gilpin gallop at the hedge,' Beaumont said shortly. 'What's the betting the boy slid his hands in the pockets at some point before mounting, and fingered the cartridges himself? It could have been accidental. On the other hand, if he's trying to cover up for someone else whom he knows killed the old girl—isn't that just what an intelligent youngster might deliberately have done?'

Yeadings stared at him heavy-eyed. 'You think the boy might have guessed his father was guilty and is muddying the water to keep us off his tracks?'

'It could explain the gravel pits business.'

'Which we haven't fully considered yet,' Yeadings agreed. 'Did he mean to get himself rescued in the nick of time, or was it a deliberate suicide attempt? Right. We've just touched on motive for Welch killing Miss Pelling. Let's look now at the note the lad left behind. Would anyone like to tell me just what he meant by it?'

They all stared at the photograph of the pocket lining.

'He hadn't considered writing a final note at the time he left hospital,' Rosemary ventured. 'He could have laid hands on some kind of paper there, even if it was only a paper towel.'

'He had proper writing materials, which his mother took in, together with books and the fresh clothes,' Beaumont told her.

'But he'd held on to his pen.' Jenner was still keen on pushing the suicide theory.

'Wore it round his neck apparently,' Yeadings said. He produced a list of the boy's belongings. 'One of those novelty things.'

'Took off his shoes,' Beaumont pointed out. 'That sounds as if he meant to give himself a decent chance of swimming.'

'Just enough to get him out to deep water?' Yeadings suggested. 'I dunno. How about the note's wording? What does "Sorry Lorely" mean?' He rubbed his chin, remembering his own attempt at note-taking in the hazy, early hours. His own cryptic words had been no dissimilar: "Lorely", then "Lonely". Or had the second one been "Lovely"—because of the picture of her as a child? Whichever, it hadn't helped him with solving her murder.

'You might apologize for standing on someone's foot, but surely not for killing him,' Rosemary doubted.

'Which leaves us the choice of being sorry *for* the old lady—her circumstances, even the way she was killed; or being sorry for not having dealt more kindly with her—the familiar regret over lost opportunities when faced by the death of someone close.'

'It's meant as a dying confession,' Jenner gave as his abrupt decision. 'The boy was short of space to write explanations, and short of words too. Taken with the next bit—"I don't know why"—it just has to mean he was mentally confused by his own guilt. When he comes round he'll confess all right. Who's going to question him?'

EIGHTEEN

'I THINK,' Yeadings had answered obliquely, 'we'd better play it by ear. There's no way we can climb on the Welches' backs at present. Whatever case we finally make out, it has to stick and it has to be watertight. I don't want any defence accusations of harassment, and with the boy's life hanging in the balance the situation's too delicate for insensitive moves. So we hold back, we let them rally—which may even serve to clarify their attitudes to each other—and when the doctors say we can talk with the boy we do just that. There's a chance he'll come clean and confess. If he doesn't, he'll have a hard time covering for someone else without making the fact more obvious.

'Meanwhile go over every detail of the investigation again. There may be further back-up you can get from witnesses already interviewed. You may consider questioning new subjects in the light of the written statements held.

'Anything you can gather on the Welch household could be relevant. The disappearance of a pair of domestic cleaning gloves may seem a small matter, but it does imply the killer had access to the kitchen quarters of Farlowes Farm. And the removal of the body to Farlowes Wood sometime during Saturday night, together with the effort to set up an "accidental death", indicates that the person responsible knew the placing of the targets used for the boys' shooting the previous afternoon.

'We know there were outside caterers, teenage guests and guests' parents swanning about the house and grounds who could have picked up enough to use in covering up for themselves and putting the Welches in mid-frame, but all inquiries into the backgrounds of these outsiders have so far failed to show any connection with the dead woman. That doesn't mean there is no link, so don't wear blinkers if there's a whisper of evidence that something's been overlooked. We all have our blind spots; anyone can make a wrong assumption.

'But, all considered, our main target must be Franklin Welch, his wife, his children and the staff at Farlowes, consisting of—' Yeadings glanced at a list on the desk in front of him—'Maureen Heath, general maid; Magda Weiss, cook; and Alec Benson, ostler-handyman. All of them live in, Alec over the stables. The cleaning-woman comes in three times a week, but doesn't work weekends, so we can probably eliminate her. And unless the ten-year-old Amanda Welch has reached Junior Olympic standard at shotgun-hefting, she goes out too.

'Beaumont, I want you to collect all press reports on the death. Make a summary of interviews and any unusual slants being followed up. See your local editor friend and get him to gossip more freely. Z seems to have picked up some unconfirmed rumours from the village on Welch's extra-marital interests. See what truth there is in them and whether Alex Welch is known to have retaliated in kind.

'Z, trot along to Welch's mother again. Insinuate yourself. If there's any long-standing trouble between the man and his wife she's likely to give you his side of it. See what she knew about Miss Pelling too.

'DI Jenner, with DC Silver's assistance, I'd like from you a written appreciation of the case against Rory Welch, separately listing proofs and assumptions. I shall be doing the same with Franklin Welch. Let's hope that in all that bumf we may find some common fact that eliminates one of them.'

Dourly he watched them dismiss, none enchanted with the task in hand. Not surprising, that. There was little that cooled enthusiasm more than the waiting game. But wait they must, until the boy was able to make a statement.

With an outsize mug of black coffee alongside, the Superintendent settled to his task. He was wrestling with an accumulation of assumptions when the internal phone buzzed. 'Curly' Foulger—bald as a snooker cue ball and not much more colourful—was speaking from his SOC extension. A civilian expert on fingerprints, he sounded positively smug. 'Those cartridges you sent in. Just had a look at them. Pretty messy, as you might expect, with them rolling about in a pocket, but I raised a beauty of a right thumb and two reasonables of the right index.'

'And how about the tumbler I dropped in today? Had time to do that yet?'

'Yes, used for neat brandy I'd say from the smell. Labelled "Welch, Franklin"; that right?'

'Yes. Get on with it, man. So you compared them. What result?'

'Negative, I'm afraid. And none of the partial smudges on the five cleaned guns had anything in common with the cartridge latents.'

And Yeadings had been so certain that Welch had been the one to wear the jacket! He nearly barked back, 'Are you sure?' As it was, he drew a breath and settled for, 'Can't win them all, I suppose.'

'No-o. Only, I thought we might as well check the cartridge dabs with CRO. And it came up a bullseye.'

'Mother Macree!' the Superintendent exclaimed devoutly.

'No, sir. Old lag of the name of Albert Summers. I checked with computer records. He did two years at Bedford, July 1977, at age of twenty-three. With the Houseman gang. They pulled a bank job. Summers was driver. The principals got five and eight.'

'Armed with what?'

'Two pump-action shotguns and a knife to tickle the throat of the duty manager.'

'And that's all we have on him? Released early for good conduct, no doubt. A slap on the wrist, so he turns out a good boy, and fifteen years later his dabs appear in a shotgun murder case.'

'There's a bit more to it, sir. The same gang hit a Securicor delivery in Hereford, January 1988. Three principals and a driver. They transferred to a second vehicle which crashed during a chase. The gunmen were held and the money bags recovered, but the original driver and a sawnoff shotgun had gone missing. Summers, who'd been in their company earlier, was pulled in three days later for questioning, clean as a whistle with a cast-iron alibi. Not charged.'

'No description of the lost weapon, I take it?'

'Just that it was double-barrelled, a sawn-off side-by-side. The wages clerk staring up its snout was a bit of a gun buff. Convinced the user was familiar with the thing; held it at hip level ready to shoot. Sprayed it round the exit passage as they left.'

'That would be a sawn-off all right. And this Albert Summers is thought to have gone off with it, h'm. What did the court in its wisdom find?'

'The Houseman brothers are still inside, also their backup. Summers didn't stay around to see how the case went. He suddenly disappeared, never surfaced again.'

'Until his dabs did, four years later on my loose cartridges.'

'That's how it looks.'

'Well, thank you, Mr Foulger. I'll get the full account and his description on a print-out.' He grimaced and waited for the line to clear, then rang for DC Silver. With two amateur suspects already to hand for the killing of Lorely Pelling, they really needed this professional as well—like an outbreak of measles in a leper colony.

Albert Summers, twenty-three years old at his first sentencing would now be thirty-eight, so his mugshots would need updating. From records Yeadings learned that he'd been five feet eight tall, weighed ten stone twelve pounds, with small brown eyes, shoulder length near-black hair, high cheekbones, lantern jaw, a large mole over the right eyebrow. Which should make him stand out in a modern crowd, except that he'd have changed not only his hairstyle and weight, but (if he'd any sense) his name too. One thing was certain, he wasn't either Franklin or Rory Welch. But he might have settled in Swardley village or hired himself out to a caterer for last Saturday's occasion.

But how had he come to be using Alex Welch's, ex-Franklin's, old shooting jacket? And even more to the point how had Rory come to get it back off Summers later?

There was one possibility staring him in the face. When he'd questioned Welch about the jacket the man's explanation had been throwaway in more senses than one. Asked who'd been given it, he'd simply said 'Alex.' But suppose, speaking elliptically, he'd meant to explain whose it was now—in fact, *'Alec's'*?

Dammit, who would know best what Welch's stable-man looked like? Beaumont had questioned him, but he was away at present interviewing his editor friend. Yeadings had himself seen Alec Benson briefly when he brought along his own shotgun to hand over to Welch for police examination.

The height could be right; if Alec Benson seemed a little
shorter it was because he slouched, dragging his left foot a
little. Greasy, dark hair, but worn shortish under a check
cap. Probably dark eyes, certainly on the small side; angular face. So far as Yeadings remembered he'd no mole; but
if he'd changed his identity he could have had that removed. Claim it's spoiling your love-life and you can get it
done on the NHS.

Yeadings rang through to Farlowes Farm. The Welches
would be away, but with any luck the cook might be able to
supply the information he required.

His call was answered by young Amanda in a correct and
demure version of an answering machine. After giving her
number she offered, 'I'm afraid Mr and Mrs Welch are unable to come to the phone at the moment. This is their
daughter. Can I take a message?'

'Amanda, hullo. This is the policeman who likes poems.
I wonder if you have a good memory for faces?'

'I remember yours.'

'What colour is my hair?'

'Very dark with a white streak.'

'Nearly black, would you say? Do you know anyone else
with hair that colour?'

Amanda thought a moment. 'My dancing class teacher.'

'Good. Any men with blackish hair?'

'Only Alec who looks after our horses.'

'I'm not sure that I've met him. Does he have a mark of
some sort on his face?'

'He's got a round scar. It shows most on cold days and if
he gets angry.'

'Where is it exactly?'

'On his forehead, over one eye.'

'I don't suppose you could say which eye?'

'Well, when you're looking at him it's on the left. So it'd be on his right.'

'I'm impressed. You really are observant. You'd make a good policewoman.'

'Thank you, but actually I'd rather work with horses.'

'That's something else you need to be observant for. I'm sure you'll do it well.'

'Did you want to talk to Mummy? She hasn't rung back yet. She went down to Ascot to see Rory. They've moved him to a different hospital.'

'Yes, I know. I was there when she left. When she gets in touch, just say I rang to find out if there's any news, would you?'

'Yes, Mr—er, Superintendent. Thank you for phoning.'

And thank *you*, he said silently when he'd rung off. He hoped she wouldn't go back over the conversation and realize she had given away important information.

He thought at first, briefly, of sending DC Silver with a uniform constable to question Alec Benson, but the opportunity of observing the man's early reactions was too tempting. He went along himself, as background, not that a pro like Summers (if it was he) would be deceived by the most mutton-headed look the Superintendent could assume. In any case he must have seen Yeadings when he visited his employers, and someone would have mentioned his rank.

'Your pleasure.' In the car he offered the questioning to Silver, adding, 'Strictly by the book, of course.'

The tips of Silver's ears went red and Yeadings observed this with grim humour.

'As ever, sir,' the man said primly.

Well, just so long as he hadn't picked up any of DS Beaumont's corner-cuttings without recognizing them as such! 'Start with the odd question or two about the leather jacket,' Yeadings briefed him. 'Never mind the Summers connection. Probe a little into his recent life, increase the innocent amazement at points where he starts to sweat, then ask if he objects to our searching the premises. If or when he does, invite him downtown and hold him while we get a warrant.'

'Right, sir. All quite casual till the end?'

'Low key, Silver. It'll read better on your report.'

'And what's likely to turn up in the search, sir?'

'Something that confirms an earlier identity, if we're lucky. Perhaps a treasured relic of the past—such as a sawn-off shotgun.'

In frosty sunshine Alec Benson was taking time off with a mug of tea and a homemade scone on the window-sill outside Farlowes kitchen. It seemed that the cook looked after him well enough, but it would probably be the horsey smell that prevented closer relations.

He swallowed the last of the drink, licked his fingers deliberately and waved towards the stable block. 'Them's me quarters, if you wants to talk.' He slouched ahead of them, unsurprised, perhaps a shade contemptuous. The two policemen followed after.

They went in by a side door, to a wooden staircase, and through a stone archway Yeadings had a glimpse of satiny haunches and restless movement as the horses sensed the presence of strangers. There was a sound of munching and hooves rustling straw, clopping on cobbles. The place smelled sweetly of hay and was only slightly ammoniac. The half-light was peaceful. For a moment Yeadings was unsure that he had the right man.

Silver turned away from the staircase and went through to the horses. Along the far wall by the harness room was a board with a set of hooks and various old sweaters and raincoats hanging from them. Alec didn't follow them all the way. He stayed in the archway, leaning against the wall, sardonic at the charade of policemen casing the joint.

'You heard about young Rory Welch?' Silver opened.

Alec nodded. 'Misfortunate, I'd say.' He narrowed his small eyes until they barely showed among his tortoise wrinkles. It was an old face for a man of thirty-eight, weather-beaten and toughened like hide.

'What did he say when he came in here for a horse that morning?'

'Found me saddling the roan mare. Said he was going after his mother. She'd taken Blanco.'

'You'd meant to follow Mrs Welch yourself?'

'She'd gone off towards the river. The mist was thick enough here. Down there she could run into trouble.'

'That would be in the direction of Battels Lane and beyond?'

Alec nodded again. 'Went by the back drive.'

'Wearing what?'

'Usual hacking clothes, with split-skirt waterproof.'

'And the boy?'

Alec almost snorted. 'Hadn't got no riding gear. Grown out of his boots and jodhpurs. Had to lend him me old jacket, didn't I? Not that he's a silly kid, mind. Got a damn sight more sense than most.'

Silver looked along the line of clothes hanging against the wall. 'Got the jacket here?'

''Course not. Still got it, hasn't he?'

Good, thought Yeadings. He hasn't heard we took the clothes away; won't yet connect us with what was left in the pockets.

Silver had grasped this and wasn't sure whether to continue on that tack. Yeadings moved across to admire the horses, keeping well out of range from any sly backward kick. 'Have you always worked with horses?' he asked.

'Since a kid. My dad was with a circus. Lost his job when that sort of thing went out of fashion. Not enough interest nowadays for more than one travelling show in the country.'

'So you never followed him.'

'Got to know a gent trained racehorses. Worked as a stable lad for a while after school, till I broke both me legs.'

'Is that when you damaged your head?'

It caught Benson off-balance. He seemed on the point of protesting, then raised one hand and rubbed at the scar over his right eye. 'Yeah, that's right. Took a tumble. Riders do it all the time, break a lot of bones, but they mend up.'

'You still have a limp,' Silver reminded him.

And there had been no mention of any deformity in the CRO file on Summers. Was that an oversight, Yeadings wondered; or had there been a later injury?

'Rheumatism,' Benson said sourly. 'Bloody arthritic knee, ain't it? You want to arst me any more?—because I've work to do.'

Silver gave him a quiet, unhurried smile. 'We have, actually. How about us going up to your rooms and doing it in comfort.' It was then that Alec began to look hunted.

The upper flat had been made quite cosy with unmatched easy chairs, partitioned shower-room and kitchen, and a single divan in one corner with a green-striped cover that resembled a horse blanket. Light streamed in from sizeable windows on two sides, and now for the first time Yeadings could clearly make out the oval scar over the man's eyebrow where he'd had cosmetic surgery. It showed up most in the cold and when he was angry, Amanda had remarked. Well, it was warm enough up here. If Alec Benson wasn't exactly angry, he was surely on the way to being very apprehensive.

'When'm I gunna get me gun back?' he demanded belligerently, going on to the attack.

'When reports on all the shotguns are complete,' Silver said calmly. 'Anyway, you've got another.

It hit the man unexpectedly. ''Corse I haven't,' he shouted, but it came too late. He had flicked a nervous glance to one end of the room. Got him, Yeadings thought.

'So,' Silver said, dropping on to one of the low chairs, 'how's the poaching going?'

He denied it at first, vehemently. Then, when Silver mentioned the jacket and the snares in its pocket, he shrugged, sat on a stool, legs splayed, hands dangling between his knees, acting casual. 'Nobody bothers about the odd rabbit round here. Nor pheasant, for that matter. We all lives off the land. Arst Mr Welch. He'll tell you.'

'Miss Pelling too? Only she can't tell us, can she? Being dead. Shot by a poacher, maybe?'

There was an ominous silence. 'Look,' said Benson rising and standing over Silver with his fist balled, 'I didn't have nothing to do with that old woman. When she got hers I was looking after the kids at their party. Dozens of people must've seen me. Eleven-hour day I worked that Sat'day, and barely time off to snatch me samwidges. And if you thinks any of those kids was up to anythink funny with the guns and I wasn't looking you're bloody lying. Air rifles or shotguns, no different. Had me eyes glued on them every minnut.'

Interesting, Yeadings told himself. Covers for the boys as well as himself. But Lorely Pelling's killer had tried to make the boys' target practice look responsible.

'Back to the snares,' Silver said equably. 'Did you ever accidentally catch a domestic animal? A cat, say.'

Benson grunted contemptuously. 'Old Pelling's moggies? One or two. Couldn't help it. They were vermin, all over the woods.'

'Mostly on her own ground, though. And that wasn't hunted as much as the other woods hereabouts, I imagine. So the pickings were better.'

Benson shut his mouth stubbornly. It was clear enough he'd set snares on the Malmsmead estate.

'I must ask you to come down to the station with me and answer some questions there,' Silver decided suddenly. 'But first perhaps you won't object if we have a good look around here.'

'You bloody won't,' declared Benson threateningly.

'If not now, later, with a warrant,' said Yeadings crisply, tiring of the preliminaries. 'Satisfy our curiosity at the station, and you can be back here before the horses need their next mucking-out.'

Benson consulted with the cook before being driven off. It concerned fetching someone in from Swardley village to see to the horses if he wasn't back within two hours. Yeadings took this opportunity to observe that the cook was decidedly cool with the man, and while Silver saw him to the car the Superintendent asked her, 'Does Benson have the run of the domestic quarters?'

'No, he does not, sir. He has his own kitchenette over the stables. I send his evening meal across by young Maureen and I see she comes back at once.'

Maybe the lady protested too much, but plainly her sense of hygiene, or of propriety, was held with old-fashioned Prussian rigour. If Alec Benson did sneak in when she was off-duty it was unlikely he would happen on the drawer where the household cleaning gloves were kept. On the other hand, he could have pocketed them if they were left about. Whichever was the case, Yeadings knew the gloves could be a red herring. If Benson had handled the cartridges in his jacket without gloves, yet gloves had been used in covering up the crime, so there could be two different persons involved; killer and accessory after the fact.

Benson was left in an interview room with a constable in attendance while Silver brought DI Jenner up to date. His expression on being presented with a third suspect for the Pelling murder struck Yeadings as little short of mean.

He left the other two to resume the questioning, and in his office found a message slip: 'W. Mount rang from Huntingdon 10.28 hrs. Please return call.' Yeadings grunted, gratified that at last his special plea had moved Ballistics. He got through on an outside line.

'Hallo, Mike,' boomed Willie Mount against a cadenza of Telecom crackle. 'Good to hear you. How's things?'

Having exchanged the expected niceties, Yeadings asked, 'What have you found for me?'

'Five well-kept shotguns, one of which fired the cartridge case. But said cartridge was no first-timer. Apart from the mark of No. 1 gun's firing-pin there were also minute crimpings caused by the claw ejector of a pump-action model. Subsequent tests confirmed that the ejector was indeed that of the pump-action shotgun forwarded as sample 3. The used cartridge had been loaded in it and ejected three times without firing.'

So, a cartridge case showing use in two individual guns, one of them Welch's pump-action. Indicating loading practice, Yeadings concluded; or possibly a demonstration of rapid pump ejection, such as Welch might have given to the four boys selected to try out the guns.

But another gun had been used to *fire* the cartridge.

He pulled towards him the detailed list of firearms. According to this, No. 1 was the only single-barrel fully choked

12-bore. In fact, Lorely's own. And that would hardly have been on loan for the boys' entertainment.

Yet the case was found in the grazing-field above the wood. Thrown there to confuse the issue, implying that it was one that accidentally killed Lorely while she was walking through?

But how could the cartridge have been demonstrated for the boys and also used to shoot Lorely? Lorely had been shot *before* the afternoon's target practice.

That left two suppositions: the pump action ejections had occurred on some earlier occasion, and the cartridge been carried around since, finally loaded and fired from Lorely's gun, probably at her; or it had been used in the boys' demonstration and fired from Lorely's gun later. Presumably to pepper the tree?

Yeadings sighed. He'd fancied a sawn-off for that, the more since Benson/Summers (if he was the same) had a connection with a missing sawn-off from the latest Houseman Brothers hold-up.

Intriguing information from Ballistics, true; but no clear indication of the villain. So back to the drawing-board with a blank sheet on it, until something definite turned up to indicate which of the three suspects was the one who'd actually used Lorely Pelling's shotgun.

NINETEEN

RORY SWAM ROUND and round in the aquarium. Sometimes its glass sides moved in on him and he was trapped in a watery coffin. At other moments he felt air all about him, rushing over him, and he half knew that he was in a lake, yet he saw his own body quite a distance ahead, mechanically moving; could even hear the in-out pumping of the swimmer's heavy breathing.

It was interminable, and this concept of going on and on could only worry him. An eternity of effort, and never reaching the distant bank, nor finally sinking either. And not knowing which of the two he really wanted, except that there should be some kind of ending.

While he endured, there were four waiting. The Sister was concerned with the equipment and his physical reactions. Two others, mother and friend, watched the grey face slowly take on colour and, part-mesmerized by the background hum, compulsively found themselves counting in time with the soft pumping. The fourth was out of sight, behind a screen, the constable due to record whatever words the boy uttered on recovering.

'Would you like to go for a drink or anything?' Alexandra Welch asked Stuart softly.

'I'm OK, thanks. You go. I'll stay till you get back.'

She looked hard at her son's drawn face, then again at Stuart. 'Maybe I will. I ought to phone Amanda. Just ten minutes, then.'

He realized he ought to have sprung up and opened the door for her. It was the sort of thing her sort of people did, but she hadn't seemed to expect it. He caught the Sister's severe eye. 'Shall I put on another tape?'

'Try it if you like. Or talk to him a bit.'

A bit of both, Stuart decided. He slid in an old Eric Clapton cassette, turned it low and said the first thing that came into his mind. 'Quite a swell affair, that rally, mate. Good nosh, too. Your Mum certainly knows what goes down well.'

A tremor went across the unconscious boy's face. His eyelids flickered but did not open. 'Ma?' he breathed.

The Sister leaned forward and nodded to Stuart. 'Go on.'

'She's round here somewhere,' he said. 'Just gone for a coffee or something. Back in a minute. She'll want to talk to you too.'

Perspiration came out on Rory's forehead. His mouth puckered. 'Ma?'

He was going into the stable block to fetch the mallet for pegging the archery target supports. In the shadowy doorway he turned at the sound of running steps on gravel, and then he saw her again, tearing along the back driveway, freakishly disarranged, her hair unfastened, eyes seeming to stand out from her desperate face. Going as if the hounds of hell were after her. From the direction of Malmsmead Hall.

He turned and went after her, caught her up in the house at the foot of the stairs. She was clinging on to the newel-post, panting and trembling. When she saw him she couldn't find breath to speak, but the look she gave him was enough. 'Leave me alone. Don't you dare to say you've seen me like this.'

He'd never been so terrified in his life. Because she—so imperturbable—was scared out of her wits. He thought she must have been attacked, raped, but then he knew it must be something quite different. It was old Lorely's she'd run from. There was nobody there who would have harmed her, and yet . . .

He found himself in the kitchen, in slow motion opening the cupboard where the Malmsmead key should be hanging, and it was gone. She had it with her still, in her pocket. He didn't know if he should follow her upstairs and insist she explain herself, or go to Lorely and ask her what had happened. But his father came in then and swore at him for standing idle with so much to do. He went back to the stable block for the mallet, as if nothing was wrong.

Later, while the others were doing laps on the go-karts, he slipped away.

In the Hall's rear garden she was lying on her back, old Lorely, her chest and the cat's body all bloody. He hadn't known why until, running towards her, he nearly tripped on the gun thrown into a patch of nettles. And then he was handling it, his own blood thumping away in his head, because he knew he had to cover the whole thing up, do something, anything, to make it seem an accident.

And it wasn't, couldn't be, because the gun was so far away from the body. Even if he laid it alongside no one who knew anything about the distribution of shot would believe she'd have killed herself by stumbling with a loaded gun.

He didn't know where to start, and he'd so little time. At any moment he could be missed back at Farlowes. He didn't consciously decide to bury the cat. It just seemed right to get it off the dead woman and dispose of it in the normal way.

He pulled off the plastic apron and handled the animal in that. There was a spade close by and he buried the bundle in a shallow grave near where Lorely had been working in the vegetable patch. Then he fetched a canvas cover from the barn and threw it over her in case anyone came by. Not that they would. Later, maybe after dark, he would come back, clear up and hide her more carefully. Later, when he'd had time to think.

'Ma,' he said tremulously again, and it started all over again, like a circular tape. A film of him at the stable block doorway, and running footsteps, his mother's terror. 'It's all right,' he whispered. 'No one knows. You're—safe now.'

ALEC BENSON HAD RUN in circles denying everything to begin with, but at last he'd broken. DI Jenner had produced the print-out from the CRO. On admitting that, yes, he had been born Albert Summers and he'd once been inside for a job with the Housemans, Benson had been given a break and a mug of strong tea. Jenner went off to see the Superintendent. Silver offered the man a cigarette and it was refused.

'Don't smoke,' he said curtly.

Silver nodded. He could see the sense in that, having been to the stables. Too much wood and straw about. Maybe horses were sniffy about smoke too. 'You disappoint me,' he said. 'You changed Albert for Alec. People often stick to the same initials. But why Benson? I thought maybe that was your favourite fag.'

Summers looked surly. 'I didn't want no more of that Houseman lot. They were in trouble again and I didn't see why I had to go along. There was this telly at the place I had rooms. The night I decided to scarper they had the snooker on; Steve Davis at Wembley. That's what give me the idea.'

'Benson and Hedges Masters tournament!' Silver marvelled. He hadn't been so far wrong; same firm, different connection. 'And then you looked around for a job with horses. Didn't you need references?'

'I had old ones from when I was a stable-lad. Had a friend change the name for me. It was typed, see. Genuine signature and date.'

'You'd have been in a fix if your new boss rang up the old one.'

'Well, she didn't. Mrs W don't have nothing to do with racing-stables. The nearest she got was hunters down in Surrey, and that was nine or ten years back. She took to me when she saw I liked her beasts.'

'Some might not have been so trustful.'

'I never done her down. I been straight all the way since I got them Housemans off me back. You only gotta look at them horses to see I done a good job.' He was flushed with self-righteousness now.

How long would that boast last, Silver wondered, when Jenner got back and started on him again, bringing up the relic he'd saved from his criminal past, the sawn-off shotgun just unearthed in Benson's quarters?

It wasn't long before the DI reappeared, his wintry features worthy of a Spanish Inquisitor. Without a word he unwrapped a narrow parcel and laid the gun on the table between them. Summers's face had gone pale and stiff.

'What yer trying to fix me up wiv? I ain't never seen that thing before, and no way you ain't going to make me put me dabs on it.'

'Don't worry about fingerprints, Mr Summers,' Jenner drawled. 'It's been through the process, and we're very happy about the results.'

'Yer bloody lying!' the man shouted. 'Yer trying to set me up. I know it's—'

'Clean as a whistle, because you did it over so carefully? But you forgot we can pick up the prints off gloves. The same fabric ones were used to clean this as wrapped the apron round the cat, and dropped the cartridge case in the field above the wood. You might as well come as clean as you thought the gun was. Unless you're going to claim the Housemans knew where you kept it, and jumped prison to

get it and do in a harmless old woman who got angry at yo□
snaring her cats!'

Benson glared back with loathing. 'I don't know nothing
about gloves or bloody cats. Yer stitching me up. Sodding
bent coppers! I want a brief!'

'TOMORROW,' said Yeadings heavily, 'is another day. You
can hold Summers until then without charging him. See he
gets a proper meal sent in. I'll be in early to read his full
statement, then we'll see what should be done next.'

'He killed her all right,' Jenner said with certainty.

'Maybe. But we've had a few enigmatic words reported
from the Welch boy, who's started coming round. I remember you once favoured him in the frame. And to cap it,
we appear to have lost sight—temporarily, I trust—of the
boy's father. Anyway, if I'm wanted I'll be at home. Beaumont and WDC Zyczynski can ring me there if there's any
unforeseen development.'

As Yeadings drove in there was frost on the tarmac, except for a darker oblong where Nan's car had stood. He
operated the garage doors and eased in alongside her blue
Allegro. The house felt warm after the chill dusk air, and
there was a welcoming smell of roasting lamb.

Luke was installed in his playpen in the hall, surrounded
by cuddly toy animals and a disjointed plastic train. Yeadings ruffled his hair in passing, evaded the groping hands
and went through the archway to kiss Nan engrossed in her
saucepans.

'Oh, good. You're back early. Pour me a bitter lemon,
love, will you? I'm quite dehydrated.'

He shed his coat, poured drinks, and brought them back
to the kitchen. Luke had ceased chortling and was now ex-
perimenting with piercing yelps to gain more attention. His

father wept across to lift him, swing him by the armpits and restore him to his toys. 'Where's Sally?'

Nan's lips tightened. 'Upstairs in her room.'

'Already?'

'Not already. *Still.* I sent her up half an hour ago. She was extremely rude to that nice Mr Vallance.'

'The plumber? What on earth did she do?'

'Threw a tantrum the instant he appeared at the door. Screamed and lay on the floor drumming her heels like a three-year-old.'

'Well, Nan, in a way she is, and always will be.'

'I know, but it's not like her. And I'm tired, and the man is so obliging. He's coming tomorrow to put the new cloakroom suite in. I don't want him thinking this is a madhouse.'

'Still, half an hour's enough. She sounds quiet now. I'll go up and see her.'

He found her face down, exhausted by weeping, asleep diagonally across the bed. Stroking back her fine hair, he touched one exposed cheek. It was hot and red.

If she slept too long now she could be wakeful at night. He lifted her and rocked her in his arms till her eyes came open, the lashes still dark with tears. She blubbered a little into his shirt-front, and when he'd helped her blow her nose he asked, 'What's all this, then?' A copper through and through, he thought wryly.

She tried to tell him, but she hadn't the words or the experience.

'Was it because of the man who came to see Mummy?'

She started to shake her head, then stopped, frowning and screwing her mouth as she thought hard.

'Something to do with our cloakroom?' His exploits there and the basin's overflow might still be disturbing her.

'N-o.' Her voice was husky and embarrassed.

'But something to do with water?'

He felt her tremble. 'Tap,' he thought he heard her say, but her head was tucked in against his chest and the word came out muffled.

'But the man's going to change the one that dribbles.'

She shook her head and dug her fingers into his flesh.

'Look, you take me and show me which tap it is that bothers you.'

'Not here.'

Well, that was different. A tap had misbehaved somewhere else; in some other child's house, or at the Friendly Club. Maybe Sally had been blamed for making a mess. In her confusion she'd connected a water disaster with the plumber, hence the outburst when he turned up unexpectedly on her own doorstep.

'Sally, where was this tap?'

She stayed quite still for several seconds before starting to loosen her grip. She gulped and then answered clearly, 'The shop.'

It took a little longer with him gently questioning until at last he was satisfied that whatever upset her had happened days ago on the occasion when they had all gone to choose the new toilet suite. Something in the showroom had scared her, and she'd connected it with the magician and his horrifying act at the Hallowe'en party earlier.

'We'll go and look at it together,' he promised. 'Early tomorrow, before I go to work. How's that?'

She nursed his big paw in her own small hands and smiled bravely, blinking several times in quick succession. 'All right.'

There I go again, he thought: building up the myth that Daddy can put everything right. What's going to happen when I'm no longer around? The dragging at his heart was more than emotion. There was physical unease.

'Now go and wash your face and brush your hair, darling. Let Mummy see how nice you can look when you try. Then we'll have something to eat.'

Their meal was interrupted by the telephone. Nan darted him a suspicious glance. 'Shall I put yours back in the oven?'

'Just cover it.' He went out to the hall and she heard the rumble of his voice with pauses between. The call wasn't a long one. When he came back he resumed eating without comment.

'Do you have to go out again?' Nan asked.

'No. That was just Beaumont relaying a message from the constable at the Ascot hospital. Rory's come round, he's breathing normally, transferred to a private room, but he refuses to talk about his exploits at the gravel pits.

'His mother phoned the good news home, and the cook told her we'd arrested the hired hand who looks after the horses. This apparently shook the boy out of his dumb act and an odd bit of dialogue ensued which will take some working out. But tomorrow. And first thing tomorrow I'm taking Sally to the Friendly Club myself. Maybe you'd ring the minibus driver, tell him he doesn't need to pick her up.'

TWENTY

SALLY PUT ON what Yeadings knew to be her brave face. Clutching his hand she went cautiously over the threshold of the builder's showroom. On their previous visit, while Nan and he had browsed through catalogues and price lists Sally had happily run free, passing through the mock bathrooms and visiting odd corners the others hadn't seen.

At this early hour only the assistant who had unlocked was there, and he was attached to a telephone, leaving them to circulate together. Sally hesitated, then led her father through a rear doorway into an open yard and across it to a shed where lengths of copper and plastic piping were laid out on racks. In one corner was a jumble of heterogeneous objects generally connected with plumbing. One of these was a curious assembly of a box-mounted enamel basin with an old-fashioned brass tap suspended above it from a sort of gibbet by a length of ordinary twine. It was at this that Sally pointed.

'Sorry, Mr Yeadings, bit of a rush to catch one of the vanmen,' said the assistant, materializing behind them. 'What can I do for you?'

'My daughter seems interested in this tap business.'

'Oh that. Did she see it working? One of the lads set it up last week for a bit of fun. Like to see what happens?'

'I should, very much.'

'Well, have a wander round while I get it ready. Then *hey presto*, eh?'

Sally blinked at the last words and Yeadings grasped their connection with magic. Possibly there was a set patter for when the ancient exhibit was put on show.

They moved away while the man transferred the box, basin and hanging tap to a different position, fiddled with it and eventually called through to them, 'Right, lady and gentleman. Roll up and see the wonder of the Edwardian age—Water Power—on tap!'

It really was quite impressive. From the unattached brass tap, which trembled slightly on its string, gushed a column of water that plashed into the bowl, spreading genuine rings on the surface and sending up occasional indisputable droplets—but having no source behind the tap itself. It was to all appearances an aqueous cornucopia eternally filling the basin, and without any water ever overflowing.

Which was impossible, Yeadings acknowledged. He looked at Sally and saw her eyes were round with disbelief, although certainly this must be what she'd seen before.

Like all parlour tricks, it had to be a phenomenon obeying the laws of physics but deceiving the observer. For Sally, desperately trying to make sense of a complicated world, this was too great a challenge. Perhaps he had been wrong in encouraging her always to look for reasons, explaining childish mysteries in terms of cause and effect. A younger or less earnest child might merely accept the magic and cry out with delight. An intelligent child like Amanda Welch could even manage to work out what had happened.

It wasn't so difficult really, once you recognized what the impossibility was. The tap had to be connected to a water supply somewhere although none was visible. So, if not at the usual end from a mains pipe, at its outlet. It was now supported not only by the string from its gibbet but also from below by a transparent column of glass which the plumber had inserted between it and the basin. Inside this tube a jet of water must constantly be shot upwards from a pump situated within the box at the base, this jet meeting a perforated washer within the tap's mouth which channelled its return down the outside of the column, giving a completely natural-looking, slightly irregular flow. The glass tube was made invisible by the water running over it, and the basin never overflowed because the same quantity of liquid was used over and over again.

'Not bad, is it?' demanded the assistant. 'It was our Mr Vallance's grandad first fitted that up. Bit of museum junk really, but it catches the eye. He used to put it in the window to bring customers in.'

Yeadings hunkered beside Sally. 'Mr Vallance's grandfather was a clever man,' he said. He nodded to the assistant who switched off the pump, and the glass rod holding up the tap became visible as the water ceased flowing. Then, as simply as possible, he explained that because of a pump the flow started upwards, through the tube and then fell back outside it. It might seem to be working backwards to someone used to seeing water pour downwards from a tap. This was really just a special kind of fountain.

It was a totally relieved, rather excited child he delivered at the Mencap centre, babbling her own incoherent version of what she had seen.

Yeadings, too, experienced some lifting of the spirits, tempted to believe that Sally's block in comprehension indicated progress. She had been alert enough to suspend belief.

The incident stayed in his mind despite the insistence of police business. He phoned a delighted Nan and when he rang off after summarizing the solution of Sally's upset for her, he was aware of a vague echo sounding on in his own mind.

Instead of the tap producing water from a mains supply
it had received it. The basin, instead of receiving, had supplied. The deciding factor had been the pump, stronger here
than the force of gravity. In some obscure way this fact had
a hidden significance for him, but short of standing on his
own hands like Carroll's Father William, he saw no practical use to make of it. Yet it persisted: a misconception over
direction.

WDC ROSEMARY ZYCZYNSKI had seen the Superintendent
arrive early and hoped he might send for her before she had
her report finally typed. She wasn't happy about her interview of yesterday with the semi-senile Mrs May Welch, and
this was one time when she would have welcomed advice.
DS Beaumont had rung in to say he was going first to the
hospital at Ascot in answer to a request from Alexandra
Welch, and DI Jenner was busy chasing up the present
whereabouts of her elusive husband. Z took her time but no
diversion occurred; at last she was obliged to deliver the
finished work to Yeadings knowing it to be unsatisfactory.

'I've missed something,' she confessed when he had finished reading it through.

It was the self-same feeling the Superintendent was himself subject to just then, but he would never have admitted
it. He glanced at the typed sheets once more and then back
at the girl. 'You're sure you've included all the dialogue?'

'Yes. But there was a feeling I had; something about the
woman herself. She seemed more than usually disturbed but
covering up. I've always found her conversation disjointed,
but this was something more. The room was in much the
same state, now I come to think of it.'

'As though she'd been searching for something and only
partly put it straight again?'

'Yes, I think you're right. She's rather a dithery old thing but she was holding on to herself rigidly, as though any thing might happen if she let go. It sounds fanciful, but—'

'But one grows antennae.'

Rosemary looked apologetic. 'I thought at one point there might be someone else in the house with her, but she said not.'

'What gave you the idea?'

'There was a soft thud from upstairs, just the once, as if a book was dropped, then nothing more. She saw me listening and said it would be the cat coming in through the landing window. Well, it might have been. Certainly it was dead quiet from then on.'

'Is it possible someone else had been doing the searching and your arrival interrupted this in the upstairs rooms?'

'It might account for her tension. I should have offered to go up and fetch the cat.'

'These things occur to one too late. But if someone was going through her things against her wishes and she'd been warned to say nothing, it may be as well you stayed out of sight.'

He glanced again at the end of the report. 'Find some excuse to go back this morning. Make sure everything's as it should be. We weren't expecting a professional criminal with a sawn-off shotgun living at Welch's place, so Swardley village may not be as peaceful as at first it appeared. Radio in when you get there.'

Rosemary had been gone only some fifteen minutes when a call came in from Beaumont. 'I'm bringing Mrs Alexandra Welch in to make a statement, sir,' he announced. 'She and the boy have been cooking up a story that almost accounts for his exploits, but not quite.'

'And neither admits to killing Miss Pelling?'

'They both say they can't imagine who would, yet the mother thought it was an accident caused by the boy, because of the way he's been behaving since. The boy thought it was his mother for some inadequate reason he hasn't yet invented. Between them they've muddied the water plenty. She's quite inclined to believe Alec Benson did it, now that he's been pulled in for questioning, but Rory went all colours of the rainbow when he heard a sawn-off shotgun had been found in the rooms over the stables. I'm wondering if there's a link there, between the boy and Benson; a spot of collusion.'

'Right. I'll leave the interview to you unless you want me sitting in on it.'

'I thought you might like to stroll in quite a bit later and be the nice guy.'

'As you wish. Don't lean on Mrs Welch too hard, that's all. In the meantime I'll run over to Ascot and get the boy's version of things for myself. Lying in bed on his own he may dream up some refinements that she won't have forewarning of.'

FOUR KNOWN SUSPECTS, Yeadings listed in his mind, leaning back with his eyes on the road. Benson, Welch, Welch's wife and Welch's son. But had any of them adequate motive for killing an elderly recluse? Just the possibility that one of them had caused suffering to her cats. So what if they had? What could she have done about it beyond bawl that person out, or threaten to make trouble for him locally? Little cause for fear, and certainly none for murder.

Lorely Pelling was the person wronged, over the dead cat; one would expect any venom to spurt from her. Spurt; the word pulled him up, reminding him of the water puzzle Sally had found so baffling. Well, it was his turn to be baffled now.

Hang on, though. The image of the unattached tap was coming through so strongly it had to be relevant. A *spurt of venom;* that was the connecting thread. A mere form of words, or was there truly a parallel?

A discharge of firearms. Shotgun deaths were rare, but the action of shooting was common enough. One pressed the trigger of a loaded gun and it simply fired the cartridge. (As unquestionable as what happened when turning on a tap.) So one tended to look on the shooting as the prime act of violence.

But suppose the shooting was only secondary violence, like the return of the water to the basin after being pumped up to the apparently unattached tap. There could have been earlier violence to which this was mere retaliation. Violence occasioned by Lorely Pelling herself?

Why not? All along he had acknowledged the strength and independence of the old woman, yet accepted that she was the victim. That didn't quite add up.

Unless the shooting had been accidental or the one who did it was out of his mind, there had to be some act of hers that had driven the killer to such lengths. So what was it that Lorely Pelling, who knew her own mind, had done to set all this in motion? Lorely, the pump that set the cycle flowing. This cat-woman *walking by her wild lone;* what was it that she had *never told anyone?* Was there a secret she'd held over her killer as a mortal threat?

Benson's true identity? Why not? But he had managed to disappear quite successfully once before, after being suspected as an accessory to robbery with violence and murder. Were his present job and its perks so valuable that he would act out of character and shoot to kill instead of simply scarpering again? His earlier criminal role had been as getaway driver, nothing more vicious. A murder in the nearby woods could only bring unwelcome attention from the police, increasing his danger rather than removing it.

Welch. What provocation could Lorely have exercised on him? She'd refused to let him take over as Squire, and all Swardley knew it. His pride had been wounded, yet he'd seemed too thick-skinned to mind much what the village people thought of him in private. When he'd wanted to expand and take on more land she'd balked him, but that was old history.

Had she worked on his family and set them against him? There was definite estrangement there. It could have been the natural outcome of a mismatched marriage, but certainly his wife and children had gone against his express command that Lorely should be ostracized. Had she mocked him when they came face to face, revealing this hitherto secret alliance, which he would see as a treacherous conspiracy against him? His brashness was meant as carapace for an underlying insecurity, but he could have believed his family inpregnable—until then. Lorely Pelling could have exposed his crucial Achilles heel, and hadn't her intention in naming the children as her heirs been an attempt to drive a deeper wedge between them and their father?

Finally Alexandra Welch—how might Miss Pelling have worked on her to make her so desperate as to kill? Had their secret friendship enabled the old woman to unearth some scandalous secret? Was it possible that the children's true father wasn't Welch at all but someone, not Lorely's kinsman but an unknown, whose hinted existence might bring Alexandra's world crashing to pieces? Was it malice that had lain behind that apparently generous bequeathing of all her goods to Rory and Amanda—creating a need to look into their siring, even as far as questioning their blood groups?

And if Lorely Pelling had intended any of the malice Yeadings was now questioning, how far had she meant it to go? What reaction had she intended to provoke? Was she, ironically, willing to face violence, even at risk of ending her long, frustrated life? Had she, in fact, died of a conscious or subconscious death-wish? It took a special kind of toughness deliberately to suffer such an end. And Lorely had been a special kind of woman. There were those in the village who'd thought her mad.

It came on him as a slight shock to discover he had arrived at the hospital. Now he must tackle the boy, and it seemed already that in this crime Rory was almost irrelevant. Yet there were questions which had to be asked and answers to be written down. He sighed, parked the car, made his way to the upper floor where Rory Welch was recovering.

Faced by the boy's slight form under the cellular blanket, Yeadings regretted for a moment that he had given up smoking his pipe. Not that tobacco was permitted here, but it would have given an excuse for keeping his hands occupied, for removing his gaze, for taking extra time to think before uttering words that could never be unsaid.

'Look,' he proposed, leaning forward from his chair, elbows on splayed knees, seeming relaxed, 'it could save time, and perhaps face, if I simply ask you *what* you did but not why. Think about it.'

Rory stared back with a kind of desperation. 'What I did when?'

'When you came on Miss Pelling shot, with the dead cat in her arms.'

'I didn't kill her.'

'You didn't shoot her, no.' Was Rory alert enough yet to notice he'd qualified the statement? Lorely hadn't been dead when the boy first saw her, but she'd appeared so, uncon-

scious and quietly losing blood. His failure to bring help or
to apply first aid could well have signed her death warrant.

'I tried to rouse her, but she'd no pulse. I was scared. I
thought I'd better bury the cat. I wrapped it in her apron
and dug a hole in the vegetable plot. It seemed right to cover
her up. I knew there was an old canvas in the barn so I used
that.' He stopped.

'Go on.'

'Then I went home.'

'And told no one.'

There was a long silence. 'You said—you wouldn't ask
why.'

'You went all through that afternoon and evening acting
as though nothing had happened.'

'I've had practice.' Bitterly.

At hiding his feelings. Yes, probably, even before being
sent to boarding-school. An intelligent, sensitive lad, he'd
not have found his father easily understood him.

'And then you decided to move the body.'

'I thought it should look more clearly an accident.'

'But you never did think it an accident, did you?'

'I didn't know what had happened.'

Didn't know, just suspected. Well, let that pass for the
moment. 'Tell me what you did.'

Carefully the boy went through the whole business, anxious to omit nothing except the terrible fear in his mind and
the motive for all the elaboration. The kitchen gloves, the
cleaning of Lorely's gun and spade and their return, the
loading of the wheelbarrow and the journey by dark to
Farlowes Wood, the masking of part of the tree with coco-
nut matting and discharge into it with the sawn-off shotgun
previously stolen from the top of Alec Benson's cupboard.
Retaining the hot cartridge case as it was ejected, but fling-

ing the one he'd found near the body towards where the boys had been shooting that afternoon.

'You know it didn't quite come off?' Yeadings asked.

'I didn't pitch it far enough,' Rory admitted. 'And the sawn-off gun didn't spread shot quite the way I thought it would. I didn't mean to get Alec into trouble, but I suppose you'll charge him now with illegal possession.'

'You can leave that to us. When did you put the gun back?'

'Early on Sunday, when Alec was setting up jumps for Amanda's pony. I don't think he can have guessed what I'd done until you pulled him in and the gun turned up during the search. Why did you suspect him?'

'Alec has a criminal record. We were looking for the sawn-off. You may like to know that if he suspected what you'd done he never mentioned it. He's staying stumm on everything.'

'But he didn't kill old Lorely, did he?'

'I ask the questions, lad. Here's my last one coming up. Now you're satisfied it wasn't your mother you were protecting, how do you feel about having done so for the real killer, whoever that may be?'

Rory shook his head. He hadn't got as far as the answer to that, but he certainly must be pondering it.

'I must have been out of my mind to think Ma would have hurt her.'

Yeadings felt stirrings of sympathy. 'We can all do surprising things in a crisis,' he said. 'Well, that's all for now. Take it easy, and see you get fit again soon. Young Stuart Beaumont's haunting the corridor outside, so I'll hand over the visitor's chair.'

His car radio was squawking vainly as he returned to the Rover. 'Cabbage Patch,' he acknowledged in code.

'Can you phone in, Cabbage Patch?' Control demanded.

Yeadings climbed out, relocked the car and went to find a public telephone. WDC Zyczynski, he was subsequently told, had run into an unexpected complication. Uneasy because there'd been no reply to repeated ringing and knocking at the cottage door, she had looked through Mrs Welch senior's windows and seen her lying on the kitchen floor. She'd broken in and summoned an ambulance. The old lady had suffered a mild stroke, probably the previous night, but there were also bruises and marking consistent with a physical assault. WDC Z was staying with her until the lady was able to give an account of what had happened. The paralysis was on the left side of her body and her speech was not affected.

'Thank you, Control. Inform DS Beaumont I am on my way back now.'

TWENTY-ONE

ALEXANDRA WELCH had made a statement of sorts. She was left alone with a cup of coffee while Beaumont consulted with his chief.

'H'm,' commented Yeadings, reading the single page through, 'that tells us little more than we'd already assumed. Rory saw his mother returning from the direction of Malmsmead Hall before 11.0 a.m. on the Saturday and later "mistakenly" connected this with the attack on Miss Pelling. If he had mentioned his suspicions she could have explained that she had taken down some of the caterer's delicacies as a treat for the old lady's lunch. Miss Pelling was alive and digging in her garden so Mrs Welch hadn't lingered, afraid her absence might be commented on back home. She ran back part of the way and probably appeared flushed on arrival.'

'No mention of what happened to the food she claims to have supplied. The contents of the dead woman's stomach were oatmeal, goat's milk, wholemeal bread and blackberry jelly. And nothing like caterer's party food was found in the house. If the cats or wild animals had snatched it there should still have been the containers.'

'I don't see Miss Pelling accepting what she'd regard as charity food, do you? No, Alex Welch went haring off down there for some other reason. I'll have a word with her myself.'

He walked through to the interview room, greeted the woman rather stiffly then went through a pantomime of removing his overcoat and folding it across the back of the empty chair. Then heavily he sat down facing her. 'What I suggest is this,' he said slowly. 'Withdraw your voluntary statement and we will forget you ever made it. Later you can't avoid giving evidence in court on oath, and it will look bad if your story has two versions. You see, by now we know a little more than you realize, and that statement has flaws.'

She looked tense. Her rapid eye movements betrayed a new nervousness at his last words.

'That s-statement is the truth, Superintendent. All Rory's stupid actions of the p-past few days were because he felt that he could somehow d-divert attention from me.'

'I wouldn't disagree with you there, Mrs Welch. What he did was stupid, although he's not a stupid lad. Instead, a mistakenly heroic one. His exploit in the gravel pits was meant as much more than diversion. Dare you equal his courage, I wonder, by telling me the truth? Withdraw your statement and I will ask you just two questions. Then perhaps you may go.'

She frowned back at him, biting her lips. 'W-what are your questions?' she asked in a low voice.

'One: what was Miss Pelling holding over your family? And two: who was she putting the main pressure on?'

'No!' Alex Welch's face was suddenly pinched and stark. She rose from her seat. 'There was nothing like that. You're quite wrong!'

'Please sit down, Mrs Welch.'

Alex crumpled on to her chair, but her hands were bunched into fists on the table between them. 'I have said all I know about this b-business. It's there in my statement and it stands the way it is. I see no reason to answer any other questions.'

'I see. That's a pity. Mrs Welch, have you any idea where your husband is at present?'

'No. He d-doesn't f-find it necessary to tell me every-thing.'

'We think he may have visited his mother in Swardley vil-lage last evening, but had left by early morning. Perhaps he has returned home. Would you care to phone and ask your daughter?'

'Amanda?' Now she showed fresh anxiety. 'Mrs Weiss is in charge there; the cook. Amanda is all right, isn't she?'

'So far as I know. Please feel free to phone if you feel anxious about her.'

She stared back at the big man's raised eyebrows. His voice had been gentle but she knew he had deliberately raised her new fears. All the time she had been worrying over Rory she had left Amanda unprotected. There were only two women there with her now. Franklin was away, even Alec was gone. Not that he'd be any safeguard, a pro-fessional criminal as he'd turned out to be.

'I'd like to g-go home now,' she said almost pleadingly.

Yeadings stood up. 'Very well, Mrs Welch. You know where we are if you wish to change or add to your state-ment. I'll have one of my men bring your car round.'

'YOU LET HER GO?' DI Jenner repeated in amazement. They were back in the Superintendent's office comparing notes. 'How did she account for the discrepancy about the food she was supposed to have taken to the Hall?'

'I didn't ask,' Yeadings said blandly. 'How are you get-ting on with the case against Benson?'

Jenner sucked in his lean cheeks. 'He admits now to be-ing Summers, gives a plausible reason for wanting to change his identity and get beyond the Housemans' reach when they come out. The sawn-off shotgun he finds more embarrass-ing. He was "asked to look after it for a friend".'

'The bank hold-up was too long ago,' Yeadings warned.
'No one is going to identify the gun after this time. There's
nothing against him that will stand up in court except a
charge of illegal possession. Let him go back to Farlowes.
He seems to have been putting some honest work in there,
and the horses still need looking after.'

'You're scrubbing him from this Pelling business? That's
two gone; only two to come. Welch and the boy, that's all
we've got left.'

'Looks like it,' agreed Yeadings mildly, reaching for his
coat again. He ambled towards the door, looking back before he closed it after him. 'Unless you count Granny Welch.
I'm trotting along to have a word with her now. Z thinks
she's as *compos mentis* as we're ever likely to find her.'

WDC ZYCZYNSKI LOOKED strained and slightly untidy.
Yeadings reminded himself she'd made a habit of spending
her nights at bedsides rather than in them. She had stayed
close to her charge all through the journey by ambulance,
the reception at Casualty and now her transfer that afternoon to a room in a nearby private nursing home.

'The old lady kept going on about her box,' Rosemary
told Yeadings. 'Every time I asked who'd attacked her she
started shouting for her box, insisting he shouldn't be allowed to take it. It was all she had left to remember him by.'

'And you thought it would be some memento of her son
Franklin Welch which he was determined to remove before
he disappeared for ever?'

'Yes, because she never mentioned any name. Always
"he" and "him". I took it she meant the same person each
time.'

'Whereas "him" covered the unmentionable name she'd
kept shut about for over four decades. The identity of
Franklin's true father. Poor little mixed up woman.'

It wasn't guesswork but insight that brought him face to face with the tragic fact. Not for the first time he felt over-whelmed when confronted by the act of one human being taking the life of another, the outrage and the futility of it. Pity for victim, and pity for killer driven to the act, bore down on him. Yet he must go on pursuing, stepping over other broken lives that were the unintended outcome.

After her passionate outbursts old Mrs Welch had re-lapsed into her earlier mental haziness and was drifting off under a dose of tranquillizer. Yeadings looked in at her through a glass panel and knew he'd get nowhere. Instead he sent Rosemary back to sit beside her, talk soothingly and offer to straighten out her house.

When she returned with with the front-door key Yead-ings nodded grimly. 'My car's outside. I'll help you search. It sounds as if her precious box has gone, but there may be something else left behind to work on.'

ALEX WELCH DROVE frantically home from her interview with the police. As she braked, flinging up gravel by the front door, it burst open and Amanda ran out. She threw herself into her mother's arms.

'Where have you been all this time? How's Rory? Daddy won't speak to me. What's wrong?'

The hall was full of spicy smells of baking; Bramley ap-ples and cinnamon. Mrs Weiss had been showing the little girl how to make *Apfelstrudel* in an attempt to restore nor-mality.

Alex loosed the child's arms from their strangling em-brace. 'Rory's going to be all right, darling. Let me just get my coat off. Then tell Mrs Weiss I'd love some coffee, will you?'

She threw her coat down and ran to Franklin's office, a small room upstairs which led off his bedroom and overooked the back drive. He was there, seated at his desk on which were scattered sheets of notepaper, torn envelopes and the black ribbons which had bound them in bundles together.

Black. For death. Death everywhere in this business. Franklin's face as he slowly looked up at her was dead too, lined and haggard as an old man's.

'His letters,' he said hollow-voiced. He made a limp gesture towards the desktop. 'My father's, to my mother.'

'Which father?' Her voice came out harsh and unfeeling.

'Pelling, of course. You knew all along. She told me that morning. She had confided in you weeks before.'

'Lorely wanted the children to inherit. She was an old woman, Franklin. She'd loved her father—your father—so much that she could forgive this folly in his sixties. Your mother had been acting-nanny for an American family in the neighbourhood. They met and were attracted to each other. She didn't tell him she was married. It just happened. When Lorely knew she hadn't many years left she wanted to enjoy them with us as her family. She was alone and lonely. She saw it as her right!'

'Pelling's daughter! You realize, she was my half-sister? That stubborn old witch, standing there threatening me, saying I was a bastard!'

'*Pleading*—or as near it as she'd ever come. I was there, I heard. I knew you'd gone down that way because when I brought some coffee for you here I found her note screwed up on your desk. I knew what she meant to say to you, how you'd react. I was terrified what might happen.'

'She said that my father—that Welch—was impotent.'

'He wasn't your father.'

Franklin shook his head heavily. 'These letters—'

She saw he had been reading through them all. Some wer
torn across. Others had been screwed up and then smoothe
out again. They had begun to speak with a dead man's voic
not meant for him. An overheard conversation of lovers
one-sided, from which he had picked up the faint voice o
his mother's responses.

'He asked her to marry him, right after it happened. M
fa—Welch, poor sod—came across a letter. He must hav
gone out of his mind, but at least he waited till after I wa
born before he wrapped his motorbike round a lamp-post
Most of these letters are from the period just after that.'

'Why didn't she accept him then?'

The man sighed. 'Guilt. She felt she had to be punished
For two years she refused to see Pelling, tried to suppor
herself and baby with domestic work; cook, housekeeper
Then she had a bout of rheumatic fever and that scared he
into submission. There's a letter here about a house conveyance. Pelling must have given her the Swardley cottage
then. The rent she got from letting it helped her take out a
life insurance in my name, in case anything happened to her
and I'd no protection. She wouldn't accept anything more.
Much later, after she'd retired and Pelling was dead, she
came here to live.'

'Then you decided to move near your mother and, ironically, bought the Home Farm from people who'd bough
if off your dead father.'

He didn't answer, but stared past her out of the window.
All his fire seemed to have gone. The ancient deceptions
burned him less now than the futility of it all, the obscenity
of his own anger.

'You killed her,' Alex whispered.

'You were there. You saw how it was. She taunted me!'
But already he was unsure. There had been such blazing
emotion, she risking all in a late appeal, he conscious only

of a crazed intrusion on his hard-won success, seeing her as a menace, a source of shame. Branded a bastard by a hated scarecrow woman who claimed instant kinship. The reaction was a devouring need to be rid of her, rid of the whole unbearable situation.

The cat's weak mewing from the wood had interrupted the tense scene, and the woman, throwing down the dibber by the drill she'd made, had stalked stiffly off to fetch the animal.

And Alex, believing the tension broken, had stolen away still unseen, appalled and fearful, breaking into a run as soon as she was free of Malmsmead grounds. She must have been almost home when the sound of the gunshot came.

'I never saw you shoot her,' Alex whispered. 'I'd gone by then. Rory saw me running back, and later—when he knew of the shooting—thought I'd done it. So he tried to save me by moving the body to make it look like an accident.'

'Yes, it had to be him. No one else would complicate things so.'

'You shot old Lorely. And you just walked away. All day long you knew what you'd done, that she was lying there dead, or bleeding to death, and you went on pretending nothing was wrong.'

He moved his hands apart, helplessly. 'It was like someone else doing it, driving me. I'd slung the old leather jacket over my tidy things, and I felt the loose cartridges in my pocket. Her gun was leaning in the scullery doorway. She must have been potting at squirrels or something. I think I only meant to scare her. I don't know. Maybe—God, I hated her so then! I wanted to kill the whole world!'

YEADINGS NEEDED only a glance at the legal document. The conveyance of the cottage, a witnessed will and several other papers were scattered on the floor in an upstairs room. A pretty rosewood box inlaid with mother-of-pearl lay nearby, its lock forced and the lid splintered.

'This proves the connection with Pelling,' the Superintendent said. 'Welch can't have read right through it, being in a hurry to get the other stuff.'

'Can we use it?' Rosemary asked.

'We'll put it back where we found it,' he said. 'It's time, I think, to follow Welch up and get the whole thing straightened out.'

She looked at him and thought he had aged by ten years since the morning.

'On second thoughts, I'll pull in Beaumont for this. You've done a good job, Z. Pop back to base and get your report typed out. Then go home and put your feet up.'

BECAUSE STUART had been peripheral to the case Beaumont felt the boy deserved to hear the outcome before it hit the television news. He shared a four of Kalibur with him while he explained how he and the Superintendent had found Rory's father down in Lorely's garden with a neat bullet hole in one temple.

Despite the boy's professed interest in pathology he didn't ask for more details. Perhaps this closeness to the real thing would put him off, if it was a genuine idea in the first place.

'I thought you had taken his guns away.'

'This was a hand-gun. An old Service revolver Alex Welch identified as having once belonged to her father. She thought her husband had got rid of it for her years ago.'

'Did he leave a note?'

'Yes. And a lot of correspondence tidily secured with black ribbon. Mr Yeadings collected that. I don't know what was in it,' he lied.

'I thought you once said the motive for most crime was either sex or greed.'

'So it is. This one was freaky.'

'So what was the motive?'

'Ask me another.' There was no way Beaumont was going to admit to his son that the way he saw it, the cardinal sin here had been respectability.

MIKE YEADINGS was folding sheets with Nan for her ironing. There was an autumn scent of the garden in them and he found it soothing.

'So will Alexandra Welch move away from Swardley?' she asked him.

'I shouldn't think so. She's a realist at heart and everything that ever mattered to her is close to hand. She inherits Farlowes and she's trustee to the children's estate. They'll both be away to school for most of the year and I think she'll want to ride it out. She's well capable of pulling everything together.'

He nodded, remembering old Lorely and her frustrated wishes. In their different ways the two women had shared something in common.

'She'll stay on in Pelling country. When all the trauma's over it will satisfy her sense of family.'

ABRACADAVER
RALPH McINERNY

First Time in Paperback

A Father Dowling Mystery Quartet

NOW YOU SEE HER...NOW YOU DON'T

A magic show at St. Hilary's one snowy night proves entertaining for the stragglers who braved the weather. Aggie Miller allows her ring to be used in a disappearing act and Father Dowling chances to notice the inscription. Oddly, the ring belongs to Frances Grice, the missing wife of a local millionaire entrepreneur.

The ring's new wearer had found it at a garage sale, but it clearly brought bad luck—poor Aggie is brutally murdered. What was the connection between the death of Aggie Miller and the disappearance of Frances Grice?

"Dowling fans won't be disappointed."
—*Kirkus Reviews*

Available in September at your favorite retail stores.

 WORLDWIDE LIBRARY®

ABRA

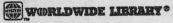

BARBARA PAUL

The Apostrophe Thief

A Sergeant Marian Larch Mystery

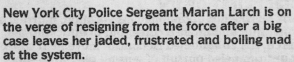
First Time in Paperback

BREAK A LEG

New York City Police Sergeant Marian Larch is on the verge of resigning from the force after a big case leaves her jaded, frustrated and boiling mad at the system.

During a cooling-off period at another precinct, she comes to the aid of her longtime friend, actress Kelly Ingram, star of the new Broadway hit, *The Apostrophe Thief*. Someone is stealing memorabilia—costumes, cups, scripts.

Marian just wants to solve the case, quit the force, finger her irresponsible boss and her incompetent partner and then...what? Holland, her ex-FBI lover, wants her to join his fledgling P.I. firm. Perhaps.

Then murder takes center stage....

"Paul is a talented storyteller...."
—The *Drood Review of Mystery*

Available in November at your favorite retail stores.

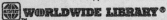

JUDAS PRIEST
RALPH McINERNY

A Father Dowling Mystery

First Time in Paperback

HIGH PRIEST OF SIN

Chris Bourke has abandoned his vocation, married a former nun and made a career out of attacking the church. His Enlightened Hedonism movement called for untrammeled pursuit of sensual pleasures—and his following was, not surprisingly, enormous.

But what does a professional apostate do when his only child announces she is going to enter a convent? He asks Father Roger Dowling for help.

Not in the business of turning away those with the call, Father Dowling agrees to speak to Sonya. But her brutal murder involves the venerable priest in a sordid tale of duplicity and deadly intent...and a clever killer with a calling of his own.

"Characterizations are excellent...."
—*Chicago Tribune*

Available in November at your favorite retail stores.